AT THE POINT OF A GUN

MAN WITH THE LAMAT

ZACHARY LANE

LEMAT BOOKS

Cover art by ClprtCo on Etsy

Cover and Interior Design by Cat & Doxie Author Services

I dedicate this book to my wife Carol. Your love strengthens me and sustains me in every endeavor.
Zachary Lane

PROLOGUE

After writing my great-grandfather's story titled *Death Rode to Lodgepole Creek*, I set his diary aside for a time. You see, it took a lot of deciphering to make sense of his 'chicken scratches' as my wife called them. There were other things to do. Gardening. Watching my grandchildren play sports. Regular household choirs every homeowner faces. Then, after about a month or two, I felt my great-grandfather's diary calling me back to it. I don't know if you've experienced anything like that in your life. The only way I can rationalize this experience is to say that my great-grandfather was calling me from the grave. Look, I'm not Stephen King. Yet, there it was, great-grandfather's diary kept calling me. And the more I resisted, the more it beckoned.

My return to the diary started subtly. At first I only read the entry or two around the spot where my great-grandfather asked Parson Abel to baptize him. You remember, don't you? I recorded the incident at the end of my first book. But, the diary was calling me to read more than that. I gave in. I couldn't help myself. Many times I found the writing illegible. At other times pages were stuck together and I couldn't separate them forcing me to skip over whole chunks of my great-grandfather's life. Maybe, great-grandfather was telling me there was little of interest on those pages. On those stuck together pages was the story of an ordinary guy growing old in the Old West.

Then one evening after my wife had gone to bed, I discovered another adventure in my great-grandfather. I couldn't put the diary down. Jess Jones was alive again speaking through the words of his diary. This was an adventure I could not resist reading. I read entry after entry until the sun showed its early morning face. Great-grandfather was pointing me to an adventure some two years after his Baptism in Lodgepole Creek. The year was 1873. Here was a new adventure coaxing me—no, begging me to write it. Here is that adventure. I call it:

At the Point of a Gun

CHAPTER ONE

War teaches hard lessons; fatal lessons. The Civil War taught Jesse Jones well. He remembered the words his sergeant drilled into his head. "Never panic. Panic kills when leaden mosquitoes fly scant inches away. Load quickly," he had said, "but pick your target well: the bigger the target the better. Aim for the chest, not the head. Take steady aim. Squeeze the trigger; don't pull it. Let the .44 do its deadly work."

Amazing how a man's training comes into play in the middle of a gun fight, Jones thought. Although his Civil War remembrances were now some ten years in the past, he could still hear his sergeant's words over and over again. They formed a habit; a habit that had saved his life many times before.

A man behind the rock lifted his head to sight his rifle. Jesse taught him a hard lesson of war. His LeMat barked and blood splattered from the gaping wound in his face. *So much for the large target idea.*

"Get behind him! Move!" Jones heard someone yell and recognized the voice of Curly Bill Barnes, a man with sandy hair with just a tinge of grey at the temples, who often ordered his men about like Jesse's old drill sergeant.

Someone behind the rocks responded. "Cover me!" Other men laid down rifle fire with the intent to keep Jones' pinned down and unable to see the direction his antagonist was running. But Jones had seen this move before, many times before. He kept his head down and then poked it out from the opposite side of the rock in time to see a figure racing toward him with gun drawn.

BAM. Again Jones' LeMat belched fire. The impact of the bullets twisted the man around and dropped him face first to the ground.

"Hey, Jonzie?" Curly Bill yelled.

"Yeah," Jones yelled back.

"You're two for two with yer shootin'. Not bad. Not bad at all. How long do you think can keep that up?"

"Depends."

"Depends on what?"

"Depends on how long you wanna keep going? I got more ammo, Curly Bill, than you've got men."

"Still got ya four to one. Kinda' likin' them odds." Curly Bill tore off his hat. A dirty hand hurriedly searched for the equally dirty handkerchief stuffed inside his sweaty shirt. The high humidity combined with the Nebraska sun made for suffocating weather, and the environment of the Sandhills only made it hotter. It was one of those days when any movement, any movement at all, brought forth sweat. Curly Bill wiped his brow, smearing dirt across his mustached face. Curly Bill ordered the Winchesters to spray lead where they last saw the smoke of Jesse's gun, but he was not there.

Two of Curly Bill's men scurried around a sandhill hoping to surprise Jones. To their surprise Jones was not where they expected to find him. "I'm right behind you!" Jones barked.

With the swiftness of an elk, the men wheeled about. Jones fired twice, each bullet slicing through its prey like a hot knife through butter; the life went out of their eyes as they pitched forward and thudded to the ground.

"That's four for four!" Jesse yelled.

That was more than Curly Bill's men could take; they broke cover and hightailed it for their horses leaving Curly Bill no choice but to follow them. He knew when he was licked. He'd have to wait for a more opportune time to do his killing.

Boothill Cemetery at the northern edge of Sidney, Nebraska is a lonely place; windswept and uncared for. Tumbleweeds make their home here; lodging as they so often do against the grave markers and staying until the next high wind dislodges them and sweeps them away like a housemaid with a broom.

Jesse Jones comes to this lonely place often, and always for the same reason; to look down upon the marker of his wife Sarah. It's a simple marker; a wooden cross. Amazing how this simple marker crowded his mind with remembrances of her embrace, her kisses, and the shattered dreams she left behind when she died.

Jones read the date he found there on her marker.

Two years. Some say that I should just get over it, but I can't. It ain't that easy. Parson Abel says that we all grieve in our own way. Some move on faster; some don't. Fer those who continue to grieve, it's like death is a scab over a wound and there's always something that comes along to rip the scab off causing one to grieve all over again.

A hand touched his shoulder and startled him. Instinctively he whirled about with his right hand drawing his revolver and cocking the hammer.

"Whoa! Hold up a little!" Parson Abel said. "I didn't come out here to get my head blown off."

"Parson, what are you doin' here? You know better than to sneak up on me like that."

"It's Thursday you know, and Adeline is holding supper for us. She sent me to find for you. I told her that I was pretty certain I'd find you here, it's the first place I looked," Parson Abel said.

"Just came up here to think," Jesse said.

"I understand."

"Do you realize it's been two years?"

"Two years--," Abel's voice trailed off as he joined Jones in the remembrance. "I can still remember the defiant look on your face when I read you the words Sarah circled in her Bible as she died. 'Revenge is mine, saith the Lord.' You looked me straight in the eye and answered, 'The Bible also says an eye for an eye.'"

Jones nodded. "I remember."

"And God did bring that about, didn't he? God kept you from killing Custus Leverette for revenge. Instead Red Hand put an arrow in his back before he could kill you."

The two men looked down at Sarah's grave. For a long time they stood there without speaking as the memories rushed over them like a flood. At last Parson Abel broke the silence. "What do you say to biscuits and gravy for dinner tonight?"

"Sounds like Adeline's baking again. There's no way I can resist her home-made biscuits an' sausage gravy," Jones replied.

"We better hurry. Adeline's invited Doc to join us and he likes biscuits and gravy every bit as much as you and I do. He's probably filling his plate right about now."

THE DINNER TABLE provided a much needed respite at the end of the day; conversations of a gentler nature take place there. Upon occasion this gentler conversation erupted into a verbal sparring match between Parson Abel and Doc. That was the case this evening.

"Had a little scuffle with Curly Bill this afternoon," Jones said as he helped himself to a generous serving of gravy with chucks of sausage.

"Now, what would that be all about?" Doc said. "Seems to me when you told him we weren't selling Swede's Mercantile that would be the end of the conversation."

"You would think that, wouldn't you?" Parson Abel said. "That doesn't seem to be in Curly Bill's nature though. Seems to me he's used to getting what he wants. Have you stopped by to talk to Sheriff Blanton about it?" He paused before adding, "By the way I want a few more biscuits. Mind passin' 'em instead of hoarding' 'em, Doc?"

"Gull-darn it! There ya go again. Needlin' me for no reason at all."Doc grabbed three biscuits off the tray before passing them on to Adeline sitting between them.

Jones replied, "Not yet I haven't. This time it was a lot more serious. Curly Bill brought a lot of men with him. They tried to corner me after I dropped off a few supplies for a wagon train waiting on the Oregon Trail. I was real lucky; dropped four of them before they skedaddled."

Parson Abel nodded. "I've heard something about George Custer heading into the Blackhills next spring. The government's tryin' to confirm whether or not there is gold there. Wonder if that ain't puttin' a bee in Curly Bill's backside."

"We already know there's gold there," Doc said while he

ladled a generous helping of gravy over his biscuits he'd split in half with his table knife.

"Can you imagine the changes that will take place in Sidney if gold is discovered there, like we all know it will?" Adeline added her voice to the conversation. "Sidney is the nearest railhead and that makes us closer to the gold fields than any other city with railroad access; closer to Dakota Territory than North Platte."

"Those hills are sacred to the Sioux," Abel added. "Riding into the hills to pan for gold is a violation of the Laramie Treaty of sixty-eight."

"There'll be no end to the number of men who will come into town. The railroad will bring them this far and they'll head north into the hills like ants streaming to sugar water," Doc said. "A merchant could make a killing."

"And more bars and whore houses will spring up for all those men who leave their families and head west. Excuse me, my dear," Abel said while turning his attention to his wife.

"No offense taken, dear," she replied.

"I'm bettin' that somehow Curly Bill's gotten wind of all of this and is makin' a play. Would someone pass them biscuits back this way?" asked Jones. "I got a hunch that ours is not the only business that Curly Bill's got his eyes on, if that's the case."

AND IT WAS. What those at the dinner table did not know was that Curly Bill was not the ringleader. A man named Cincinnati Culver was, and he had a brother in Washington, D.C. who alerted him of upcoming events. Custer was headed into the Blackhills in the spring of seventy-four alright and he had already reported that there was no doubt he would discover gold. The plan was for Custer to trek into the hills and afterward stick around to provide military escort for the thousands of miners making their way into the hills, forcing the Sioux into a fight for their existence. Swarms of men would come by train to Sidney, Nebraska the closest train stop to the Blackhills, some two hundred miles further north.

While Parson Abel and Adeline were gathered with friends around their kitchen table, Cincinnati gathered accomplices; men like Curly Bill Barnes, his chief lieutenant, and Jimbo Livingston who enjoyed doing Cincinnati's devilment, and four or five others depending on the job to be done. These men met in the back room of the Last Chance, a run-down, seedy tavern on the north edge of town. Cincinnati liked this place because he knew there'd be no interruptions when he met here; after all, he owned the joint.

"Custer'll start out in the spring," he said while striking a match on the corner of his desk. "Gentlemen, the U.S. government is declaring war on the Sioux." Cincinnati lit his cigar, took a deep draw and blew out the match with the smoke. "Says so right in this here telegraph. Everything begins in the spring. Yep, things are a-poppin' and the Sioux don't even know it."

Jimbo Livingston liked the sound of that. As an experienced Indian fighter, he showed no-quarter to those he fights. Standing six feet-five and weighing in at three hundred pounds, none survive who venture to go toe-to-toe with him. Jimbo wasn't much for talkin'. Twin pearl-handled .45 pistols rest in his belt with gun butts facing forward. Jimbo's draw is smooth and across his belly; right hand to the left revolver and left hand to the right. He has ridden with Cincinnati ever since Cincinnati tugged his wounded body out of the reach of the flames during the Battle of the Wilderness.

"Ya like that, don't ya, Jimbo?" Cincinnati said. "Well, you, me, Curly Bill and the boys here, got a lot a work to do in the meantime. There's lots of money to be had and I'm aimin' to get more'n my fair share. Never been rich, but I think I can get used to it. I don't want to be rich. I want to be bodaciously rich. I want to own all of Sidney by this time next year."

Jimbo agreed with a contented grunt.

CHAPTER TWO

Adam Potter greeted the day in his usual fashion; pouring cold water from the pitcher into the wash basin and splashing it into his unshaven face. He took a second handful in an attempt to tame his matted hair; hoping somehow to keep it in place. He was unsuccessful.

There was more than a day's work ahead of him as he came down the stairs of Swede's Mercantile. Ever since Swede's murder and the subsequent purchase of the store by Jesse Jones, Parson Abel and Doc, he has served as General Manager, making his residence in the upstairs apartment once occupied by Swede and his wife.

It was a daily occurrence for wagon masters on the Oregon Trail to send a supply wagon into Sidney. Such was the case already this muggy morning, for Potter heard a wagon pull to a stop in the alley behind Swede's just as his left foot hit the bottom of the stairs. He made his way to the front door and flipped the sign there from 'Closed' to 'Open.' Through the glass in the front door he watched the town around him came to life. Edgar Martin, the town drunk, emerged from the Sheriff's Office, where he'd slept off his booze, much to the satisfaction of his beleaguered wife.

The pounding on the alley door drew Potter's attention back to the tasks of the day. "I'm coming!" he pronounced while weaving his way through the neatly arranged crates, boxes, and barrels of the storeroom. "I'm coming!"

The stubborn latch finally gave way and Potter opened the door. A young man in his late teens stepped in. He was slightly-built and sported a rather scraggly goatee in an attempt to show his manhood.

"I've been sent from the wagon train to get supplies. The Major said to bring back some axle grease, three barrels of flour and sugar. Got cash to pay for it," he said in a voice that cracked.

"Need any salt pork? Just got some in yesterday," Potter said.

"Yeah. That wouldn't hurt if ya got it. An' some beans, too," the young man replied.

"Won't take long to load ya up if you'll give me a hand," said Potter.

"You got it," said the young man.

He and Potter bent to the task of loading the supply wagon. As they worked Potter made conversation. "How old are you, son?" he asked.

"Seventeen and a half," came back his answer. "This is my first trip west and I'm working as a cook's assistant." He told Potter that he had seen several, what he called 'savages' from a distance, and wasn't looking forward to meeting them up close.

Potter tried to straighten out the young man's perception that all Native Americans were savages, but he was not very successful.

Sometimes those dime novels do more harm than good, Potter thought. Soon the conversation ended and the young man began his return trip.

Potter closed the back door and latched it. Removing his pocket watch as he returned from the storeroom, Potter noted the time: seven thirty a.m. That's the last thing he remembered until he woke with a terrible headache with Doc, Parson Abel, and Jones all huddled over him.

"Whoa there," Doc said preventing Potter from sitting up. "Just stay down there for awhile. You've got quite a knot on the back of your head."

"Whaaa happened?" he asked.

"Thought perhaps you could tell us," Doc said. "We found you lying here on the floor."

"I just got done helping a young fella load up some supplies for the wagon train and I came back in here from the storeroom." He paused to think. "That's the last thing I can remember." Another pause. "That was about seven thirty. I remember 'cuz I looked at my pocket watch."

"You don't remember seeing anything or hearing anything? That was over an hour and a half ago," Jones said.

"Nope. Came in here and it was lights out." Potter looked at Doc. "Can I get up yet? I got work to do."

"I'm going to have a couple of men carry you upstairs. I want you to stay in bed the rest of the day. You got a bad bump on your head. Rest, but don't sleep. I've heard about men who went to sleep after getting a hit on the head like that and never waking up." Potter rubbed his hand over the knot on his head. "And keep yer dad-blamed hands off it. I'll be back later this afternoon to check on ya."

Jesse recruited a couple of men to take Potter upstairs as the three owners of Swede's talked over what do to next.

"Is there anything missing that you can tell?" Abel asked.

"Don't think so," Jones replied. "Ms. Jenkins said she came

in about eight fifteen and found Potter on the floor right where we found him."

"That's forty-five minutes unaccounted for. Somebody must have snuck in while he was in the backroom and just waited to conk him over the head when he came through the door," Abel commented.

"But who would do something like that?" Doc said. "It doesn't make much sense to whack someone over the head for no reason."

"Sorry, I'm late," said Sheriff Blanton barging into the room. "Somebody shot a young man driving a wagon load of goods north of town. Left him fer dead, but he ain't hurt too bad—"

"I'll be the judge whether 'er not he's hurt bad," Doc interrupted. "Everybody thinks they're a doctor around here." He slammed the door on his way out.

"What's going on here?" Blanton asked.

"Somebody cold cocked Potter about seven thirty this morning." Jones said. "Doesn't look like they stole anything, but they about killed him."

"Can I talk to him?" Blanton asked.

"Just had a couple of guys carry him upstairs. I think I'd wait 'til this afternoon sometime. But I'd ask Doc first, if I were you," Abel said.

"That's a good idea. Wouldn't want to find myself in the crosshairs of Doc's temper. I'm in enough hot water with Doc already."

IN THE BACKROOM at the Last Chance Saloon, Cincinnati sat at his desk twirling a pencil in his left hand while two of his men filled him in on the results of their morning's work. Curly Bill was one; Jimbo Livingston the other. Curly Bill was talking.

"—and before Potter even knew what hit him, Jimbo belted him in the back of the head with his fist, an' he dropped to the floor. I thought he'd killed him." He turned to Jimbo. "Didn't I say, 'I think ya killed him?'"

Jimbo grunted.

Cincy smiled as Curly Bill continued. "Then we followed the kid out of town and ambushed the wagon, just as you said we should. We took the wagon to the hideout. I think I killed the kid. He took a bullet and it tore him right off the wagon and onto the trail."

"And you're sure nobody saw ya?" Cincy asked. "I don't want any loose ends."

"Nobody saw us boss," Curly Bill said. "Me and Jimbo was careful. Real careful. Weren't we, Jimbo?"

Jimbo grunted.

Cincy thought a moment. "We're gonna make Swede's so hot that nobody's gonna want to do business there. We'll put the squeeze on Jones until he's gotta sell and we'll hurt anybody who gets in our way. Today was just a warning. I want you two to get back to the hideout and stay there until I send fer ya. Go out the back way and I'll have Mitchell bring your horses around back. Good job today. I got a little bonus for ya."

Cincy went to his safe and opened it. A black notebook popped out and fell to the floor. Cincy retrieved it and put it back in the safe. He pulled out a roll of bills. "Here's a hundred for each of ya. Now, the two of ya, get out of town and stay out of town. Go to the hideout. Do you understand me?"

"Yes, boss," Curly Bill replied.

WITH DOC HOVERING OVER HIM, Sheriff Blanton pulled a chair up next to Potter's bed. "What can you tell me about what happened this morning?" he asked.

Potter tried to sit up but found it too difficult. His head throbbed like a herd of buffalo had stampeded over it.

"Not much," Potter said. "Some kid from the wagon train knocked at the back door. The train needed supplies and I helped him load them. I put the money in my pocket—." He reached into his shirt pocket and found the money still there. "After the kid left, I came out of the backroom." His voice fell silent. "I think that's all I remember, Sheriff. Next thing I know I'm waking up with a whopping headache and Doc's telling me to lay still."

"Someone shot the young man you sold the supplies to," Blanton said.

"Is he hurt bad?"

"He took a bullet in the arm, but Doc here says he's going to be fine," said Blanton.

"Good thing he's so young. Had he been your age, we'd be planting him in Boot Hill," Doc said. "He lost a lot of blood before someone found him."

Blanton added, "Can't find the wagon though. Had a posse lookin' fer it this morning. Found some tracks but lost 'em. The ground's rock hard out there."

"When can I get up, Doc? My back's lame from lying here all day," said Potter.

"Stay in bed 'til tomorrow and we'll see," Doc said.

Jones stood in the doorway. "How ya feelin, Potter?' You were white as a ghost this morning."

"Better," Potter replied, "but it still feels like my head was squeezed in a smithy's vice."

Doc moved the Sheriff out of the way and felt the lump on the back of Potter's head. "Ya got quite a goose egg back here. Yer lucky whoever it was didn't kill ya. That makes fer two of ya; you and that young man from the wagon train." Doc put a stethoscope to Potter's chest and listened. "Now, all of ya, get out of here so he get some rest!"

SHERIFF BLANTON KNEW ONE THING; a wagon weighed down with supplies does not disappear. Late that afternoon he set out to retrace the steps he and his posse had taken. He found the original tracks easy enough, but as before as he traced them north toward the Oregon Trail they vanished. Blanton considered the possibility of another path leading off into the Sandhills somewhere.But, where?

Settlers populated little plots of land, putting up sod houses and shanties in years past, many of which they abandoned when the ground failed to deliver as the eastern papers had promised. That supply wagon could be anywhere, so instead of veering off the trail as he done before, he stayed on it riding a mile or more north and it was there in the dirt he found wagon tracks again.

They didn't leave the trail, they stayed on it, but the cross traffic covered it up.

He stayed with the wagon tracks for a couple more miles until they disappeared a second time. By now it was late enough that picking up the trail again was impossible. It would be dark soon. Blanton determined to return to Sidney for the night and bring fresh eyes with him to search again tomorrow. A full moon lit the path and before long, Sheriff Blanton was riding past Fort Sidney to the sound of "Taps."

Those inside the fort settled in for the night, but the night life of a bustling frontier town was just beginning.

CHAPTER THREE

Most nights Sheriff Blanton slept on an old army cot in the corner of his office. That meant he was available when the town was its most rambunctious. As usual he locked the front door, blew out the lamp, and stretched out his five-foot eight-inch frame for what he knew would likely be a night of interruptions.

Like a child reaching puberty, the town of Sidney suffers growing pains. Construction of bars and brothels outstrips the construction of businesses and homes at a rate of three to one. Civilization, it seemed to Blanton, comes to town only when wives arrive with their husbands, and not when men come to town alone. Right now there were few wives. In Sidney, the bars and brothels made sure that when men arrived alone they could find women, but no one dared call these women *ladies*.

What this meant was that Sheriff Blanton would not sleep again that night. An array of occurrences kept him awake late into the night. Friends brought in a drunk to 'sleep it off.' There were two brawls and a stabbing. Two men shot it out in the Lodgepole Saloon, each claiming the same prostitute for the night. Blanton put both men in jail. Fortunately, neither man was a good shot. The only injury suffered was a bullet hole punched into the painting that hung behind the bar.

JIMBO LIVINGSTON WAS the first man awake. While the others spent the night in the lean-to hideout Cincinnati won in a card game, he slept alone in the barn, guarding the contents of the wagon stolen in Sidney. What Cincy's intentions were for these contents, he did not know; but what he did know was that he was going to guard them until Cincy made up his mind.

Tossing off his blanket, he rolled up his bedroll the best he could and then tossed it near his saddle before trudging down the path to the lean-to where the others slept. His giant fist hammered the door like a monstrous woodpecker.

Curly Bill opened the door and he was not smiling. He did not appreciate an early morning wake-up call and his words bore a hostile sarcasm to them. "Why do you always get up so early?" he asked. "The boss ain't around or did you forget?"

Jimbo shrugged him off, pushed him aside and sat down at the small wooden table in the center of the lean-to. The table and its two chairs accounted for all the furniture in the place, save the stove. At the opposite end of the lean-to, two men, awakened by Jimbo's pounding, yawned, and stretched in their makeshift beds in a weak effort to wake up.

"What time is it?" one of the men asked.

"A little after five," Curly Bill shot back after taking a blurry-eyed look at his watch. "Jimbo's hungry. Which one of you two knows how to cook, 'cuz ya sure don't want me to do it." Neither man answered.

"Well, this is a mess," Curly Bill said. "Cincy sent us out

here without a cook when he knows how angry Jimbo gets when he's hungry."

SHERIFF BLANTON SAT down for breakfast at the Sidetrack Café, so named for its nearness to the railroad station. He had wanted to be in the saddle about now, but his night of interrupted sleep meant that a cup of strong coffee was needed prior to the coming events for the day. Had it not been for Jones' continual pounding on his office door, he would still be asleep.

He picked up his coffee cup with two hands and lifted it to his lips. A sigh of satisfaction followed as he swallowed the warm liquid. Jones had Potter with him. Blanton did not mind the extra gun.

"Who knows what we'll run into out there," he said when Jones told him of Potter's presence.

Doc and Parson Abel had welcomed Blanton and Jones to their table and they were soon joined by Adam Potter still rubbing his head where someone had clubbed him and left a knot on it.

"Well, you three aren't gettin' a very early start on the day," Doc noted. "How's yer head this morning?" The last question was aimed at Potter who nodded as if to say, *Better*.

"We have a little unfinished business," Blanton said as he set his coffee cup down. "I took another ride out of town yesterday to see if I could find where the wagon tracks led. I got to the spot where we lost the tracks and rode a little further north and picked 'em up again. Then I lost them again and it was gettin' dark so I thought I'd see what I could find this morning."

"Potter and I said we'd ride along if he wanted us to," Jones said.

"Just don't go wanderin' around and getting' yerselves shot, that's all I got to say," Doc said.

"Ya wanna ride along, Doc? Is that what 'yer sayin'?" Parson Abel asked.

"Dad blame-it! There ya go again, tryin' to put words in my mouth," Doc fired back. "That's not what I'm sayin'. What I'm sayin' is that they should be careful and not get themselves all shot up!"

"Ah, Doc, I didn't know ya cared!" Abel said. "I didn't know you had a sentimental side."

"I don't. I mean, I do! Ah, ya got me so flustered I don't know what I got anymore." Doc turned his attention to his steak and eggs and ignored the laughter.

"So, what do you think you'll find out there?" Abel asked returning the conversation to the lost wagon.

"Not sure," Blanton said. "How's our young friend doing, Doc? The young man they shot and left for dead?"

"He'll live," Doc said. "Recovery will take time. I'll ride out with you. We need to let the wagon master know what happened."

A train whistle interrupted their conversation. Across the street from the Sidetrack Café carts and wagons jockeyed for position to receive supplies unloaded from the train. Other wagons stood in line to load it. Individuals who'd delayed their ticket purchases until the last minute, scurried about the depot like so many ants on an ant hill, and passengers lined up to board the west bound train.

The locomotive came to a jerky stop, the engineer released the steam and for a few minutes everything around the train was enveloped in a foggy haze giving the place a surrealistic quality as if all this occurred by magic.

Parson Abel checked his watch. "Eight o'clock on the dot," he said as he returned the watch to his vest pocket.

Sheriff Blanton recognized the man walking through the mist carrying a valise. "That's Bill Hickok," he said.

"Dang," Potter said turning his head in the direction Blanton was looking. "It's gotta be. Shoulder length hair, handlebar moustache. And do you see those two pearl-handled revolvers with the butts facing out. Yeah, that's him alright."

"Well, I'm gonna welcome Wild Bill to town. Anybody care to go with me?" Blanton asked.

"Ya got my attention," Potter said as he stood at the Sheriff's side. "You comin?" he asked Jones.

"Nope. I'm finishing my breakfast before I do anything else," Jones replied.

"Are you Bill Hickok?" Sheriff Blanton asked.

"I am. And who might you be?" Hickok said not stopping to visit.

"Sheriff Isaiah Blanton. And this here is Adam Potter." Blanton extended his hand. Hickok ignored it.

"Nice to know ya. Can you point me to the hotel and a place to eat? I'd like to freshen up a bit and have some breakfast," Hickok said.

"The Moore Hotel's down the street about a block. They have a restaurant, but I'd recommend the Sidetrack Café. They serve up the best breakfast in town," Potter said.

"Thanks." And without another word Hickok headed in the direction of the hotel.

"I heard Wild Bill is a man of few words," Potter said as he shrugged and walked back to the Sidetrack.

Blanton watched Hickok sidle down the street and disappear into the hotel.

THE TRAIN CREW scurried about the locomotive preparing it for departure. Some scaled the heights of the engine to fill the boiler with water. When the tender box was heated, using coal or wood as fuel, the water turned to steam. That steam propelled the tons of metal forward along the steel rails. As the crew hurried about their business, they had no time to notice a young woman staring out the window of one of the passenger cars. She would have remained unnoticed had it not been for the Conductor making his way through the train.

"Ma'am," he said. "This is your stop. This is Sidney, Nebraska."

The young woman continued to stare out the window, watching as a growing western town came alive. Shopkeepers hurried by to open their stores, buckboards carried families from one place to another and then there was the sound of a school bell calling children to their studies of readin', writin,' and arithmetic. She did not see anyone she knew.

"Ma'am," the Conductor said a second time. "This is as far as your ticket carries you. You'll have to get off now. Ma'am?"

"I'm looking for my brother. He promised to meet me and I don't see him," she replied.

"Ma'am, you'll have to do your waiting somewhere else. We're getting ready to leave. You can wait in the depot. I'm sure your brother will be along. But, you can't wait here."

With reluctance the young lady gathered herself. It was this whole idea of coming west after twenty years of living in rural Ohio that frightened her. But the passing of her mother had left her with few options.

CHAPTER FOUR

Sheriff Blanton led the party of men to the spot where the wagon trail veered to the northwest. Blanton, Jones, and Potter were each astride their horses while Doc drove a team of horses pulling a buckboard behind. The young man from the wagon train sat next to him with his right arm in a sling.

"The Oregon Trail is about a mile or so north of here, Doc," Blanton said.

"I know good and well where the trail is," he responded to the laughter of his friends.

"Just thought you might want to—"

"I can think for myself, thank you," Doc interrupted. "I'm riding with you. Never know when one of you might need a doctor. You could be riding right into a trap, you know."

"No use arguing with him, Blanton. 'Ole Doc is gonna do what he wants to do and to hell with anything you might want him to do otherwise," Jones added.

"Alright, Doc. If you want to ride with us, it's okay with me," Blanton said.

"Don't need yer permission but thank you anyway."

For the remainder of the ride no one spoke a word. They slowed their pace a bit as they approached the base of a tall sandhill. Observing that the wagon tracks continued over the hill, Blanton dismounted and crept to the top for a look. A half-mile in the distance stood a lean-to and a ragged building he reckoned was a barn.

"See anything?" Potter asked.

"A lean-to and a make-shift barn about a half-mile away," Blanton said. Potter and Jones climbed the hill and joined Blanton.

"Give this a try," Jones said offering Blanton his field glasses.

Blanton first focused on the lean-to. There was movement inside, but he could not be sure how many. He moved his focus to the barn. This time he did not see anyone, but he could trace the outline of a wagon inside.

"I think I've found our wagon."

"Where?" Jones asked. In response Blanton handed him the field glasses.

"In that barn to the right of the lean-to. I think I see the outline of a wagon in there. Give it a look."

Jones agreed that a wagon was inside the barn. Like Blanton before him, he could see its outline. He gave the lean-to his full attention, in particular the view through the window. "I got two, maybe three men in the lean-to," he said. "I'm thinkin' we need a diversion; something to keep everyone inside the lean-to while a couple of us sneak in and retrieve the wagon. The set-up is perfect."

"I'm a thinkin' somebody's gonna get shot. That's what I'm a thinkin'," Doc added as he joined the group near the top of the hill.

Everyone's attention came to rest on Doc.

"Gentlemen," Jones said. "I think we found our diversion."

"Hold on. Let's not get carried away," Doc answered. "I'm not here to be a 'diversion.' I'm a medical doctor." He fidgeted. "I fix things when someone else provides the 'diversion'."

"C'mon, Doc," Potter said. "All ya gotta do is ride in and keep the men in the lean-to busy while we steal the wagon right out from under their noses. It's easy."

"If it's so easy why don't you ride in and keep the three men in the lean-to busy, huh?"

"Doc, you're the obvious choice because if we ride in there's libel to be some shooting," Blanton noted.

"Right!" Doc said. "That's when I ride in. I ride in *after* one of ya gets shot. Not before."

"Okay. Okay. It's no use arguing anymore. Let's all go back to the trail so Doc can deliver his patient to the wagon train. We'll just have to wait for another opportunity," Jones said. He started down the trail to the horses.

"I thought you said that the set-up was perfect," Doc replied.

"It is," Jones said turning back to Doc. "But if you don't want to be a diversion; then you don't want to be a diversion. We'll just have to wait for another time. That's all."

Doc grabbed Jones by the shoulder. "Wait a minute. Do you really think we can pull this off?"

"Yep," Jones said. "And right now you are the only one who can make this work. Chances are pretty good that the men in the lean-to would recognize one of us—especially the Sheriff, if we went riding in. But, if you drove the buckboard in and struck up conversation we might all come out alive and return the wagon, too. What do you say, Doc? Are you up for a little adventure?"

Doc stroked his face. "I couldn't go in there with him sitting next to me," Doc said with a nod to the young man in the buckboard.

"Of course not," Potter said as he and Sheriff Blanton joined Jones and Doc at the bottom of the hill. "He'll just have to stay here until you come back to get him. Can you imagine what everyone in the wagon train will think when you ride up in the supply wagon with the kid? Why, we might even have to get in touch with Ned Buntline and have him put your story in one of his dime novels. What do ya think, fellas?"

"It's entirely possible," Sheriff Blanton said.

Doc thought about his prospective hero status. "Alright, I'll do it. I'll be yer diversion."

"Here's the plan," Jones began. "Doc will ride up to the lean-to. If anyone asked what he was doing there, he will to tell them that he was on a regularly scheduled visit to the wagon train when he remembered the man who lived in this lean-to and decided to check on him first. "Doc," he continued, "you will keep all the men inside the lean-to *and* away from the window while Potter and Sheriff Blanton get into the barn. Once they're inside and ready to drive away, Potter will whistle like a meadowlark. When you hear that whistle it's time to leave, so you won't get hurt in case there is gun play. I'll keep my Sharps trained on the front door just in case someone inside figures out what was going on outside."

With the young man out of the wagon, Doc drove his buckboard over the hill. He was surprised when no one came out to meet him. Surprised but pleased since his goal was to keep everyone inside. He got down from the buckboard and walked to the door and knocked.

"Mr. McNolte," he shouted. "Are you in there?"

"What do you want?" someone inside yelled. The door opened a crack.

"I'm the doctor from Sidney. But, who are you? You don't look like old man McNolte."

"The name's Curly Bill and I don't need no doctor. Who sent fer you?"

"No one sent fer me. I'm out making my regular rounds and I always call on old man McNolte when I'm in the area. Mind if I come in?"

"Yeah, as a matter of fact, I do mind. There ain't no one here by that name. So you just hop back on yer buckboard and ride away."

Doc was about to give up and ride off when someone from inside the lean-to started to cough. "Well, it sounds to me like someone inside needs a doctor. Get out of my way!" With that Doc pushed his way into the lean-to and Curly Bill slammed the door behind him. Everyone was inside just as they had planned it.

Jimbo continued in a fit of uncontrollable coughing. Doc raced over to him. "When did he start coughing like this?" Doc asked as he looked into the three faces of the men he found there.

"Just now," Curly Bill noted.

"Well, sit him down so I can have a look at him." Doc was careful to gather the men as far away from the window as possible.

THROUGH THE FIELD glasses Jones saw what Doc was up to and sent Potter and Blanton off on a roundabout trip to get behind the barn.

Jones watched them enter the back door of the barn and heard the faint sounds of Blanton calming the horses. Soon

Potter was at the barn door to give a 'thumbs up' that they had found the wagon.

On the hill, Jones put a bead on the front door. If there was trouble, he was ready for it.

INSIDE THE LEAN-TO Doc poured an elixir into a filthy glass and gave it to Jimbo to drink.

"This should tame yer cough," he said. "Don't know what it is about this time of year, but it seems lots of people come down with a cough when the warm weather passes and the cooler weather sets in."

Doc heard a meadowlark. That was his cue to finish what he was doing and escape the lean-to. "Is there anything else any of you need while I'm here?" Doc said as he packed his medicine bag and prepared to leave. As he took hold of the door latch a strong hand grabbed his and turned him around. It was Jimbo staring him face-to-face.

Jimbo grunted.

"Hope he didn't scare ya none, Doc," Curly Bill said as he joined Jimbo at the door. "He just wants to say 'thanks' in the only way he knows how. He can't say much, but he wants to know what he owes ya."

"Nothin," Doc replied. "I was expecting old man McNolte and he can never pay me anything. I'll just call it good."

"Jimbo always remembers when someone has done him a good turn," Curly Bill said. Jimbo grunted.

"Glad I came by when I did," Doc added as he climbed aboard his buckboard. "Next time yer in Sidney, stop in and say hello. You can pay me by buying me a drink. How does that sound?"

Jimbo smiled and nodded.

IN THE BARN, Blanton and Potter waited until Doc was out of sight before opening the rear door on the barn and driving the wagon off in the opposite direction. No one in the lean-to offered any resistance and within a half hour the three conspirators reunited with Jones to discuss their success. The center of attention was Doc who had kept everyone inside preventing any gunplay.

Only one thing remained to do and that was to return the wounded young man and the supplies in order for the wagon train to continue its westward journey to Oregon.

Jones waited until the foursome rode home to discuss what he thought would happen next. Someone would not be pleased with Doc's bravery, nor of anyone else who had participated in the 'liberation' of the supply wagon. Who this someone was Jones did not know, but he vowed to be ready if and when any blame pointed in Doc's direction.

CHAPTER FIVE

The young woman from the train sat forlorn in the Sidetrack Café. Her brother had not arrived as scheduled. She had read and reread his most recent letter and then stuffed it back into her valise. All she could do now was wait. She found the table near the window favorable to her waiting. From here she could see the main thoroughfare, such as it was, that dirt road, which cut Sidney in half from east to west. She could also see the train depot where she had waited for her brother who never came.

"Can I bring you anything, sweetie?"

The young woman looked up into the toothy grin of the third waitress she had seen in the past thirty minutes. "No thanks," she replied. "My brother will be here soon to pick me up."

She had said the words so many times that she failed to notice that the inflection behind them had gone from eager anticipation to hopelessness. The waitress moved on to a paying customer.

"May I join you?" a man's voice asked.

This time the young woman looked down in an attempt to ignore him.

"Been watching you for the better part of an hour," he said. "Is there anything I can do to help? The name's Abel. Parson Abel."

"I'm Martha Belt," the young woman said.

"Pleased to meet you," said Parson Abel.

Martha put her face into her hands. "My brother was supposed to pick me up this morning," she said. "I don't know what to do. He and his wife have a little place northeast of town. I don't know what's keeping him."

"Out here it could be anything. How about this? How about I have the waitress bring you a little something to eat while we wait together? How does that sound?"

"I'm not hungry."

"Beth?" Parson Abel said to draw the attention of the waitress who only moments before had hovered over Martha. "Would you happen to have any of those cinnamon rolls you made earlier this morning?" Beth nodded. "I'd like two, if you please. And two cups of coffee?"

Parson Abel turned his attention to Martha. "Well, Martha Belt," he said. "Tell me a little about yourself. How you came to be in Sidney." His smile and caring manner assured her that he was a man she could trust.

With his gentle coaxing, Martha revealed her story.

"I've come west to live with my brother and his wife after our mother died. He's eight years older than me. I'm the surprise my parents had later in life after learning they couldn't have any more children."

"God does have a sense of humor," he said.

"My father died when I was eleven from complications from a wound he suffered when a Confederate bullet tore through his right shoulder. There never had been much money in the family before the war, and afterward when my father could not work, there was even less. That meant, that like a lot of other wives of disabled veterans, mom took to cleaning homes, mending ripped clothing; anything she could do to put food on the table and a roof over our heads."

Tʀʏ as they might to explain how the wagon they were supposed to be guarding was stolen from them, their excuses rang hollow to Cincy. His fisted left hand smashed down on his desk in anger. "Where is my wagon? And don't be givin' me any more of your tripe about it disappearin' neither! You was either watchin' it or you weren't. Which is it?"

He grabbed Curly Bill by the front of his shirt and glared into his eyes. He was so close Curly Bill could smell the booze on his breath. After what seemed an eternity to Curly Bill, Cincy relaxed his grip.

"Like I was sayin'," Curly Bill began again. "Jimbo was guardin' the wagon but came in for some breakfast. Then along came this doctor from town. Said he was lookin' fer someone named McNolte. We said he wasn't here. But then Jimbo started coughing and the Doc gave him some elixir. After that the Doc left and Jimbo went back to the barn and found the wagon missing. It just disappeared."

"Were there any tracks to follow?" Cincy butted in. "Wagons don't 'just disappear'."

"We didn't think about that, did we boys?" Curly Bill said looking about the room for any support; any at all.

Cincy rolled his eyes. "Can't you get it through yer thick skulls that Doc was a diversion to keep you busy while someone stole the wagon right out from under yer noses?"

Boss?" Curly Bill interrupted. "What's 'a diversion'?"

"'A diversion' is somethin' done to take yer attention away from somethin' else." Cincy said. Looking about the room he could tell that a lack of understanding still remained so he continued his explanation. "Do you guys remember the magician I hired last year?" They nodded. "Remember how he made stuff disappear and reappear? Everyone in the room wondered how he did it. I told you to keep your eye on the hand away from where he was doing his trick, right?"

"I remember that," Curly Bill said. His cohort near him nodded. Jimbo grunted.

"The hand out front is the diversion, a distraction, taking your eyes away from where the magic is really done," Cincy said. "It wasn't really magic, but sleight of hand."

"Got it," Curly Bill said. "So Doc was a distraction so we wouldn't notice that someone was getting into the barn to steal the wagon?" He thought a moment before asking, "So, what are we gonna do to this 'distraction' to keep him from 'distracting' us again?"

"Let me think about that fer awhile. What I want the three of you to do is to go back to the barn and see if you can find out where the wagon tracks lead.There's gotta be tracks. Follow them and then report back to me."

"In other words," Curly Bill said, "you don't want us to stay here 'cuz we might be a distraction." He hurriedly gathered his friends and was gone, leaving Cincy alone.

"What have I done?" Cincy asked himself.

DARKNESS SHROUDED THE SANDHILLS. Artificial lights countermanded the darkness as hundreds of kerosene lanterns illuminated rooms throughout Sidney.

In the Last Chance, the lanterns lit Bill Hickok as he played poker, facing the door as he always did because of a premonition that one day someone would shoot him in the back.

In the back room, Cincy was well lighted as he planned his future without the 'distraction' of his minions who rode in the moonlight back to their hideout.

In the Moore Hotel, Martha Belt uneasily slipped between the sheets, praying that her brother and sister-in-law were safe. She had not anticipated the events of the past few days; nor did she care for them. But, here she was, alone in a city where she knew only one other person, Parson Abel. She had refused his invitation to join his wife and a few friends for dinner, believing that her brother's arrival was imminent, although her heart kept telling her otherwise.She leaned over and blew out the lantern at her bedside and just like in the Sandhills darkness shrouded her room.

Sheriff Blanton and his wife had long ago blown out the lantern in their bedroom. They had not seen much of other the past few days and they were soon busy making up for lost time.

Parson Abel went about his drawing room lighting the lanterns, which, in turn, drove the darkness into the corners. A discussion underway about how best to protect Doc migrated from the dining room table to the chairs and sofa of his parlor. After dinner cigars in the hands of Abel, Jones, Potter, and Doc gave off a red glow, to be sure, but contributed nothing to the room's brightness.

"What makes you think that I'm the one they'll go after?" Doc asked as he plopped down in a chair.

"Well, for one thing, you are the only face Cincy's men saw that day," Jones said. "They know that the wagon was in place when you arrived and that it was gone after you left. His men can put two and two together."

"That's not very assuring," Potter said.

"Especially from where I sit right now, it ain't," Doc added.

"We went through all this at dinner," Parson Abel said. "My question is: What do we do about it?"

"Let's talk through a couple of options," Jones said as he held his cigar to his lips. "One of us could stay with Doc at all times. Kinda like a personal bodyguard. That's one option. A second would be that Doc stays home and sees only patients who come to him."

"I'm a doctor. I can't stay in my office. I swore an oath to help people. How can I do that if I'm a prisoner in my own home?"

"Or," Parson Abel said, "you and your wife could move in here. We have a spare bedroom and you could use this room as your office. Then, if you have to go out, one of us will ride along with you. How does that sound?"

"Like I'm a kid who can't be trusted, that's what it sounds like, and I'm having none of it." He stormed out.

"Well, that didn't go well," said Potter.

CHAPTER SIX

Two weeks of calm followed the explosive conversation in the Abel house. Doc continued to see patients in his office above Swede's; unaware that Curly Bill had been sent to watch his every move. This was a tedious assignment for Curly Bill who longed for action or gunplay; anything other than the mundane task of watching Doc's office hour after hour.

It took only two days of drudgery before Curly Bill modified the assignment Cincy gave him. Curly Bill put Jimbo in charge of watching Doc and he spent his time at the faro tables down the street.

Cincinnati was furious when he found out.

"I got tired of waiting, boss," Curly Bill confessed. "I'm not good at standing around waiting for something to happen. I want to make it happen. Waiting is something for the weak in the head, like Jimbo."

"I gave you an assignment," Cincinnati excoriated. "I figured you could talk your way out of any situation arising if someone came along and started asking questions. Did you ever think of that? Now, you've got Jimbo standing across the street from Doc's office; sticking out like a sore thumb, attracting all kinds of attention. You are more subtle. You, at least, *could be* smart enough to keep an eye on Doc's place from the restaurant across the street. I should shoot you right here; and I would, too, if I didn't have a bar full of people. Go get Jimbo before someone figures out what we're doing. Then get back to your post. Do you understand me?"

Curly Bill retraced his steps to retrieve Jimbo. His steps took him past the Sidetrack Café where he noticed Jesse Jones engaged in conversation with a man he recognized at once as Wild Bill Hickok. *Those dime novels I read are good for something.*

Hickok's auburn locks flowed to his shoulders and his moustache curved at his upper lip and made its way to either side of his chin. The melancholy look on his face belied the malicious nature of his profession; just as Ned Buntline described it. Curly Bill turned his attention to Jimbo standing across the street and kept walking until he reached his destination.

"The boss wants to see us."

"In a minute." Jimbo's angry reply caught Curly Bill by surprise. Up to now he had never heard Jim speak. His attention was no longer on the entrance to Doc's office but on a brunette across the street.

"You can take in the sights of Sidney another time," Curly Bill insisted.

"I said, 'in a minute.'" Jimbo forcibly removed Curly Bill's hand from his shoulder. It was not until the woman entered the Sidetrack Café that Jimbo gave Curly Bill his attention. "Don't ever interrupt me like that again," he threatened.

"Yer serious, aren't you?"

"You better believe it. Next time, I'll kill ya."

Jimbo's glare sent shivers down Curly Bill's spine. He recognized the killing lust in the big man's eyes. Curly turned away in time to watch Doc exit his office and climb into his buggy. With a gentle tug on the reins, he drove away. "That there might be what we're looking for," he said.

Curly Bill led the way back to the Last Chance and the waiting Cincy. But not before Jimbo pressed his face against the window to the Sidetrack Café to take in one more look at the young woman who had previously attracted his attention. She stood at the table where Jesse Jones and Wild Bill Hickok sat.

"Sheriff Blanton said you might be able to help me," Martha Belt said.

"And just how might I do that?" Jones asked. He stood and offered her a seat.

She took it.

"I'm trying to find my brother and sister-in-law. They were supposed to meet me at the train depot a couple of weeks ago, but never came. Sheriff Blanton rode out to their place. He said there's no one around. There's spoiled food on the table. It's like they disappeared."

"Or someone took them," Wild Bill said without looking up from his breakfast.

Martha's countenance fell. "Why would anyone want to do that?" she said.

"Allow me to introduce my friend Wild Bill Hickok," Jones said. "Wild Bill this is—. I'm afraid we've not been formally introduced, but I believe you are Martha Belt. Am I correct in saying so?" She nodded. "Bill, this is Martha Belt."

"Glad to make your acquaintance. Jones was telling me about the things going on in town; that someone wants to control all the dry goods stores and outfitters in town. So, that's where my mind went when I said 'someone took them.'"

"My brother wouldn't be involved in anything like that."

"Maybe he saw something he wasn't meant to see," Jones said.

"Like what?"

"I'm sorry, Mrs. Belt, but I don't know."

"It's Miss. I'm not married."

"Did your brother tell you about anything he was doing?" Hickok asked.

"Just that he was trying to farm a patch of ground northeast of Sidney. Having a pretty rough go of it, too."

"The land out here is good fer' grazin' cattle and that's about it," Jones said.

"That doesn't mean he's doing anything illegal."

"No, it doesn't mean that at all," Jones said.

"Will you help me or do I need to look somewhere else? Sheriff Blanton said perhaps you might be available to ride out to my brother's place sometime and have a look around and that you might see somethin' that he overlooked."

"What do you say, Bill? Want to keep me company while I ride? We'll stop by the Sheriff's office and ask for instructions on how to find the place and head out."

"I'll ride with you, but what about taking that Potter fella you've told me so much about?" Hickok said.

"Well, miss, it looks like you got three sets of eyes instead of one," Jones added.

Curly Bill entered the alley behind the Last Chance Saloon and knocked at the back door. Cincinnati let him in. Jimbo followed.

"Brought Jimbo like you told me to, boss. I thought you might be interested to know that we saw Doc ride out of town and hurried right over."

"That's exactly the news I've been waiting for. I want you two to ride after him.Hold him hostage and take him over to our new hide-out; the Belt place. Got Smitty and Hays there now making the place comfy and secure. Want ya to meet someone." Cincy pointed to a young man about thirty years old in the far corner of his office practicing his fast draw. His black hat was cocked over his right eye. "The name's Ben Roach. I just hired him. He's come in from Tucson."

Curly Bill nodded in Roach's direction.

"Liked the old hide-out," Jimbo grunted ignoring Roach completely.

"I know you did," Cincy said, "but we can't stay there anymore. It's been compromised, remember? 'Sides, when we take Doc hostage, that's the first place everyone will look."

"Liked the barn," Jimbo said. "No one bothered me in the barn."

"There's a barn on the Belt place, too. You can hang out in there if you'd like."

"By myself?"

"By yourself."

"Can I bury someone in there?"

"Look," said Cincinnati, "if you'll do this for me, I'll give you Belt's wife to play with. You can have Doc, too, if you want; if Jones doesn't give me what I want."

Jimbo grunted. "Don't want Doc," he said. "I like him. He made me better. Don't want Belt's wife. Want girl in the Sidetrack."

Curly Bill said, "I saw Wild Bill Hickok in town. He was in the Sidetrack this morning talking with Jones."

"So, Jones has hired a shootist, huh? Stay away from him. He's fast. Real fast."

"I ain't afraid of Hickok. Ain't a gunman alive that I'm afraid of," Roach announced, putting his hand on the hilt of his Colt .45. Roach let out a chuckle. "Hickok don't scare me none."

Cincy confronted him at once. "You better be afraid of him. Heard he outdrew a man in Abilene and put two slugs in him before the guy cleared leather."

Cincy went to his safe and withdrew three one hundred dollar bills and held out a hundred to each man.

"Now, do what I told you. Get Doc and take him to the Belt place." He withheld the money and asked, "Do I make myself clear?" When they nodded their reply he put the money into their hands, but when they turned to leave through the bar, Cincy stopped them in their tracks. "Not that way," he said. "Go out the back way so you don't arouse suspicion."

DOC'S MIND drifted to the appointment ahead of him, checking up on Tootie Belle Watson, the youngest daughter of a freed slave couple who settled six miles east of Sidney on land sold to them by the railroad. His diagnosis earlier in the week was that Tootie had contracted the flu and he rode to make sure that her fever had not led to dehydration.

"Be sure she drinks plenty of water; dehydration is far worse than the flu," Doc had told her parents. He played that conversation over in his mind as his horses trotted along a dusty, narrow, one-lane path a mile or so from the lean-to where the Watson's lived.

Out of nowhere Doc was surrounded by riders with kerchiefs over their faces and guns drawn. He looked about him and noticed one man of incredible size among the riders. *These are the men from inside the McNolte place.*

"Hold it right there," one of the men shouted. It was a familiar voice, the man Doc recalled had tried to keep him out of McNolte's house.

"What's the meaning of this?" Doc asked. "The Watson girl is sick over yonder and you're interfering with my ability to treat her."

"She'll just have to wait awhile longer, 'cuz your comin' with us," said one of the men.

"What for?" asked Doc.

"Let's just say that you were at the wrong place at the wrong time and leave it at that for now." The man grabbed for the reins of Doc's horse.

Now, Doc knew for certain these were the same men he'd met at old man McNolte's. In a single motion Doc removed a whip from the side of his buggy and lashed it across the man's face. The man's gun went off putting a bullet hole in the leather fabric of Doc's buggy seat scarcely two inches away from Doc's left shoulder.

The welt on the side of the man's face oozed blood and he cursed aloud as Doc wheeled his buggy around and thundered back to Sidney ahead of a cloud of dust. Behind him Doc heard the report of a Winchester, but never felt the sting of lead.

I gotta get back to town.

He lashed his horse, praying for additional speed. He got it. However, the price of that speed was more than Doc bargained for as he raced headlong into a tight right turn. With all his strength he pulled hard on the reins. His horse turned and in the process the buggy separated from its rigging and went rolling into the trees; tossing Doc to the ground. He came to rest at the bottom of a gully.

WHEN HE REGAINED CONSCIOUSNESS, Doc found himself in a chair facing a lap-board wall. Doc blinked his eyes a couple of time to clear his aching head. Not only did his head hurt but his body as well. He wasn't a young man anymore and his body told him so. He hurt all over; especially his shoulders, which were pulled back behind a chair with his wrists tied. He could feel the wooden chair with his fingers, but there was no way he could find the knot to untie it.

Where am I? He glanced about the room in an attempt to orient himself.

He heard distant voices from somewhere behind him. *What are they saying?*

He strained to understand the words and could not, but the intensity of the words were quite clear; they were arguing over something. For all he could tell, they were arguing over what to do with him. Doc didn't scare easily; but he was feeling very uneasy about his situation.

Suddenly the arguing stopped. Dead silence followed by footsteps getting closer and closer. A doorknob turned. A door creaked.

Doc closed his eyes and feigned unconsciousness. The footsteps drew near.He felt hot breath on his neck and calloused hands checked the knot that secured him.

"Still out!" a voice shouted beside him.

Doc did not recognize the high pitched, nasally voice.

"How long do you think it will be until he wakes up?He's been out three hours."

Other footsteps. Two sets.

"Don't know," a second voice answered. "I'm not a doctor."

"Very funny, Curly Bill. Very funny," said the voice near him.

Doc thought for a moment. *Curly Bill. That's one of Cincinnati's gunmen.*

The man with the nasally voice slapped Doc's face in an attempt to wake him."Wake up, will ya?" he shouted.

Doc bit down on his tongue to keep himself from responding.

Curly Bill responded with a reprimand. "Don't do that, Roach. He'll wake up sooner or later. Leave him alone. Jimbo likes the guy and you don't want to make Jimbo mad." He paused. "'Sides, Roach, I need you to write a ransom note. I hear you can write."

Roach left Doc's side and ambled to the door. "So," he said with pride, "yer tellin' me that I didn't make it all the way through fourth grade fer nothin'. Is that what 'yer sayin'?"

Roach's voice squeaked with delight.

CHAPTER SEVEN

A tall, broad shouldered masked man lifted Doc into the saddle as easily as someone might lift a bag of flour. The man tied the leather straps that secured Doc's wrists around the saddle horn. Doc knew in an instant that it was the man named Jimbo whom Doc had helped back at the McNolte place.

Doc leaned to his left and whispered, "Let go and I'll make a break for it."

"Can't. But don't worry I won't let no one hurt you," Jimbo answered. Doc could almost picture his smile behind the bandana he wore as a mask. "You made me feel better. I won't forget ya for that."

A man Doc surmised was Curly Bill walked up to where Doc sat high in the saddle. He inspected the knot Jimbo had tied.

"How about loosening these ropes?" said Doc.

"That ain't gonna happen. Don't want ya to get no ideas about escapin'." Curly Bill chambered a round in his

Winchester and said in a voice that Doc thought soul-less: "Cuz if'n ya did I'd have to shoot ya."

There was a slight pause before Curly Bill spoke again. "Now that I think of it, maybe it'd be better if ya did try to escape. I'd just as soon shoot ya then mess around with all this hostage note bull. I'm in favor of shootin' you, Jones, and that Potter fella, and takin' yer business."

"But, that ain't what Cincinnati wants," Roach squeaked out behind him. "And we're gonna make sure Cincinnati gets what Cincinnati wants." His laugh reminded Doc of the stories of African hyena's laughter.

"Don't you ever sneak up on me like that again," Curly Bill snarled at Roach.

"I didn't mean nothin' by it," Roach hissed. He giggled as he mounted.

Curly Bill turned his attention to Jimbo. "He's secure?"

"Yep."

"Well then, let's mount up. We got us a little ride ahead of us. We're travelin' the back roads so as ta keep from gettin' spotted. I'll hold Doc's reins until ya get mounted and then you'll lead the way," Curly Bill told Jimbo. "And Roach?"

"Huh?" he replied.

"I want you to follow after Jimbo and Doc here. I want you in front of me and not behind me. I don't trust ya any further than I can toss ya."

"What'd I do?" Roach asked, all the while his giggle never quit.

Jimbo turned in his saddle long enough to break his silence with some advice. "Roach," Jimbo said, "someday that stupid laugh of yers is gonna get ya killed."

Roach mounted in silence.

He knows better than back-talk Jimbo, a man twice his size and as tough as nails, Doc thought. He felt the tug of Jimbo's iron fist on the reins and feared the force of the pull would remove the bit in his horse's mouth. Soon the foursome rode single file north along the back roads and into the sandhills.

Jesse Jones came down the steps in front of Parson Abel's home. Parson Abel joined him, accompanied by Martha Belt.

"Do you think you can find the Belt place?" Abel asked.

Jones unfolded a piece of paper and looked at it. "We'll follow the map Martha's brother sent her."

"Any idea of what you might run into out there?" Abel added.

"Not exactly sure, but the three of us should be able to handle it. If not, we'll be back for reinforcements," Jones said as he reached the last step and he walked to his horse. Potter and Hickok had already mounted, and Jones quickly did the same.

"By the way," Jones said, "thank you for the breakfast this morning."

"Don't thank me. That was completely Adeline's doing. We'll keep an eye on Martha while you're gone. Let me offer a quick blessing on the three of you."

The three riders removed their hats and Parson Abel prayed. "Dear Lord, Bless these three men today. Give them success in finding the whereabouts of Martha's brother and sister-in-law. May they still be alive. I pray this all in Jesus Name. Amen."

With that Martha put her hands over her face and began to weep.

"We'll do everything we can, ma'am, but what's already happened is out of our hands," Jones said.

Between her tears Martha replied, "I know that, but the unknown frightens me."

Parson Abel put his arms around Martha shoulders. "That's where prayer comes in."

"Parson Abel is right, you know," Jones added. "We put ourselves in God's hands."

He wheeled his horse about and rode through town with Potter on his left and Bill Hickok on his right.

CHAPTER EIGHT

Parson Abel ushered Martha into the house where Adeline met them.

"Oh, child, you've been crying," Adeline said. "Come on into the parlor, let's all talk awhile."

"I'm so scared about what they'll find."

"That's understandable, child. This fear of the unknown afflicts all of us at one time or another." Adeline's warm hands surround Martha's as the older woman lead her to the settee where they sat. Parson Abel sat nearby in the overstuffed chair. Martha noticed that his deep blue eyes were almost a perfect match with the color of the chair itself.

"Parson Abel and I were talking about this earlier this morning," Adeline continued.

"And we concluded," Abel interrupted, "that God has His hand in all of this.We don't know how and we don't know why, but He does. So, we turned to Scripture this morning and we found what we think is a perfect verse for us to talk about." He took up the Bible from the table nearest him and found the slip of paper he'd placed to mark the page. He read aloud,

"'Trust in the Lord with all thine heart; and lean not unto thine own understanding. In all thy ways acknowledge him, and he shall direct thy paths.' A reading from Proverbs 3, verses 5 and 6."

"That's a hard lesson," Adeline joined in. "Trust is hard enough and when you put 'not to lean on our own understanding' on top of it; it's even more difficult."

"I don't understand any of it," Martha said. "I don't understand why anyone would want to hurt my brother." Her eyes begged someone, anyone for an answer.

"We don't know that someone *hurt* your brother. Our minds often want to go to the worst case scenario," Abel noted. "All we know at this point is that your brother and sister-in-law are missing."

"And that's way beyond my understanding."

Adeline again gathered Martha's hands in hers. "Of course it is, my dear," she said. "That's where trusting in the Lord to see you through comes in. We pray and we trust. Those are the only two things we have to rely on as we wait for answers that God will provide."

"Will I ever get to that point that I trust God so completely?" Martha asked.

Parson Abel let a smile cross his lips. "That's a great question and to be quite honest with you, one I'm still working on myself." He chuckled. "I'm better than I once was, but not nearly as good as I will be."

Martha felt the warmth of Adeline's hands as she gently patted her own hands. She saw aged hands; seasoned hands along with the wrinkles on her brow and grey hairs at her temples. *All of which bespoke of wisdom that time spent walking with God gives,* she thought.

"Trust comes in time," Adeline said. "Give God the time to work out the details."

AT THE EAST edge of town, and very near the new Fort Sidney, a riderless horse trotted by Jones and his men. A set of long reins stirred up the dust behind. The animal paid no attention to the men, its eyes were set on the livery stable. Reaching it, the horse trotted inside.

"That sure looked like Doc's horse," Potter noted.

"I thought so, too." Jones turned his horse and rode in the direction of the livery. There he dismounted and walked inside. "Is that Doc's horse?" he asked the attendant.

"Yep," a young man in his early twenties replied. "Somethin' must have happened for Sheba to come home without him." He ran a curry brush down the animal's sable coat. "She must have come unhitched somehow. She's full of thistles, so she's been off the road some."

Hickok swaggered in. "What do you suggest?" he asked Jesse.

"I suggest we angle south a bit and see if we can't check up on Doc before we ride on over to the Belt farm."

"Yeah," Potter added. "I don't like the thought of Doc lying along the road somewhere without a doctor to help him."

Jones chuckled out loud.

"What? What'd I say?" Potter asked.

Jones reached over and pulled the brim of Potter's hat down over his eyes in a light-hearted gesture. "Nothin' really." He swung his leg over his saddle and mounted. "I say, let's ride."

An hour in the saddle brought the riders to the spot where slide marks in the road disappeared into the brush. Potter followed the marks on foot to the spot where Doc's buggy had smashed to pieces, but did not find Doc.

Jones and Hickok joined him and scoured the spot.

"Looks like someone laid here in the grass." Jones pointed to a matted down spot some twenty feet from the crash site.

"And by the looks of it several men drug whoever it was back up to the road.The toes of his boots traced a line in the dirt," Hickok added. He walked along the road until he found where the riders entered the brush. "They rode in that direction." His right arm pointed to the northeast.

"Doc's out there somewhere and these hoof prints will lead us to him," Jones said, "and they seem to be heading in the direction of the Belt's place. Too coincidental, I'd say. It's gotta be the same men Doc saw at McNolte's last week."

"You mean they figured out that Doc diverted their action while we took back the supply wagon?" Potter asked.

Jones said, "That's what I figure."

"The only way we're going to know for sure is to follow their tracks and they will lead us to Doc," Hickok added. "I'm game if you are."

"Well, it's for sure that we won't be any use to Doc back in town," said Potter."If we don't follow they'll kill him fer sure."

The three men mounted and followed the tracks left for them. "This is too easy," Jones noted. "They're making no effort to cover their tracks."

Wild Bill gave him a sideways glance. "Neither would you if you didn't think anyone would follow you."

Jones nodded.

CURLY BILL FOUND the Belt place much to his liking. What he didn't like was that Smitty and Hays were not there as Cincy had said. He also didn't like Roach's backtalk when he handed him a note with Cincy's instructions for the ransom note.

"Write it yerself," Roach barked. He sat across from Doc, the kitchen table separated them. "I don't much feel like writin' today!"

A sharp 'click' and the cold steel of Curly Bill's .44 pressed against his temple persuaded Roach to knuckle under and comply.

"And I don't much feel like listening to yer mouth," Curly added.

Doc watched the entire scene play out within feet of where he sat hog-tied to a chair.

"Let me tell ya," Doc said, "there isn't anything in my bag for the head wound yer about to receive."

"Shut your pie hole, old man!" Sparks flew from Roach's eyes and Doc felt their sting.

Without warning, Jimbo swung a mountainous hand down on the table inches from Roach's face. The table heaved under the blow and ricocheted off his chin. Blood splattered when Roach's teeth penetrated his tongue.

"Don't hurt Doc!" Jimbo yelled.

Curly Bill shoved Roach's face into the table. "Write the gull-darned note," he said, "or I'll have Jimbo dig a spot for you in the barn. Do we understand each other?" Curly Bill took his hand away letting Roach raise his head. Roach nodded, but it was a defiant nod.

"Ha. Ha," he laughed. "I was just funnin'. No sense ta gettin' so bent out of shape." He eyed the paper he was to write on. "There's blood on this paper."

"That makes the note look all the more urgent, don't it? Write!"

Doc looked about. He wasn't going anywhere with his hands tied behind him.Delicate laced curtains hung from the windows. *Obviously a woman's touch*, Doc thought.

"Don't worry, you ain't going anywhere." Curly Bill

checked the knot behind Doc's chair and patted him on the cheek. "We've got ya just where we want ya."

Curly Bill stepped outside.

Doc watched as Curly Bill took in the lay of the land. Through a window Doc could see him pace off the steps between the house and the barn, a new structure with fresh red paint. Curly disappeared inside the structure only to reappear one story above in the hay mow.

It would be easy to get intruders into a cross-fire. He's taking no chances. Doc thought.

Just the thought of it brought back those dark days with the Grand Army of the Republic and he realized a possible ambush when he saw one.

"There's a killing field. Anyone riding onto the place faces enfilade," Doc said under his breath. He struggled to free himself only to feel a huge hand on his back.

The look in Jimbo's eyes said it all—I may be your friend but that don't mean that I won't kill you.

Roach dropped the pen and scanned the blood spattered paper before him. Satisfied with the results, the word "Done!" escaped his lips. He stood dwarfed by Jimbo's girth and height. A wry smile crossed his lips.

"Think I'll go outside. It's kinda stuffy in here," said Roach.

Curly Bill met him on his way out. "Are ya done?" he asked

"What yer lookin' for is on the table!" Roach replied. "I'm takin' a walk."

Curly Bill snagged him before he could take another step.

"While yer takin' yer walk, grab your rifle and get yourself perched up in the hay loft. I'm expecting company."

Through the window Doc watched Roach practice his draw. Each time his right hand moved like a whip, never taking his hand higher than his belt buckle. Twice. Three times he drew.

"Ya forgot somethin', Roach," Curly Bill's voice chased after him as he neared the barn. Roach froze in his tracks, then wheeled about to face Curly Bill. Feet apart. Right hand placed for a quick draw. "What did you say?" he barked.

Curly Bill walked to Roach's horse drew Roach's rifle from the scabbard and held it at arm's length in front of him.

"I said, 'You forgot something'."

Defiant. Roach stood his ground. "Bring it to me!"

Curly Bill obliged. He walked at an even pace until he stood at arm's length from Roach.

"You forgot your rifle." With his left fist wrapped around the gun barrel, Curly Bill held it out for Roach to take.

Roach extended his right hand and grabbed it.

That was all the opening Curly Bill needed. With lightning speed, he gave a powerful tug on the barrel. Roach stumbled and Curly Bill's clenched right hand crashed full force just below his left temple. His knees buckled. His limp body slammed hard into the dirt. The air pushed from his lungs wheezed out like the sound of an accordion. He was knocked out; but not dead.

Roach never heard the words Curly Bill spoke over his sprawled out body but back at the house, Doc and Jimbo did.

"DON'T YOU EVER STAND AGAINST ME! EVER!"

CHAPTER NINE

Three men rode on in silence. A silence broken only by a temporary pause for spurs to signal a dismount and one man to search for a trail hidden among the rocks, and finding it, mounting again.

On they rode with the tenacity of a bloodhound combined with the caution of seasoned trackers.

At last Potter broke the silence with an utterance just above a whisper. "Any idea how much further?"

Jones pulled a crude map from his pocket. "By the look of things we are about two miles away from her brother's place if this map is accurate."

An autumn moon hung like a lantern in the southeastern sky, while the sun took its final fluorescent bow in the west.

Hickok grabbed the watch fob dangling from his vest pocket and found the watch at the end of it.

"Almost nine. I suggest we dismount, remove our spurs and go the rest of the way on foot."

"Agreed," Jones replied. "The one thing we don't want is to ride headlong into an ambush."

"Or have our spurs give us away," Potter said.

With spurs silenced and stuffed in saddlebags, they proceeded on foot; each leading his horse. Soon the trail wound around a sandy hill and at a quarter mile distant, the object of their search came into view. By now the sun had hidden itself and stars salted the darkened sky. For the benefit of the three men making their way in the darkness, a full moon illumined a house and nearby barn.

By the moonlight, Jones again looked at the map with Potter and Hickok peering over his shoulders.

Jones said, "Gentlemen, it looks like we found the Belt place."

Hickok removed a pair of field glasses from his saddlebag to take a closer look. "I can make out two men inside. No. Wait. There's three. One is tied to a chair," he said.

"Gimme a look," Jones said. Like Hickok, he focused on the house. "It's Doc alright."

"Any sign of Martha's brother?" Potter whispered.

"No. Just two men. One's a mountain of a man. Doc's their prisoner."

Jones handed the field glasses back to Wild Bill. "No one around the entrance to the barn," he said. He raised his eyes to the haymow where a brief red flame caught his attention. He refocused his field glass to look again. "There's someone standing in the hay loft." A pause. "And he's got a rifle. Must be from the city; he's smoking up there. Evidently he's got no sense that he could start a fire."

Potter said, "Can I see?"

Hickok handed him the field glasses.

"Sure enough," he said. "City kid alright."

Jones took a moment to study the scene the moon so generously lit for him.

"It's gonna take more firepower than we've got to set Doc

free. If we go a-chargin' in there, the white picket fence in front of the place will stop us before we can get to the house. And if we stop at the fence to regroup, the rifleman in the barn'll cut us to pieces in a cross-fire."

The sound of distant hoof-beats caught everyone's attention. They stood statue-like as two riders came in from the northwest and halted a pistol shot from the house.

"Hello, in the house!" one of the figures called out.

The house went dark. Jones watched. After a few moments the front door opened and a shadow appeared there.

"Who is it and what do you want? We're about to bed down for the night." the shadow at the door answered.

A tiny red glow descended from the haymow as the man cast off his cigarette in preparation for a fight.

"Is that you, Curly Bill?" a figure on horseback asked.

"Who's askin'?"

"It's Smitty!" he replied. "We're here to help ya secure yer new hideout."

"Come ahead," the figure in the door replied. "Okay, Roach, you can put yer rifle down."

"I hear ya!" the sentry in the haymow shouted.

Jones took another look with the field glasses. Two men rode up to the picket fence with two more riders between them.

"You're late," the man at door announced.

"Ya, we got a late start. Cincy told us to bring the Belts back here for safe keepin'."

Someone inside the house lit a lamp. The man at the door stepped aside as the two riders brought a man and a woman inside. The man from the haymow scurried across the yard and joined them all. The door closed.

"We're outnumbered five to three *and* they have three

hostages," Jones noted."No sense to be stupid about it. A willy-nilly attack'll get Doc or someone else all shot up."

"The good news is that Martha's brother and sister-in-law are still alive," Potter added.

"The bad news is that they are all held by desperate men and desperate men do desperate things," Wild Bill said. "We've got to come up with some way we can separate them from their hostages."

"And we aren't gonna get that done tonight," Jones responded. "So, let's make our way back to town. Gotta think this through."

With that thought on their minds, Jones led the three back to Sidney; a trip made easier by the light of an autumn moon.

Jones stayed the night in town, sleeping in Doc's office above Swede's Mercantile. The ride home along Lodgepole Creek would add an extra hour; the lateness of the hour dictated the change.

Fact is, he thought, *the place really hasn't been home since Sarah died.*

He'd done some work; cut trees, pulled stumps and, in general, enlarged the grounds, but the garden he took such pride in while Sarah was alive, was long abandoned and over-grown with weeds. The house needed a woman's touch, and at the present time, he had no interest in finding a second Mrs. Jesse Jones.

High, wispy clouds greeted the sun early the next morning with the smell of rain blowing in on a west wind. To the south, the tops of thunderheads stretched upward as high as one could see, bearing silent witness that somewhere rain fell and watered fields of ripened wheat.

Jesse Jones loved the smell of rain in the air. This morning the smell stirred memories of his childhood hundreds of miles back east long before the Civil War devastated his family and lots of others like his across five Aprils. He navigated the six block distance to Parson Abel's home on foot, arriving at 7 a.m. in time for breakfast.

Parson Abel greeted his arrival.

"Were you successful?" he asked.

"Yes and no," Jones replied following the Parson to the kitchen where the aroma of fried bacon, eggs, and coffee delighted Jones' olfactory.

"That's quite the non-committal answer," Abel interjected. "I'm sure Martha was expecting a more definitive one."

"I wish I had a better answer. What I can say is that her brother and his wife are still alive."

Martha arose from her chair at the breakfast table upon hearing the last. "You saw him?" Jones felt her grab him by the shoulders. He saw pleading in her eyes that matched that of her words.

"From a distance of forty yards, yes, I saw him."

"And...?"

"I wouldn't get my hopes too high just yet. Your brother is being held by five men. His wife is with him and by the looks of it; I'd say she has a little one coming."

Martha turned her joy toward Adeline Abel who was plating the eggs. "Did you hear that? I'm gonna be an aunt?"

Abel motioned Jones to seat himself, which he did.

"Now, let's not get the cart before the horse, dear. Jesse said your brother is held by some very vicious men," said Adeline.

"They are. These are five of Cincinnati Culver's men," said Jones.

Abel joined everyone around the table. "Cincy owns the

Last Chance Saloon at the east end of town. He's been going around trying to buy out everyone along Main Street."

"Including the business we own, Swede's Mercantile," Adeline announced. She handed a platter piled high with bacon to her husband and turned her back to the table to retrieve the eggs. "Start the bacon, if you please," she told him.

"To complicate things further, they've got Doc, too."

The shock of what Jones said did not take long for Adeline to absorb. "What?" she said.

Abel explained the business dealings to Martha. "Doc's a silent partner with the three of us here, along with Adam Potter. Few around town know that, but it seems Cincy does or else he would not be so anxious to include Doc in all of this. That does complicate things a bit."

At this point in the conversation everyone in the room heard a monstrous THUD!

"What on earth was that?" Martha inquired.

"My guess is that a bird found our picture window. Sometimes when the angle of the sun is just so, a bird flies into the window. I'll go take a look," said Adeline.

Moments later she returned with a puzzled look on her face. "Nothing," she said. "I don't understand."

Jones unholstered his LeMat. "We may have visitors," Jones said. "I want all of you to wait here while I check the front of the house." He pulled a small handgun from his boot and handed it to Parson Abel. "Know how to use one of these?"

"Been a while, but yes," he said. He gave the cylinder a spin to check his ammunition.

"Use it if you have to," Jones said. "I have a hunch Cincy is playing another card in his bid to get hold of Swede's."

With that Jones maneuvered through an unlit, narrow hallway, past the living room, where Adeline had moments before examined the plate glass picture window for a bird strike. He walked past Parson Abel's study, past the stairway, to the front door. Only silence greeted him.

No intruders, Jones reasoned. *That's a good thing.*

At the front door, Jones slid back the curtain a couple of inches and peaked around it for a view down the street. Nothing he saw looked out of place or unusual in any way. Holding his gun in his right hand, he reached for the doorknob with his left.

Someone's headed this way, he thought. *Someone's running.*

The sound of hurried footsteps drew nearer. Someone bounded the steps.

Jones ducked behind the door and waited. His body tensed for action. The doorknob turned in his hand and whoever was on the other side slowly pushed the door open. Jones crouched and backed up. He was coiled like a rattler ready to strike.

A hand. Jones saw a hand; a man's hand. He holstered his gun. *Better to take him alive.*

As if shot from a gun, Jones grabbed the hand, yanked the man inside and at same time spun him around. He pulled back his fist and smashed his gun hand into the man's face. There came a second THUD, not as loud as the first one, but a thud nonetheless, as the man fell to the floor, knocked senseless by Jones' fist.

Jones stood in the doorway before moving outside onto the veranda. No one else was there. No gunfire, just silence. He turned about to reenter the house when he saw something out of the corner of his eyes; an object embedded in the door. A knife not unlike the Bowie knife Custus Leverette once used to strike fear in the hearts of Sidney residents. There was a note slid up its blade. Jones grabbed it and pulled off the note and stepped back inside.

Parson Abel knelt beside the body of the man Jones had slugged.

"Help me roll him over, will ya, Jesse?" Parson Abel said.

Jones obliged and together the two rolled the man onto his back.

Abel raised the lantern he had brought to the scene and they stared in disbelief at the victim of Jones' wrath.

It was Adam Potter.

POTTER LAY on the settee with arms folded across his chest, looking like the occasional bad man displayed in the front window of the city morgue.

The good news was that he was not in the city morgue, but in the Abel's parlor. More importantly, this man was not dead but unconscious from Jones' hay-maker.

Adeline Abel held a cold wash cloth to Potter's forehead.

"He'll wake up soon enough, no sense fretting about it," Jones said.

"I'm trying to think of what to do now that Doc isn't here," she answered.

"Doc would use smelling salts," Parson Abel replied.

"Of course. Why didn't I think of that?" said Adeline.

Jones watched Adeline gather up wash cloth and basin and scurry from the room. Martha followed.

Abel's attention shifted to Jones and the note that an hour ago he plucked off the end of a knife. "Read that note again, will ya, now that the ladies are gone?"

Jesse read,

> *"Just so ya know we are holdin' Doc hostage. His release alive depends on what you do next. We're watchin' ya, so don't go blabbin' any of this to Sheriff Blanton. If you do, Doc's a dead man.*

And so is the couple whose house we're stayin' at. Do as we say and nobody gets hurt. First, sign over the deed to Swede's Mercantile to Cincinnati Culver. Second, bring the deed and one thousand dollars cash to the Belt homestead by three tomorrow afternoon. If'n you don't we'll kill each hostage one-by-one startin' with Doc. Remember, we're watchin' you, so don't try no dirty tricks."

A broad grin crossed Abel's face.

Jones noticed. "What's that grin for?" he asked.

"I find it amusing that the note warns us that they'll kill everybody and then warns *us* not to try any 'dirty tricks," Abel answered.

"Not finding it half as funny as you," Jones replied.

Parson Abel regained his composure. "The Lord will work things out to His glory. There's no doubt in my mind."

Jones made his way to the window and pulled back the curtains. "Sure enough," he said. "There's someone keeping an eye on the place."

Jones tipped his hat and the man in the street tipped his in return. "It's one of Cincy's men," Jones said.

"Why would anyone be watching our house?" said Adeline as she and Martha reentered the room. Adeline knelt beside Potter to apply smelling salts.

"You said earlier there was a note," Martha joined in. "Did it have anything to do with my brother?"

Her blue eyes implored Jones for an answer. She was so close to him now that there was no escaping her gaze.

How can I find the right words to tell her? Then, instead of fishing for the right words to say, he reached into his pocket, drew out the ransom note and handed it to her.

The room was silent except for Martha's sobs.

Adeline embraced her. "What is it, child?" she asked.

"They've got my brother and his wife Cynthia," Martha replied. "And they're threatening to kill them."

"Who is?"

"They've got Doc, too," Jones added.

"Who does?" Adeline asked. "Who's got Doc? Will someone please give me some answers?"

Martha handed the note to Adeline. Her mouth popped open in disbelief as she read.

"I've got to tell Doc's wife," she blurted out. "She's got to know about this."

Jones stopped her in her tracks. "This house is being watched," he said. "Better wait a minute or two."

"You are going to do something aren't you?" Martha asked.

"Yes, I'm going to do something, but I can't go running off half-cocked or someone's going to be killed. I need time to think this through."

"Ohhhhhhhhhh. My head." Potter moaned.

"The smelling salts are working their magic," said Abel.

Potter tried to sit up. "What happened?" he said.

"It's a long story," said Parson Abel. "Perhaps it would be best if Jesse explained it to you."

CHAPTER TEN

"So, you're saying that you thought I was trying to break in. Is that what you're saying," Potter snapped in disgust. "Couldn't you at least have looked and made sure before you belted me?"

"I couldn't take that chance. What if I'd opened the door and gotten a face full of someone's .44. Look, I can only say 'I'm sorry' so many times," said Jones.

"Gentlemen, let's cool our heels a bit," Parson Abel said interrupting the verbal feud. "I want you two to forgive each other and put this whole thing to rest. Jones, you're the one who whacked him. Apologize, and Potter you forgive him.

An indignant Jones replied. "I did that already!"

"I know," said Parson Abel. "Humor me. Do it again."

"I'm sorry." Jones fired off the words with no emotion behind them.

"That sounded more like you're sorry you got caught, rather than a real apology."

"C'mon, Parson," Jones pleaded. The stern look on Abel's face never changed.

"Alright." Jones faced Potter. "I'm sorry."

"Sorry for what?" Abel asked. "Tell him what you are sorry for?"

"I'm sorry I whacked ya."

"It's alright," Potter replied.

Abel stopped Potter short. "No, it isn't alright. That's not how you forgive someone."

Potter cast his eyes toward Adeline to seek her intervention. She turned away.

"Alright then, what do you want me to say?" Potter asked.

"You say, 'I forgive you as the Lord Jesus has forgiven me.' It's not that hard, you try it."

"I forgive you as the Lord Jesus has forgiven me," Potter said. "Is that better?"

"Much better. This town will never be civilized until we treat each other with value and respect," Abel noted.

"The only thing Cincinnati respects is the point of a gun," Jones noted.

"Let's pray that changes before someone else gets hurt," Abel added.

"In the mean time, we need to come up with a response to his ransom note."

"And my brother and his wife are right in the middle of all this," Martha interjected.

"And so is Doc," Potter said.

"And our very existence in the store," said Jones.

"I'm going to go out on a limb and say the very existence of Sidney as an entity.If one man can take over a city, then we're in big trouble," Parson Abel added.

"Parson, would you mind checking to see if our friend is still hanging out across the street?" Jones said.

Parson Abel made his way to the window and pulled back the drapes.

"He's not paying a whole lot of attention right now.Too busy rolling a cigarette. But, yep, he's still there."

Bam! Bam! Bam!

Pounding on the back door caught everyone except Abel off guard. He alone didn't panic. "I'll see who it is," he said.

"Here," Jones said, "take my pistol with you."

Abel waved him off. "I'm a man of the cloth, not a gunfighter."

Everyone in the Abel's parlor hid throughout the room. Jones mounted the stairs in the hall and secured himself a place on the landing; a place where he could watch the coming in and out of the parlor. He heard the sounds of conversation in the kitchen one flight below. The tone of the conversation was cordial. Moments later he heard the sound of two sets of footsteps moving down the hall and he peered over the banister to see Abel return with Bill Hickok. He joined them in the parlor.

"Ya got someone watching the place from across the street, so I thought I'd come in the back way," Hickok began. "They've got a lookout out front, but no one's covering the alley, 'cept someone's alley cat that I stepped on."

"What are you doing here in the first place? I thought you were leaving town on the morning stage," said Jones.

"I was, but as I was having breakfast in the Last Chance, I overheard talk of a ransom note. I thought maybe you could use some help."

Potter came out from hiding and sat on the settee. "You're right about that.We did get a ransom note. The deed to our store and a thousand bucks in exchange for Doc and the Belt's."

"So, what's the plan?" Hickok looked around from face-to-face—Jones, Parson Abel, Adeline, Martha, and Potter. "You're not thinking of giving in to their demands, are you?"

"I don't think we have much choice," Potter said. "We can't

exactly storm the Belt place. Going in with guns blazing is libel to get someone killed."

Martha was quick to endorse Potter comments. "My brother and sister-in-law for instance."

"You saw the place," Jones noted. "There'd be guns at every window as well as the rifle we saw in the barn to get us in their crossfire."

"What other choice do you figure we have? Well, I'm glad you asked. I could sneak in and take out the sniper in the barn," Hickok said.

"Still too risky," Jones answered him.

"What if..." Martha's voice trailed off into silence. Everyone eyed her and waited for her to finish the idea forming in her mind. "What if..." again she paused, but this time she finished her thought. "What if we had a hostage too?"

"By golly," Parson Abel joined in, "that just might work."

Jones put an arm around her shoulder. "This, my friends, is a woman with *brains* as well as beauty."

"ALRIGHT THEN, we're all agreed. The plan is to take Cincy hostage, ride him out hog-tied to the hideout and exchange his life for those of the others," Jones pronounced after an hour of haggling.

"Sounds simple enough," Adeline noted.

"It's like a lot of things in life. They sound simple in the saying, but are difficult in the doing," said Potter.

"Can we go over everything once more?" Jones asked. "Wild Bill, what's your assignment?"

The man thought for a moment and Jones thought he saw a twinkle in his eye as he spoke. "Sneak out the back and strike up a conversation with our *friend* out front and find out if

Cincy's in his office. If he is, light a cigarette as a signal to go after him."

Jones turned to Adam Potter. "Potter?" he asked.

"Get around to the stable and get our horses. Lease an extra horse for Cincy. Make my way to the back door of Cincy's office to join you there."

"What about me?" Martha asked.

"You're not going along," Jones said. "It's too dangerous."

"This whole thing was my idea, remember?"

"I remember," Jones said. "But you stay here and out of harm's way. I don't want to save your brother at the cost of your life."

Jones turned back to Hickok. "There's an additional part for you to play. After you're done out front, make your way to the Last Chance. Once inside, start a fight. That ruckus will be our cue for Potter and me to bust in the back door and take Cincy."

"Before everyone leaves," Abel said, "I'd like to ask God's blessings." Everyone stopped in their tracks and bowed their heads. "Oh, Lord, on what's about to happen, we ask for Your mighty hand of protection. Keep us safe and those for whom we care for but are hostages against their will. Amen."

HICKOK LEFT the house the way he came; through the back door and into the alley, and then took the long way around. He soon found himself a block south of the watchman in front of Abel's home. Hickok strolled past the man but was halted by him.

"Hey, yer Bill Hickok, ain't ya? I heard you was in town."

"I am. And who might you be?"

"My friends call me Curly Bill."

"Well, Curly Bill. I'm just passing through Sidney on my

way north. Heard there was action in a town up there called Deadwood."

"Heard of the place. But, we've got plenty of action here. Ever heard of the Last Chance?"

"Been there a couple of times, but the stakes aren't high enough for me. Ain't no fun taking money from farmers and businessmen who don't know how to play cards. I'm afraid I'm gonna have to ride north."

Hickok started to leave but was stopped again by Curly Bill. "My boss likes playing high-stakes poker. Maybe I could ask him to play you. What do you say? I mean, what more have you got to lose than another day in this little stink hole?"

"And who might yer boss be?"

"Goes by the name of Cincinnati Culver. He owns the Last Chance."

"Never heard of him. 'Cides, I doubt if he has the kind of money to put up a stake that I like to play for."

"Well," said Curly Bill, "let's just go over to the Last Chance and ask him. Ya ain't out nothin' fer askin'."

Hickok reflected on the offer for a moment. "Alright," he said, "Let's do that.Assuming he's in town." He turned to face Curly Bill. "So help me if yer leading me on a wild goose chase and this--what did you say his name was?"

"Cincinnati."

"If this 'Cincinnati' fella of yours isn't available and I find you've wasted my time, you and me are gonna have it out right here in the streets of Sidney. Do I make myself very clear?"

Curly Bill let out an audible gulp. "He's here. I saw him in his office not more than two hours ago."

Hickok answered. "A lot can happen in two hours."

Curly nervously reached for his tobacco pouch and paper. All the while Hickok monitored his every move. Suddenly, a smile flashed under his moustache to reveal the scar on his upper lip.

"Would you mind rolling one of those for me?" he asked.

Curly Bill's match lit more than Hickok's cigarette. It lit an invisible fuse that set in motion the second phase of the plan Martha conceived in Parson Abel's parlor.

MARTHA WATCHED Potter and Jones exit through the back door and disappear in the alley, Potter turning right and heading to the stable and Jones to the left to cover the back door of the Last Chance. She closed the door and bolted it.Even so, she moved the curtains and maintained her gaze upon the alley.

"Come away from the window, my dear. You can't help them and it does no good to worry when men go off to fight."

Martha came to the table and sat beside Adeline. "I'm concerned for my brother," she said.

"As we all are. We have to trust that God provided the plan and He alone will see to it that everyone is safe." Adeline poured tea and sat a cup in front of Martha, who added sugar and stirred.

After taking a sip Martha asked, "What kind a man is Jones?"

"I'm not sure what you're asking? Are you asking if he is dependable?"

"I guess so?"

"Then my answer would have to be yes. He came to us a few years ago having spent time in the army. He was married once, if that question has crossed your mind. His first wife was murdered. He and Potter rode after the murderer."

"Did he kill him?"

"No, my dear, he didn't. Fought him in the street just a few blocks from here.Had him on the ground, too, choking him to death, when my husband called him to remember the words 'Justice is mine,' saith the Lord.'"

Martha was confused and her confusion caught Adeline's attention. "It's a long story, Martha. I'll tell it to you sometime. Anyway Jesse let the man go and walked away, but the man pulled a knife and was about to throw it into Jesse's back when a Cheyenne warrior put an arrow into him."

"He's never remarried?"

"Nope. He and his first wife had a place along Lodgepole Creek, but I don't think he's been back there in a while. Too many memories, I suppose. Since her death he's stayed mostly in town working as an owner and shopkeeper at Swede's and occasionally helping Sheriff Blanton keep the peace. I'd say that if there is anyone who could rescue your brother and his wife, it would be Jones. To say nothin' about our cantankerous and beloved town quack."

Adeline sipped her tea. "Does that answer your question about Jesse's dependability?"

Martha nodded.

BILL HICKOK FOLLOWED Curly into the Last Chance. The seedy exterior of the place gave way to an even seedier interior. Two-bit ladies of the evening prowled the place like coyotes on the hunt. For some reason Hickok noticed things that he had not noticed when he was there earlier. Tonight the ambiance was different; the kerosene lights were lowered to create a trance-like hue. Cowboys of every size, shape and complexion dotted the room and occupied every nook and cranny from bar to gambling table. A tinny upright piano, riddled with bullet holes, gave musical underscore to the bar and the events within.

"Wait here and I'll see if Cincy can break away to appease your appetite to lose money," Curly barked out over the noise. "Tell Fred at the bar that I said it's ok to pour you a whisky." Curly exited through a side door and disappeared.

At the end of the bar a young man kept fooling around with his six-shooter.He drew and pointed it at everyone. Hickok strolled in his direction. The nearer Hickok got the louder the young man's laughter toward those who cowered when he pointed the barrel of his revolver at them. The spot next to the young man was open at the bar and Hickok filled it.

"Fred?" Wild Bill said. The sound of his name brought the bartender. "Curly Bill says that it's ok for you to serve me a whiskey. I've got an appointment with Cincy to play cards."

Fred obliged. He poured a shot glass three-quarters full and slid it in front of Hickok.

"Thanks," said Hickok. He tossed back the drink. It ran warm down his throat.

The young man noticed him, exactly what Hickok wanted to happen when he chose this place at the bar. Hickok turned his head to his left and found himself nose to barrel with the young man's revolver. Above that barrel hazel eyes laughed.

"Bill Hickok ain't it?" the youngster said.

"It is, son," said Hickok. "I'd appreciate it if you didn't poke your gun in my face. It could go off."

"Naw, it won't." This reply came with a loud laugh. "It can't go off. I ain't cocked it. What ya scared of?"

"Didn't your pa teach ya nothin' about guns? Don't point them at anyone unless you're prepared to use it," Hickok said.

"So, yer sayin' that my pa never taught me nothin.' Is that what yer sayin', mister fancy vest?"

With an easy swipe Wild Bill removed the weapon from his face. In anger the young man holstered his gun.

"Now, if you don't mind, I'd like another drink." Fred responded with a second pour like the first, but before Hickok could put it to his lips, the young man's left arm swatted the shot glass to the floor.

The shattering glass drew attention just like Hickok hoped it would. With lightning speed Hickok unleashed one of his ivory-handled Colt Navy revolvers and pressed the barrel into the young man's forehead, cocking it as he did.

"You owe me a drink, son!" he shouted.

Beads of sweat formed on the young man's hairline. Hickok saw a barmaid scamper through the door where Curly had disappeared mere moments ago.

"Don't shoot," a voice with authority yelled. A man's figure loomed in the doorway. It was Cincinnati. "Don't shoot," he barked. "I don't want blood on the floor in here!"

Cincinnati walked toward Hickok.

Cincy's back door burst wide-open behind him.

Jones shouted, "Grab Cincy and let's get out of here."

The young gunman knocked Hickok's gun away. A bullet slammed into the ceiling.

Confusion reigned. In the gun smoke, Cincy and the young gunman sprang through the front door and into the street.

Hickok did not fire for fear of hitting an innocent bystander.

Jones and Potter emerged holding someone between them—the stranger who once stood across the street from the Abel's—Cincy's taskmaster, Curly Bill.

CHAPTER ELEVEN

Outside the Belt home a rooster crowed to welcome a splinter of light in the east.

Inside, Doc stirred. His arms and legs ached.

"Don't you think you can untie me now?" Doc asked. "My hands and feet are going numb. That means you're cutting off the circulation."

"Untie Doc!" Jimbo commanded. He stood to add emphasis to his command.

A knife flashed and for the first time in hours Doc felt the blood surge to his extremities. He clinched his fist several times to restore the feeling. Trying to stand was much more difficult. He pushed off on the side of the chair and wobbled his way erect.

"Thought there for a second that I'd become a permanent part of the chair," Doc chuckled. "How about untying the couple you brought in last night? My guess is that they've been tied up even longer than I have."

"Roach, see to it, will ya? I'll keep my gun on Doc, so he won't go nowhere," one of the men ordered.

Doc noted that the man he called Roach wore a droopy moustache and had steel-grey eyes. He wore his gun low on his hip and the straps of his holster were tied around his thigh.

A gunslinger.

Roach complied with his order and soon a man in his early thirties by Doc's estimation, and a woman emerged from what Doc guessed was a bedroom. Both found it difficult to stand after spending the night strapped to chairs.

Jimbo plopped back down at the table. "Breakfast!" he barked.

"Any of you men know how to cook?" the man in charge asked.

"Don't look at me, boss," said Roach. "'Sides, I got hired for my gun, not my cookin'.

"Ma'am," the man in charge said, "this is your place. How about rustlin' up some grub?"

"Cynthia," her husband responded. "You don't have to cook for these men."

Roach patted his revolver. "This says she does," he said. "What do you say, Snider? You're the man in charge here."

"Ma'am," Snider said. "I ain't orderin', but I am asking."

"If you're askin'," Cynthia said, "then I need some eggs. Got layin' hens out back."

"Roach, take the lady out to the hen house," said Snider.

The young man made a move to protect his wife, but Jimbo stopped him.

"And Roach?" Snider said.

The gunman turned to him.

"Keep yer hands to yerself. Do I make myself clear?"

"Yes, boss," Roach replied.

Doc watched Cynthia take a wire basket from near the door and go outside. Roach followed. His gaze remained fixed on her backside.

"If I were you I'd keep my eyes on that one," Doc noted.

Snider moseyed to the door then out onto the porch. It was obvious to Doc that Snider felt the same way he did. This was no time to have the fox guard the henhouse.

Jimbo left his place at the table to scour the cabinets for food. He was hungry and impatient.

"You must be Doc Hardesty," said the young man.

"I am," Doc said. "And if I can venture a guess, you must be Martha's brother."

"You know my sister? How is she?"

"Fine. Fine. She's doing just fine. Got to Sidney about a week ago."

"Cynthia and I were supposed to meet her, but these thugs took us hostage. Oh, by the way, my name's Brody."

They shook hands.

"Well, Brody. It looks like we're all in the same predicament."

"I've been thinking," Brody whispered. "If we could just get to the storm cellar."

"What do you have in mind?"

"Got food in there and a secure lock on the inside. We could hole up for several days until help arrived. Dug it to protect us from tornados and strong storms. Used it once last year."

"Yeah, and these men are equally as dangerous."

"I was thinkin' the same thing."

"Is there another way out of the house besides the front door?" Doc asked.

"Out the bedroom window. That might be a good option if they leave us untied tonight."

"Wouldn't count on that," Doc said.

The screen door flew open and in walked Cincinnati Culver and the kid.

"What are you doing here?" Jimbo asked. "Did Jones give in that fast?"

"Wish that was the case, but it ain't. Me and the kid have been on the run since about nine last night. Jones raided my place and took Curly Bill hostage. We had to hoof it in the dark and we nearly lost our way. Thought we'd never get here."

Cincy took in the scene and noticed something missing. "Where's the girl?"

"Gatherin' eggs for breakfast," Jimbo replied. "I'm hungry!"

"When aren't you hungry, my friend?" Cincy laughed out the words.

Cincy sat at the table, took off his boots and rubbed his aching feet. "What about Roach and Snider?"

"Roach is watchin' the girl. Snider's watchin' Roach," Jimbo said.

"That makes sense when it comes to Roach and women," Cincy said.

Doc couldn't help but take advantage of the situation that faced him and poked the bear by asking Cincy, "What are you gonna do with us? Your plans been shot full of holes. Now what? Jones is coming after ya, you know?

"If he does and the shootin' starts you'll be the first to die. I'll see to it," Cincinnati said.

"What happens to me is the least of your worries with Jones on your tail."

"Jimbo, will take these two into the other room? I can't deal with this right now," said Cincy.

Jimbo did as he was asked, putting Doc and Brody in the bedroom.

"That worked out rather well," Brody said.

"Better than I thought. But let's not get our hopes up too high. There are two of them outside and they still have your wife."

Brody went directly to the window and raised it. Fresh morning air flowed in.

"Cindy and I agreed that if there was any trouble the first thing one or both of us would do was to get into the storm cellar and lock the door," Brody said. "I'm not sure how she'll do it, but I'm guessin' she'll find some way to get into the cellar."

Brody climbed out the opening and then helped Doc to do the same.

"I'm getting too old for this," Doc said.

Brody stopped him short. "Keep your voice down, if we get caught chances are you won't be getting' any older."

"Guess I never thought of that," Doc replied in a whisper.

JONES TURNED a couple of crates over in the backroom of Swede's and sat on one of them. He motioned his captive from the Last Chance to join him, but the man had little interest in doing so. He glared back at Jones and stood with arms folded across his chest.

Potter grabbed him by the shoulders and forced him down.

"You know," Hickok said. "We could all get along a lot better if you'd cooperate."

No answer.

"We know that you work for Cincy," he continued, "and that he's holding Doc and a young couple by the name of Belt hostage."

Still no answer.

Potter drew his revolver and snuggled it beside the man's temple. His right thumb pulled the hammer back and clicked it into place.

"Adam, there's no need for gunplay."

"Curly," the man said. "They call me Curly Bill."

"Now you see, Adam. There was no need to draw your gun. Curly Bill here intended to cooperate, didn't you Curly Bill?"

He nodded.

Potter withdrew his pistol from the side of Curly Bill's head, eased the hammer down and holstered it.

"Tell us about Cincy's hideout, Curly Bill." Sarcasm dripped from Hickok's words.

"Cincy's holding the hostages on the Belt's farm several miles east of town. It's a two story house so he'll have gunmen on both levels and across the way in the hayloft. Anybody walks on the place will get cut to pieces. Ride in with guns drawn and the hostages get it first."

Hickok leaned in, his face inches from Curly Bill's. "You are our ticket in."

"Cincy will kill me if I do."

"And we'll kill you if you don't. Where I come from in Kansas it's called a Mexican standoff," Hickok said.

Jones joined in. "It's kind of like yer dead if ya do or yer dead if ya don't." He took Curly by the collar and stood him up. "Potter, would you do me a favor and escort our friend here to Sheriff Blanton's office? I'm sure he'd be delighted to keep him for us overnight. Tell him that we'll come by in the morning and ask him if he'd like to ride out to the Belt place with us."

After Potter led Curly away, Jones and Hickok continued to talk.

Jones led off. "Curly's familiar with the Belt farm alright. He described everything like we saw it a couple of days ago."

"Sure 'nuff did," Hickok added. "Right down to the rifleman in the barn."

"And by now Cincy's gotta know that we have an ace up our sleeve in Curly Bill," Jones said. "That is, of course, unless Curly is expendable."

"Do you think Cincy would kill his own foreman?" Potter asked.

"Cincy's a desperate man and he's just seen his plan blown up in his face," said Jones.

"Then," Hickok began, "the question is how we convince Curly that he's expendable and his life counts for nothing in Cincy's eyes."

"I think we start by getting word to Cincy that Curly's in jail and seeing how he reacts."

"While at the same time protecting Curly's life and doing it so neither party knows what we're up to," Hickok added.

The corners of Jones' mouth curled up into a smile. "What do you think of this? Why don't you go back to the Last Chance for a beer and casually let it slip that Curly's singing like a magpie, while I set everything up in the jail."

"I'll meet up with you at the jail in a couple of hours," said Hickok.

DOC FOLLOWED Brody to the northeast corner of his home. There, between the house and the barn stood a hen house surrounded by fencing to keep out the foxes so prevalent in the area. From there the two men saw Cynthia had completed her egg gathering and emerged basket in hand from the hen house under the watchful eye of Roach who had situated himself inside the fence. Snider stood twenty yards away. Doc could see that his mind was elsewhere and not really on Roach at all.

"Let me help you with them eggs," Roach insisted and took the basket.

To Doc's surprise a quail whistled nearby, with its distinctive 'bob-white' call. Doc turned to find the source. Not a real quail but Brody's imitation and *a darned good one,* Doc thought.

Cynthia heard it too and like Doc turned in the direction of the whistle. Thankfully, Roach didn't. He walked through the gate and closed it behind him.

Brody peered tentatively from behind the house. Doc saw him mouth the words 'storm shelter.' Cynthia nodded in reply.

"I'll be in in a minute to cook breakfast," Cynthia yelled at her captors, "the privy is calling my name."

"I'll wait out here for ya," the men heard Roach call back.

"No, ya won't either," barked Snider. "Can't a lady even go in peace? For Pete's sake what's come over you?"

"Come down here and say that to my face," Roach yelled. "Do you hear me? Come back here and slap leather. No one yells at me!" he screamed.

Snider must have overheard everything. His voice rang clarion clear. "Roach, you get yer butt in here! That's enough of you always wanting someone to draw down on ya!"

That was the break Cynthia needed. She raced into her husband's waiting arms.

"Let's skedaddle to the storm cellar," Body said. "We'll be safe there."

In minutes the three were down the steps and behind the bolted door of the Belt's storm shelter where a single candle illuminated the space.

"We'll be safe in here until help arrives," said Brody.

"Won't we run out of air in here?" Doc asked.

"Already thought of that, Doc," Brody said. "Dug an underground tunnel and vented it about a quarter mile away near the creek. No one will find it unless they know exactly where to look."

Cincy's entire body shook with anger.

"What do you mean you can't find the girl?" he growled. "She didn't just disappear."

"All I know," said Snider, "is that Roach has looked for her everywhere."

"Did you check in the barn? In the chicken coup? Are all of our horses still tied in the front of the house?"

"Yes," Snider answered.

"To which of my questions are you answering 'yes'?"

"All of 'em. The missus can't be found."

"Jimbo, go grab her husband from the other room. We'll make her come out of hiding or I'll kill him," Cincy said.

"What about my breakfast?" Jimbo asked.

"I know you're hungry and the sooner we find the girl the sooner you can have your eggs," Cincinnati said.

With reluctance Jimbo left the others and entered the bedroom. Cincy noticed the suddenness of his return.

"There ain't no one in there," Jimbo said.

"What do you mean, 'there ain't no one in there?'" Cincy asked.

"Well, there just ain't. No husband and no Doc neither," said Jimbo.

Cincy went to see for himself. The result was just as Jimbo's words described it—there wasn't anyone in the room. Cincy felt his knees buckle under him and he did everything he could to prevent himself from dropping to the floor. His carefully devised plan of hostage-taking and deed-getting evaporated like fog on a sunny day.

One moment it was all within easy reach. Now, all my leverage is gone. How is this possible? People don't just disappear.

"Spread out," he told his men, "Don't come back until you find all three of them."

The men hesitated not knowing where to start.

"Out, I said. Do your jobs or you're all fired."

Late that afternoon Cincy watched a buckboard come over the ridge about a mile from where he stood on the Belt's front porch. It wove its dusty way onto the property and swung around in front of where Cincy stood.

"What are you doing coming out here, Nellie?" he asked.

"Got news from the bar for ya," she replied while pulling up on the front of her dress that had sagged to reveal her ample bosom. "Bill Hickok was in the place a while ago and let slip that the Sheriff's holding Curly Bill and that Curly's throwin' you under the wagon, so to speak."

"Doggone it. It's always somethin' that prevents a guy like me from making an honest living."

CHAPTER TWELVE

Darkness shrouded Sidney in its nightly cocoon. Jones noticed that, per usual, only the lights from inside the plethora of taverns and brothels illumined the street giving ample light to walk, if one chose to do that. Gunfire occasionally lit the street as well. When horseplay turned to gunplay blood spilled and men died at the point of a gun.

This will be another busy night for Sheriff Blanton and his deputies; riding herd on a town that grew up too fast. Someday Sidney will grow up and settle down thanks to men like Parson Abel. Men like Cincy can only hold the reins for so long.

Jones rounded the corner and made his way to Blanton's office and knocked. The deadbolt clinked and the heavy door squeaked open.

"Might want to oil those hinges," Jones pronounced as he entered.

"'Fraid I got bigger fish to fry," Blanton replied from behind his massive desk. "Rumor has it that one of Cincy's men is back in town. A man named Roach. My sources say he's tossing down whiskey at the Last Chance. Sounds like he's liquoring himself up for what Cincy's sent him to do."

"Sounds like..." Jones replied. "Best get a move on then before he does what's he's come into town to do."

"You still think he's comin' after Curly Bill?"

"I'd stake my reputation on it. Saw Nellie ride out of town in a buckboard this afternoon."

"So, if Roach is back in town that means that Cincy's taken the bait."

"Yep."

Blanton came from behind his desk. He stopped only long enough to draw his handgun and check the cylinder. Five cartridges stared back at him.

"Ya got only five in there?" Jones asked.

"Sure do. I like my hammer to rest on an empty cylinder so I don't shoot myself in the foot. Then when I cock the hammer the cylinder rolls to a live round. Somethin' my daddy taught me when I was a kid. Noticed that you still pack a LeMat."

"Firing nine rounds before I reload comes in handy sometimes, and I like the added wallop of a shotgun round," said Jones.

"Hope neither of us has to light these candles tonight," Blanton said.

"Wouldn't count on it," Jones replied.

Blanton removed the cell keys from their peg near the oak door that separated the front of his office from the jail cells. The key turned and the lock clicked.Blanton turned the doorknob and opened the door sending what little light there was in his office scurrying down the hallway.

"Time to get up, Curly. We're movin' you to a safer location," Blanton commanded.

A form stirred on the bunk in the second cell from the door.

"What's the big idea of wakin' me up?" the form asked.

"Time to move ya, Curly Bill," Blanton said. "One of yer friends is in town and I'm betting that he's here to put a bullet in you."

Curly sat up. "Cincy would never do that."

"He would if he thought you were spilling yer guts and telling us everything he's got planned," said Blanton.

"And that's exactly what he thinks. We've already seen to it," Jones added. "That's why Roach is in town liquoring himself up at the Last Chance."

Curly Bill stood up and grabbed the cell bars. "Still say that Cincy wouldn't send someone to gun me down in cold blood."

Blanton turned to Jones. "Keep me covered while I get him outta here."

Jones obliged and leveled his La Mat at Curly's chest. Blanton opened the cell, handcuffed Curly's hands behind him, and led him past Jones and into the outer office. Jones took a few minutes to remake Curly's bed. He arranged the covers to look like Curly was snuggled under them before he pulled the cell door closed and locked it.

"That should do it," Jones said when he rejoined Blanton and Curly. "Let's get him out of here."

"Where are you taking me?" Curly asked.

"Across the street to the Moore Hotel. Got a room for you up on the second floor," Sheriff Blanton answered.

Jones doused the lone candle that lit the room, drew his LeMat, and opened the front door. He stepped out alone and surveyed the street. He found no one in sight except Potter whose rifle barrel came into view on the second floor balcony of the Moore Hotel. The moon shone on it when wispy clouds moved out of the way.

"All clear," Jones said.

A few moments later Sheriff Blanton followed Curly

through the door. They walked at a brisk pace through the street and into the hotel lobby.

"Keys!" Blanton said to the night attendant. The man fumbled for the key, found it, and tossed it to Blanton who snatched it out of the air and responded with a polite, "Thank you."

Blanton's revolver urged Curly to climb the curved stairway that led to the second floor. Jones covered their rear, his revolver aimed at the lobby and the front door as he did.

Once in the room, Blanton forced Curly to sit on the bed. Only the light from the gas lantern in the hall illuminated the room. Blanton removed the handcuff from Curly's right hand and locked it around the bedpost. When he finished securing Curly, Blanton bent down to his level and said, "Now, I want you to be as quiet as a church mouse. One scream...just one... and your brains will be splattered all over this room.

"Understand?" said Jones.

"Now all we can do is wait," said Blanton. Blanton sat the chair nearest the window and watched the ebb and flow of life on the streets of Sidney.

Jones left the room and closed the door behind him. He asked the night attendant to dim the lobby lights and he pulled up a chair by the window. His eyes scanned Blanton's office across the street. In his right hand he held his pistol.

The chime of the hotel's grandfather clock marked the passing of each hour; one o'clock and then two. Jones was sure that by now the local bars had announced "last call" for he saw them empty their human contents into streets and alleys. Cowboys rode away. Gamblers grabbed their earnings, the winners, that is. The losers snuck home with their tails between their legs confessing that for some reason Lady Luck had not smiled on them tonight, but certainly she would tomorrow. Bar owners locked their establishments and doused their lights deepening the darkness, although ten-thousand stars twinkled above. All the while, 'the man in the moon' smiled down.

A single chime marked half past two when a shadow slipped into the alley between the jail and the nearby leather goods store. Jones could not make out the identity. Whoever owned this shadow had slid the brow of his Stetson over his eyes. Jones' body went from one of leisure to high alert in an instant. He rose from his chair, went to the door, and opened it slow enough that the bell over the door did not jingle.

Two gunshots, one after the other broke the silence. Moments later the shadowy figure returned from the alley and scampered down the wooden sidewalk in front of the leather goods store.

Jones fired three times. Two bullets thudded into wood. Jones could tell by the distinctive sound each made. The third smashed glass. Three shots. Three misses.

Overhead Potter's Winchester opened up with the same results as Jones—close but all misses.

Townsfolk jarred awake by gunfire flowed into the street.

"What the heck is going on out here?" someone clamored for answers.

Sheriff Blanton ran down the stairs and into the street ahead of Jones and Potter.

"It's alright folks. Go on back to bed. We just had someone shoot into the jail."

Satisfied with Blanton's answer the people seemed to evaporate before Jones' eyes; all but Ned Blankenship who was not at all happy that a bullet had shattered his window and damaged some merchandise. Blankenship erupted into Blanton and only relented after the sheriff promised to come in tomorrow and make restitution for Ned's property.

"Did anyone get a good look at who fired the shots into the jail?" Blanton asked at last.

"I only saw a shadow," Jones replied.

"Me, too," said Potter.

Pounding hooves nearby signaled that the intruder had mounted and was making a hurried get away.

"Too late!" Jones noted.

"Well, we sure played our cards right tonight," Blanton announced. "We would have a dead hostage on our hands had we not taken Curly to the Moore Hotel for the night."

"Toss me your handcuff keys," said Jones. "I'll go get Curly Bill so he can see first-hand just how popular he is with Cincy now that he's in our custody."

Jones found Curly Bill wide awake, his eyes as big as saucers. "Were those first two bullets meant for me?" he asked.

Jones unlocked Curly from the bed and clamped the open cuff around his own left wrist, keeping his gun hand free. "I'm gonna say they were, but let's go get a looky-see to be sure." Jones watched as Potter slid down the alley where the shots had come from.

It did not take long before Blanton's keys granted access to the cell where Curly had once laid. In his place a bedroll with two bullet holes in it.

Potter appeared at the window opposite of what had been Curly Bill's cell."Whoever did the shooting moved a rain barrel into place and climbed on it," he said. "Looks like whoever it was twisted his ankle when he jumped down. He's dragging his left leg."

"Aren't you glad we moved you to the hotel? The bedroll took the bullets meant for you," Blanton said.

"Had I not cooperated," Curly Bill replied, "the bedroll would have been me."

Curly Bill sat at the table in Sheriff Blanton's office. All hesitation to discuss Cincinnati's plans to control Sidney vanished with gunshots in the early morning hours. Jones and Blanton asked the questions. Potter wrote everything down, and Hickok served as lookout in case any of Cincy's men came back to check on the results of their assassination attempt.

"Cincy's got relatives back east," Curly said. "Whoever it is must be high up in the government or Bureau of Indian Affairs or somethin'."

"What makes you say that?" Jones asked.

"Because whoever it is knows the when and where of Custer and the Seventh Cavalry and their planned ride into the Badlands in search of gold."

"Some of us already know there's gold there." Blanton shot a look toward Jones who nodded.

"Yea, but can you imagine the impact such an official announcement will have?" Curly Bill continued. "Miners and prospectors will flock to the Hills. They'll arrive by train, the quickest way west, and ride the rails to the closest railhead to the gold fields...Sidney, Nebraska."

From the front window Hickok saw the town waking up. The seven o'clock stagecoach rattled by only a few minutes late. Wild Bill joined in the conversation. "And owning a saloon or store of any kind will be a license to print money."

"Cincy's been talking about a freight line and a stage line between Sidney and Deadwood. And I've heard talk of an engineer named Henry Clarke planning a bridge over the North Platte River. If he made that a toll bridge, think of the money that would roll in."

"How do you know all this?" said Blanton.

Curly said, "Know it first-hand. Clarke talked to Cincy last week in his quest for investors. I was in Cincy's office when they met. I saw Cincy give him fifty thousand dollars as a down payment on a ten percent stake in the bridge."

"It's no wonder Cincy's desperate to get his hands on Swede's and any other business in town," Blanton said.

"He already owns a stake in the Moore Hotel across the street and a couple of the other saloons in town," Curly said. "He's wasting no time in getting ahead of the game. He aims to control half of the town by the end of the year and all of it by seventy-four when Custer heads into the Black Hills."

"So, what do you think Cincy's next move will be with the hostages now that we have you?" Hickok asked.

"I think the hostages are safe as long as Cincy thinks he killed me. If he thinks I'm dead he'll reopen negotiations. As long as I'm alive I'm the fly in his ointment."

Jones turned to Potter. "Are you thinking what I'm thinking? We need to arrange a funeral so that everyone thinks Curly Bill is dead. It's the only way we can keep our advantage."

"Then the fly in Cincy's ointment becomes the ace up our sleeve," Potter noted with a grin.

"I like your turn of a phrase," Jones said. "Now all we have to do is convince Parson Abel to do a funeral for a man who isn't dead yet."

Adeline Abel led Jones into the parlor where they found the Parson hunched over his desk. "Someone you know to see you, dear," she said. "I'll leave you two men alone, I'm sure you have business to discuss."

Abel pushed away from the desk and extended a hand. "Jones, what a pleasant surprise."

"Good to see you too," Jones said. "Am I interrupting anything?"

"Only a sermon that doesn't want to be written quite yet." He motioned for Jones to sit down. "Sit. Sit," he said. "Any word on the hostages?"

"You knew we have Curly Bill, Cincinnati's right hand man?"

"I heard," said Abel. "I also heard there was some gunplay at the jail this morning."

"Curly's still alive, but I don't think we want Cincy to know that. We want him to think he still has the upper hand. That will keep the hostages alive," Jones said.

"Where do I fit in? You wouldn't be here if I did not have some role to play in this little drama," Abel said.

"Have you ever done a funeral for someone who wasn't dead?"

Abel thought a moment: "Not that I can think of. Why?"

"We were thinking that if we want Cincy to think Curly Bill is dead, then the best way to do that is to have a funeral for him."

"Well, if I was looking for a new adventure, this would certainly be it...doing a funeral for someone who isn't dead." He paused for a moment. "I like it. I like it a lot."

Martha Belt burst into the room and confronted Jones.

"What's the latest on my brother and his wife?"

"The information we're getting," Jones said, "is that both are still alive. The same goes for Doc. Right now, Parson Abel and I are working on a plan to keep them all alive. Your brother's place has been fortified and if we ride in there we'll all be killed. For that matter, Cincy would most likely kill all the hostages first. We've got to come up with a way to lure everyone away, so we can make a rescue on our own terms."

"Trust in the Lord, Martha," Parson Abel said. "We've all got to pray to God for His deliverance from evil."

CHAPTER THIRTEEN

Inside the cellar Doc shivered from the cool, dampness of the earth surrounding him. His mind played back memories of younger days in rural Ohio before the War. His grandfather and uncles had joined his dad in digging out a root cellar where his mother stored potatoes and hung up freshly pulled onions.

"I remember the worst spanking I ever got in my life was on account of a root cellar like this one," Doc said aloud.

Cynthia Belt pressed Doc for more of the story and Doc warmed up to it at her invitation.

"I was about seven or eight, as I recall. My mother had cold packed some beef—we called it 'canned beef'—and set it in the cellar with a warning to my older brother and me not to get into it."

"But you got into it anyway?" Cynthia chimed in.

Doc nodded. "Yep. We got into it anyway." He paused to let the recollection catch up with his words. "Ma went into town a couple of days later. Pa had hitched up a team to bust up a new ten acres of sod. A long about noon Ma had not returned yet and Pa was still in the field, and my brother and I were hungry. So he talked me into going to the cellar to retrieve some of the canned beef. We pried open the jar and helped ourselves. Days later, Ma went to root cellar to get some onions and happened to notice a jar of beef missing in one of the stacks. Ma kept track of everything she put down there. She confronted my brother and me. There wasn't any sense to lie to Ma. Although I put the blame on Edgar, my brother, both of us got paddled that day."

"Yer ma didn't say, 'Wait 'til yer father gets home' like my ma used to? You got spanked on the spot?" Brody asked.

"Ma never waited. She took discipline into her own hands. When Pa got home she told him what had happened and we got it again."

"Would you like some canned beef now?" Cynthia offered.

"I'd love some," Doc said. He took the jar from Cynthia. "Just for old times' sake."

The room filled with laughter which they quickly stifled at the sound of approaching footsteps.

Brody put a finger to his lips. "Shh," he said. He blew out the lone candle, plunging the room into complete darkness.

The doorknob turned, but the door did not yield.

In the darkened chamber, Doc heard breathing quicken.

He whispered, "Don't panic. Breathe through your nose and don't move."

Thud! Thud! Thud!

Someone pounded on the oak door—*the dividing line between life and death,* thought Doc.

The doorknob turned repeatedly, followed by the sound of a heavy body slamming against the door.

It did not yield.

From the other side of the door came Roach's voice. "If

they're in there, all we gotta do is wait 'em out. They ain't goin' nowhere."

The sound of footsteps disappeared and quiet returned.

For what seemed hours, no one in the root cellar dared move. Nothing was heard within but their breathing; nothing was smelled but their own sweat.

Doc broke the silence with a whisper. "Is it ok if I have my canned beef now?"

Brody struck a match and the flickering flame lit a candle to push back the darkness. "I built this cellar to withstand a storm and it did," he said.

Cynthia hugged him like she would never let him go. "Let's not have another storm like that," she said. Brody kissed her forehead.

"We ain't out of the woods yet," Doc said. "But the good news is that we are safe for now. They don't know for sure that we're in here. And that's a good thing."

The sun completed its trek across the sky and gave way to darkness not unlike what Doc experienced in the root cellar. Before it gave way, however, streams of purple, orange, and brilliant red shot skyward to produce a sunset of magnificent beauty.

Jesse Jones watched the sunset from the front porch of the Abel's home. Like Doc, memories stirred within him as he rocked back and forth, alone, on the front porch swing.

It was here Sarah and I fell in love. If only she were here to see this sunset. And our baby, the one Custus stole from me when he killed my sweet Sarah—would be about two years old. A single tear raced down his cheek.

Martha Belt joined him on the porch.

"They told me you'd be out here," she said. "May I join you?" Martha did not wait for Jesse's reply. She sat beside him. "Would you look at that sunset. One of the most beautiful I've seen in a while."

He answered without taking his eyes off of the sunset. "It is."

"Do you sit out here often in the evening?"

"Not very often. Too many memories," Jesse said.

"Am I interrupting those memories? Do you want me to go back inside?"

"It's alright," he said. "I don't mind the company tonight."

They rocked in silence and watched the sun finish its light show.

Martha broke that silence. "Would you mind me asking what happened? The Parson says your wife was murdered."

"She was. A man named Custus Leverette took her life and the life of the baby she was carrying."

"I'm so sorry." She gently touched his arm.

Jesse pushed back his hat and rubbed his chin. "It still hurts."

"I can't even imagine," she said. "I heard that you didn't kill the man?"

"Parson Abel prevented it."

"He never told me that part."

"Not by stepping between us, if that's what you mean. I had Custus on the ground, choking the life out of him, when the words the Parson spoke to me came flooding in. I'll never forget his words. 'Vengeance is mine,' saith the Lord. I let Custus go. When I turned to walk away Custus picked up his Bowie knife to kill me when a Cheyenne brave named Red Hand put an arrow in his back."

Stars commenced to dot the black sky overhead and a cool

wind kicked up from the southwest. Martha drew her shawl around her neck.

"Getting a bit chilly," she said. "Can't stay out here too much longer."

Jesse stopped her. "Been thinking about a way to get Brody, Cynthia and Doc back."

"You have?"

"We captured one of Cincinnati's men. Curly Bill. Now we have a good idea of what he's up to and why. Cincy thinks another one of his men killed Curly Bill in his jail cell, but he didn't. I think we can get Cincy back into town and off your brother's place by faking a funeral. With fewer men on the place we have a better chance at a rescue."

"Do you think my brother is still alive?"

"He's Cincy's bargaining chip to take possession of my store. I'd bet he's still alive. Your sister-in-law, too," Jones said.

"And Doc?"

"And Doc."

"I don't know Doc very well," Martha hesitated before adding, "He seems a bit gruff."

"I guess you just have to get to know him better."

"I have no reason to doubt you." Martha stood. "I think I'll go back inside before I take a chill."

When she reached the door she turned back to see Jesse looking straight ahead in the same position she found him.

"Jesse," she said with great affection. "Thank you for looking out for my family."

He looked her direction and smiled.

Cincy was at the opposite end of the emotional spectrum from

Jones when the sun rose the following morning. With hostages no longer in his grasp he felt out of control.

"Are we goin' into town for Curly Bill's funeral tomorrow?" Roach asked. He fastened his gun belt and joined Cincy at the table.

"Yeah. I think it will give me the lay of the land," Cincinnati replied. "I'm guessing that thanks to yer incompetence, we'll find Doc and the others back in town." His fist hammered home his point. "And that is exactly what I didn't need!"

Cincy watched Jimbo's feeble attempt to make coffee. "Gull-darn it will somebody give Jimbo a hand?"

"I got it, Jimbo," Snider said. "Why don't you go out to the well and draw some water and let me put the coffee in the cloth for steeping."

"Never could get the hang of keepin' the beans in a bag and tyin' them," Jimbo said to himself on the way out the door.

"Snider," Cincy said, "I want you to ride into town with me tomorrow. I'm takin' Jimbo, too."

Roach pulled up a chair and sat next to Cincy.

"What about me, boss? What do you want me to do? Snoop around town tomorrow while yer at Curly's funeral? Or do you want me to find a spot and take care of Jones for ya?"

"Yer stayin' here. I don't want you foolin' around and getting us all killed."

"But, I'd be more useful in town," Roach responded.

"You'll be more useful where I say you'll be more useful. And I say yer stayin' here. There's an off chance that Doc and the others are hiding in that root cellar. If they think we're all gone they may sneak out. I want you here to make sure that if they do come out, I regain my bargaining chip. Is that understood?"

Roach stood. "C'mon, let me ride with you." He drew his

revolver, pointed it at Snider and laughed as he spun the gun with his trigger finger and holstered it.

Cincy nodded to Snider who crossed the room and stood toe-to-toe with Roach. "Can I see that again?" Snider asked.

Roach obliged and drew his gun. When he did Snider gripped the barrel with his left hand and shoved it aside and his right hand crashed into Roach's face sending him to the floor.

Roach bounced to his feet. "Don't you ever do that again," he shouted. "'Cuz if you do, I'll kill ya! Do you hear me? I'll kill ya."

Snider bent down and picked Roach's hat off the floor, dusted it off, and handed it to him with a smile. "That'll be the day," he said. Snider turned his back on Roach and returned to the task of readying the coffee.

Roach appealed to Cincy. "I'm gonna kill him. That's what I'm gonna do is kill him, ya know?"

"Instead of being so mouthy," Cincy said, "why don't you check on the horses?And while yer at it, maybe make a little visit to the root cellar to see if you can hear anything inside."

Knowing he was licked, Roach gathered up his hat and stormed out the door, banging it closed after him.

"That kid's up for a huge awakening. He thinks he's fast with a gun, and he is, but when it comes to gunplay there's always someone faster," Snider said.

"Yep, and a bullet in the chest is certainly a rude awakening. I hope he settles down before he discovers that," Cincy added. "Wish Snider would hurry up with that water. I've waited long enough for my morning coffee."

Inside the livery stable Wild Bill cinched his saddle tighter, slipped a borrowed Winchester into its scabbard, and prepared to ride.

"Sure was nice of Parson Abel to loan me his mount," he said.

"You don't have to do this, you know," Jones said.

"I know that and I wouldn't if I thought there was a better way."

"My guess could be all wrong, but I'm thinking that Cincy and his gang will leave their hideout tomorrow to attend Curly Bill's funeral. They may give you the perfect opportunity to rescue the hostages. The element of surprise will be with you."

"How is Curly Bill?" Wild Bill asked.

"Since walls often have ears, Sheriff Blanton said we shouldn't keep him in the Moore Hotel since Cincy is part owner. So he's alive and well in an upstairs bedroom at the Abel's. Potter is sittin' outside his door in case he has an idea of escaping and rejoinin' Cincy," said Jones. "Are you sure you don't want me to ride with you out to the Belt place?

Hickok put a foot in the stirrup and mounted. "Nope. I think it best if I handle this alone. I'll do a little nosing around to locate the hostages and when everybody leaves for town in the morning, I'll bust 'em out. That will take the slats right out from under Cincy's plan."

Wild Bill extended his right hand and Jones shook it.

"See you in a day or two," Hickok said. He pulled the reins tight and rode east.

Several hours in the saddle put Hickok exactly where he wanted to be, on the far side of the Belt property and away from any chance at all of any crossfire.He dismounted and walked his horse to a spot where he could see the back side of the house. In front of him, at a distance of about fifty yards he saw a rise in the earth and surmised this rise a root cellar.

He tied-off his horse to a clump of grass, squatted down and snaked his way to the root cellar which gave ample protection from any eyes that looked in that direction.

It was not long before Wild Bill saw a man come around from the front of the house. The man walked with intention toward the root cellar. The closer the man came the surer Hickok was that this was the same man he had bested in the Last Chance. The man nicknamed Roach.

Wild Bill heard voices from inside the cellar.

Roach neared the door of the cellar and the sound went still.

Roach tried the doorknob, but the door did not open. He beat on the door with his fists.

"I know you're in there. You might as well come out," he yelled. For the next ten minutes or so, Roach tried everything he could think of to coax those inside to come out. "Got my eyes on you," he said. "You gotta come out sometime and when you do, I'll kill ya."

Roach drew his revolver and fired two shots at the door in anger.

Around the corner of the house, a man Hickok pegged as Cincy came, screaming at the top of his lungs. "Roach, what in tar nation are you doing? If the hostages are in there and you killed 'em, they're no good to me. Would you do somethin' for me? Start thinking with your head and not what you sit on!"

Roach stomped back toward the house.

Wild Bill Hickok waited. It wasn't long before he heard voices inside the cellar again.

CHAPTER FOURTEEN

Cincinnati Culver admired himself in the mirror. At forty-five years of age he had developed a bit of a paunch. He cinched his belt tighter in a vain attempt to hide it. "Except for the wrinkles around my eyes and forehead, I'm as good lookin' as I've ever been," he said to his reflection.

He took a brush to his hair, slicked it back, and slipped on his suit coat to hide his gun belt before stepping into the room.

"Wow, Cincy, yer a sight fer sore eyes," Snider chided. "Looks like yer all dressed up for a funeral or somethin'." He let loose a laugh.

"Shut up, will ya? And go bring our horses around. I want to be on time to mourn the dearly departed."

Roach laid his revolver on the table. "It's just too bad that ol' Curly Bill had to die such a quick death from lead poisoning."

Cincinnati drew up a chair and sat as close to Roach as he could. "Remember," he said, "I'm leaving you here in case Doc and the others are hiding in the cellar. I don't want you to try to flush them out, smoke them out or anything like that. Go down there and sit by the cellar door. If you hear anyone talking, guard the door and wait until I get back."

Cincy waited for Roach's reply, but it never came.

Roach sat there staring at his gun.

"Do I make myself, clear?" Cincy insisted.

Again no response.

Jimbo brought his massive fist down on the table with a jarring thud.

Roach went for his gun, but Jimbo covered the pistol with his hand and held it in place against the table.

"One of these days yer gonna get yours!" Roach glared up into Jimbo's face.

"One of these days," Jimbo answered, "yer gonna learn not to draw on people. But for you I'd say it's a lesson you'll die learnin'."

With little emotion whatsoever, Cincinnati added. "Now, why don't you run along like a good boy and take your place outside the cellar door."

Roach stood up. Cincy saw his eyes beg Jimbo for his revolver.

"You can give him his gun, Jimbo," Cincy said. "He ain't gonna try nothin'."

Roach gathered his gun, holstered it, and stormed out the door.

"Want me to bring the horses 'round now?" Snider asked.

"Do that," Cincy replied. "And Snider?"

Snider turned back.

"Don't pick on Roach while yer doing it. I don't want him dyin' before he grows up."

Jimbo went to the stove and fetched the coffee pot. He poured Cincy a cup and poured one for himself, too.

"Do you think we'll see Doc in town?" Jimbo said.

"Nah, I think they're all hidin' in the cellar. It's too far to walk into town and all the horses are accounted for. So, they're around here somewhere and the root cellar is as good a place to hide as any. And it's just as well, 'cuz they ain't goin' anywhere with Roach guarding the entrance."

Snider stepped inside. "Brought the three horses up out of the barn," he said.

"Well, gentlemen," Cincy said on his rise from the table. He looked at his pocket watch and snapped the cover closed. "It's seven o'clock and it's time we mounted up and rode into Sidney to pay our last respects to Curly Bill."

"Yeah, it's a shame that he had to die so young," Snider opined.

"Yeah," said Cincy. "There's two things in a man's life that he can't control. When he is born and when he will die."

BILL HICKOK WAS AWAKE LONG before he saw mounted men ride in the direction of Sidney. He'd already taken a breakfast of hardtack and corn dodgers, foregoing lighting a fire and giving his presence away.

He watched Roach make his way to the front of the cellar and hammer on it like he had the day before.

"Open up!" he shouted. "I know you're in there. Ain't no use in stayin' in there and starvin' to death."

No answer.

From his hiding place behind the cellar, Hickok heard it all, including the cocking of a pistol. He anticipated a shot that never came.

"Ahh," Roach said. "I'd better not. If I do Cincy'll hightail it back here and I'll have to kill him." He thought a bit and said, "There's too many of 'em for me to handle, if they all ride back."

Roach stood with his eyes fixed on the door.

Hickok could barely see him from his hiding place. *I need some kind of distraction, but what? I've got to get him away from the door. Don't want to have to kill the kid in the process.*

Roach just stood there, eyes transfixed.

Then Roach broke the silence. "Coffee. What I need is coffee. I do my best thinkin' with a cup of coffee in my hand." He turned and sauntered toward the house.

That was the cue Hickok had waited for. With Roach out of sight, he scrambled from behind the cellar and approached the door. He knocked three times and said in a hushed voice, "It's Bill Hickok. Open up!"

Nothing.

"Open up, Jesse Jones sent me to retrieve ya, but ya gotta hurry before Roach comes back," he said.

Hickok heard a stir inside the cellar and then a male voice at the door. "This is Doc Hardesty. Are you really Bill Hickok?"

"Look," Hickok answered. "You're just gonna have to trust me. Staying in there is not an option. Roach has gone for coffee, but he won't be away long." He glanced over his shoulder to assure himself that Roach wasn't already on his way.

The door opened and three people came out.

"Shut that door and lock it," Hickok said. "Make for that tree line over yonder. We can get acquainted later."

The younger of the two men locked the door and they all scrambled for cover along a tree line some fifty yards away.

They hadn't found shelter for very long before they all observed Roach, coffee cup in hand, ambling back to the cellar door and perching himself on a dead log nearby.

For security reasons, Hickok moved everyone further into the brush.

"Keep it quiet," he intoned. "Let's head further in. There's a clearing ahead where my horse is tied up." Hickok led the way.

When they reached the clearing, he stopped and took inventory of his three refugees.

"Is everyone alright?" he asked.

"I'm Doc Hardesty," the older man told him. "And thanks to the careful planning of this man here, we're all safe. He had plenty of food and water stored away in the cellar."

Brody introduced himself. "The name's Brody Belt and this here's my wife Cynthia."

Cynthia took it all in. "Are you really Bill Hickok the famous Marshal of Abilene?"

Hickok took her hand in gentlemanly fashion and bowed. "One and the same, ma'am.

Hickok straightened. "Let's get down to business. I need to get you back to Sidney. We have four riders and only one horse. That means I gotta get to the barn without being seen."

BRODY BELT TOOK Hickok back to the place where they entered the trees.

"If you follow this tree line it takes you all the way around my property and leaves you off on the back side of the barn," he said. "I got an old plow horse and a mare in the barn."

"And I'm guessin' the kid sittin' over there has a pony there as well," Hickok added. "And that makes three."

"Want me to come with you?" Brody asked.

"Don't think so. This is something for me to do alone. Wouldn't want to be responsible for you, you being married and all."

"If I had my Henry from inside the house, I could keep you covered," Belt added.

"I don't suppose you've ever fired a Winchester then?" ask Hickok.

"Cut my teeth on a Winchester."

"Let's do this. You grab the Winchester off my horse and keep me covered as I make my way to the barn. I'd prefer not killin' the kid, but if it comes down to it and it's him or me—I'd rather it be him."

Brody extended his hand and Hickok took it. "Glad I got to meet you, Wild Bill."

"Just call me Bill. Never did like the 'Wild' part. Dime novelist Ned Buntline gave me that name at the insistence of Bill Cody and Texas Jack," he replied. "Cody and me go back a long ways to our days with the Pony Express, but that's a story for another time."

"Follow the trees and keep the barn on your right and you'll get there."

Bill Hickok followed Brody's instructions. By keeping the barn on his right he reached a clearing on the lee side of the barn. He also kept a wary eye on where Roach sat sipping his coffee. From a distance he looked quite comfortable on the log. When Roach stood and cast the last of his coffee to the wind, Hickok ducked behind a tree and waited. The next time he looked Roach was nowhere to be seen.

Hickok marked time for five minutes before he journeyed away from the tree line and into the open expanse between the trees and the barn. He presumed Brody stood with rifle in hand one hundred yards to the north.

I'll just have to chance it.

With even steps Bill Hickok approached the barn and found the back door wide open. He sneaked inside. Not far from where he entered, he saw two horses, one in each of two stalls on his left. Roach's saddled horse was tied to one of the support beams at the far end of the barn. He found a couple of bits and leads in an area of the barn reserved for tack and readied Belt's two horses.

Roach's horse whinnied and stomped its hooves when he approached. Through the front door Hickok saw Belt waving frantically.

The warning came too late. The whinnying of his horse had drawn Roach to the barn. He now stood there framed by the open front door.

"Hold it!" He yelled, waving the pistol in his hand. "Why if it ain't Bill Hickok. Or would you prefer Wild Bill?"

"Bill Hickok is fine," Hickok said with all the ease of an experienced gunfighter.

"You got the drop on me in the Last Chance, so I guess turnabout is fair play."Roach holstered his revolver. "If I don't ask ya to slap leather, I'll always wonder who was faster."

"Not in here," Hickok announced. "Ya might hit a horse."

"I'll oblige ya," he said. "Although I ain't about to miss."

Roach turned his back on Wild Bill and wandered to a spot where an errant bullet would not strike inside the barn.

Hickok moved to stand thirty paces away.

"You don't have to do this, you know. You can just let us ride out of here," said Hickok.

"Us? Did you say 'us'?" Roach asked.

"I did."

"So where were they hiding?"

"In the storm cellar."

"I knew it. I'll have to tell Cincy that I was right after I get done with you."

"If this is the way you want it..." Hickok said.

"It is."

"On your count then."

"We draw on the count of five," Roach said.

Hickok nodded his agreement.

"One...Two...Three...Four...Five."

Roach made a play for his gun, but before he cleared leather, a shot rang out. Roach swayed. Looked down at the bloody hole in his chest. Dropped like a stone, face up, eyes open.

Jones, Potter, Sheriff Blanton, and his deputies all sat in the front row for Curly Bill's funeral. Martha Belt and Adeline Abel finished out the row. Curly Bill's casket, empty of course, rested on a bier between them and the altar area from which Parson Abel preached.

Cincinnati Culver and his men sat at the back nearest the door.

"It's a tragedy," Abel began his sermon, "when anyone is cut down in the prime of their life. Curly Bill was well known as a scoundrel, but no man has a right to deprive another of his life. Who can say what may have happened later in Curly Bill's life had he had opportunity to repent of his sins and come to Jesus.St. Paul teaches us it is God's desire that everyone come to the knowledge of the Truth. That's a come to Jesus moment, for Jesus is the Way, the Truth and the Life."

Behind Jones someone shouted a loud "Amen!" which found an echoing voice in other congregation members gathered there.

"Yet, someone had the audacity to end Curly Bill's life as he slept in Sheriff Blanton's jail. It's not right! It's just not right, I tell you."

"Amen!"

"Why isn't it right, you may ask yourself? Well, I tell you

why. Because right here in the Good Book..." He raised his Bible high. "It says 'Thou shalt not murder,' and Curly Bill was murdered. Someone intentionally put a freight box up against the side of the jail house, climbed on top of it and with deliberateness fired two shots into Curly Bill. That, my friends is murder.Intentional murder. Deliberate murder. First Degree murder. And that's wrong.It not only trespasses man's law; laws we passed to maintain order as any good community will do, but it trespasses God's Law as well."

"Amen!" came the congregation's reply.

"It's time for law and order in our community. It's time we stopped all the killin,' and gamblin' and all the prostitution. It's time we settled down and became respectable and law abiding."

"There are some in our community, and many of us know who they are, who would steal from us the opportunity to be civilized, to raise our families, to send our children to school, and live peaceable lives. It's time we stopped the killing in the name of decency so there will be no more tragic killings like that of Curly Bill. May it be so. Amen."

When the final "Amen" sounded and Parson Abel offered a prayer and blessing, the pallbearers placed Curly Bill's casket in the horse-drawn hearse that stood at the ready to take Curly's mortal remains to Boot Hill for burial.

Cheering erupted up the street from the church. Jones stepped into the street to see Wild Bill Hickok riding into town towing a second horse behind him.Doc rode by his side and Jones could soon make out a fourth horse with a man and woman riding tandem.

Martha took to the street shouting, "That's my brother."

Hickok pulled up behind Curly Bill's hearse about the time Cincinnati and his gang exited the church.

"This one belongs to you," Hickok proclaimed to Cincy while he dismounted.

Cincy separated himself from Snider and Jimbo and walked to the body draped over the horse. He lifted the head and stared into the dead man's face. "Roach," he said.

"Next time," Hickok said, "don't leave a boy to do a man's job."

CHAPTER FIFTEEN

The reunion of the brother and sister Belt occurred in the middle of the street.

"I was so worried about you," Martha began.

"Had it not been for Bill Hickok we'd still be holed up in our storm cellar," Brody began.

Cynthia cried for joy. "He stepped in and led us to safety. I've never been so scared in all my life. Not even the tornado that swooped through our place last summer threatened our lives like this."

Bill Hickok received congratulatory handshakes but shook them off. "Hold on a minute," he said. "This was all Jones' idea. He planned it."

Cincinnati, who was leading Roach away draped over his own horse, turned to listen.

"Jones put the whole idea together of sending me alone to rescue everyone."

"And it worked, too," Doc added.

Jones noticed Cincy paused in the middle of the street and

whispered to Parson Abel who interrupted the reunion. "Adeline," he said, "why don't you take everyone over to the house? I'll be there as soon as I've done the committal service." He singled out Doc for his next comment. "Why don't you join them, Doc?"

"I thought you'd never invite me," Doc responded. "I'm gone for four days and you act like you never once missed me."

"You know, I was so busy that I hardly noticed you were gone," Abel said with a smile.

"Don't let him fool you, Doc. He missed you a lot," Adeline joined in.

"The only time I missed you was last night when you weren't there for me to beat you at checkers." Abel turned and walked to the hearse.

"You never beat me in checkers," Doc fired back.

This remark caused Parson Abel to turn back. "Why, Doc," he said, "it's not wise to lie to your pastor."

JONES DELIBERATELY AVOIDED ALL the reunion chatter. Small talk never was his forte, especially in situations where people talked over each other like what was going on inside. At his first opportunity, Jones slipped out the front door, sat on the porch swing and rolled a cigarette.

He had finished half his cigarette when Martha found him.

"Parson Abel said I'd find you out here," she began. "I want to thank you for your part in all of this."

"Glad you got your brother back," Jones answered. "I understand it was because of Brody's quick thinking that Wild Bill rescued them."

"Yeah," Martha said. "Taking everyone out the window and into the storm cellar was a stroke of genius."

"And having the foresight to have the cellar well stocked and secured from the inside didn't hurt either," said Jones. "You must be very proud of your brother.

"I am," she said as she made her way to the where Jones sat rocking. "May I sit down?"

"Help yourself," Jones answered. He finished his cigarette and cast it aside.

Martha Belt joined him on the porch swing. Without looking at Jones, she said, "I am also very proud of you."

"What for? You asked me to help you and I said I would. It's as simple as that."

"You dreamed up the plan to take Curly Bill captive and to fake his death and funeral. You dreamed up the plan to send Bill Hickok out to my brother's place in an attempt to find him, Cynthia, and Doc. To me that's every bit as important as my brother's foresight with the cellar."

"Maybe so, but I don't think of things that way. I think of this as a job I agreed to do and I did it."

Martha put her index finger to his lips. "Call it foresight or just doing your job, I owe you a big thank you." She took her finger away and replaced it with her lips.

Memories of his wife Sarah flooded in. It was on this same front porch on a cool evening that they fell in love. When Martha tried to kiss him again, he pulled away and held her at arm's length.

"I can't," Jesse said. "As much as my heart says to let go, I can't. Do you understand?"

"Is there something wrong?" she asked.

"I'm not sure that I can explain it."

"Will you try for me?"

"Something feels all wrong," Jones said. "I fell in love with Sarah right here on this same porch swing."

"Your wife."

He nodded.

"Adeline has told me a little about her."

"Yes. And when you kissed me just now everything came back. I hope you won't be offended, but I can't." He paused. "Does any of this make sense to you?"

"Of course," she answered. "My intent was not to force you to abandon your wife's memory for me. I can't ask you to do that. But what I want you to know is that I love you. For whatever it's worth. I love you and I can wait until you feel comfortable letting someone back into your heart."

"Right now Cincinnati Culver is still on the loose. Being in love with me could put you in danger and I really don't want to lose you like I lost Sarah. I feel guilty enough as it is that I wasn't home the day she died. Let's put all this talk of love away for a time."

"For how long?" she asked.

"Until Cincinnati's somewhere where he can't reach out and hurt you. Maybe then my memories of Sarah will let you into my heart."

THERE WAS no reunion at the Last Chance. With Roach dead, and as far as Cincy knew, Curly Bill dead as well, he had little to rejoice in. Jimbo was still alive, and that was a good thing since Jimbo once saved his life. Then there was Snider and Stevens. With only these men, Cincy's plans to control businesses in Sidney now and the trade into the gold fields of Dakota Territory later were quashed.

"Well, Jimbo," Cincinnati began, "it looks like old times, doesn't it? Old times like when we came west together."

Cincinnati plopped himself down in a rickety chair behind his well-worn desk. "Sit, down, why don't the three of ya?"

Jimbo grabbed a chair and sat across the desk from Cincinnati. Snider did likewise. Stevens stayed at the half-open door; his eyes on a dancing girl in the saloon.

Cincy withdrew a bottle of whisky from his desk along with four shot glasses and poured while he commiserated. "So close," he said. "So dad-blamed close."He drained his glass and watched Jimbo and Snider do likewise. Stevens never took his eyes off the dancing girl.

Cincinnati poured a second round.

"Whenever I get close to getting what I want," Cincy continued, "Jones comes along and pulls the rug right out from underneath me. There was that raid where Curly Bill had Jones pinned down, but he got away. There was the theft of the wagon, but Jones busted that up. Then we held Doc and that sod-buster and his wife, and Jones recruited Bill Hickok." Cincy shook his head as he reflected, and then downed his second shot. "I told Roach that his temper would get him killed. Didn't I say that, Jimbo?"

Jimbo grunted.

"Why can't Jones just die?" said Cincinnati. "It would make my life a whole lot easier."

Snider held out his shot glass for a refill, but Cincy ignored him, shoved the cork back in the bottle and put it back where it came from.

"Maybe we've just been too nice about it," Snider said.

Cincy folded his arms behind his head and leaned back in his chair. "I'm listenin'."

Snider held out his shot glass a second time. This time Cincy retrieved the bottle and poured. Snider gulped it down and continued his thought. "What if we hired a gunslinger to come in and take care of our little problem?"

"Ya mean bushwhack Jones?"

"And Potter, too," Snider added.

Cincinnati pondered the idea. The more he pondered, the more he liked it.

"What do you think, Jimbo? Should we eliminate the competition altogether?"

"Don't care," said Jimbo. "Don't care as long as you leave Doc alone. Doc helped me."

"Yes, I remember," Cincinnati replied. "We'll leave Doc out of it."

Jimbo grunted a contended grunt.

"And what about you, Stevens?" Cincy asked.

No answer. To his chagrin the door to his office stood open and Stevens was gone.

"Jimbo, would you help Stevens find his way back in here?" said Cincy.

It wasn't long and Jimbo returned with Stevens held by the scruff of the neck like a mother cat might carry her kittens. He plopped Stevens into the chair he had moments ago occupied. Snider closed the office door.

"You've got a one-track mind like Roach had. His was guns, yours is girls. Keep your mind on yer work." Cincy pounded his fist on his desk for emphasis. "Do I make myself clear?"

Stevens nodded. "Yes, boss."

"You'd better understand, 'cuz if I catch you distracted again, I'll turn you over to Jimbo," said Cincy. "Now, where were we? Oh, yea, we were talkin' about a hired gun to get rid of Jones and Potter."

Snider interjected, "I think it's the best way to go. You want Jones gone and what better way to do it. With him and Potter out of the way you can intimidate the rest of the business owners into seein' things yer way."

"I'm assumin' ya got someone in mind, Snider?" Cincy asked.

"I do. I've been hearin' about a guy from Wichita who goes by the name of Fitz.He's a lefty. They say he's as fast as Bill Hickok and meaner. Likes to ride the gamblin' circuit; Denver, Dodge City, Tombstone, and Abilene. Hasn't visited Sidney yet, so why not invite him to try his luck," Snider said. "Give him a grub-steak and I'm sure he'd come."

"Snider, go on down to the telegraph office and invite this fella, Fitz. Offer to pay his way plus five-hundred dollars when he gets here and another five-hundred when he completes the job I've got for him," Cincy said.

Jesse found Potter keeping a watchful eye on Curly Bill. The upstairs bedroom of the Abel's home was the perfect place for that.

"Untie him and let him go," Jesse said. "We've got no more need of him."

"What do you mean you got 'no more need' for me?" Curly Bill asked.

"Well, in case you hadn't heard by now," Jones continued, "Wild Bill freed all the hostages. We faked your death and your funeral and that drew Cincinnati and his men into town giving Wild Bill ample opportunity to set everyone free."

"One of Cincy's men didn't make it. A kid named Roach. He died of lead poisoning when he drew down on Wild Bill," Jones added.

Potter took out a knife and sliced through the ropes behind Curly Bill's back and set him free. Curly Bill sat on the edge of the bed for a few minutes rubbing his arms to relieve the pain.

"So, what's gonna happen to me?" Curly Bill wondered aloud.

"We're turnin' you loose," said Potter. "We've got no more need of you."

"Where do you suggest I go?" said Curly Bill. "I can't stay around here. If Cincy finds out I'm alive, he'll kill me."

"And we can't afford to feed you any longer, so you can't stay here," Jones said.

"Don't you have relatives somewhere?" Potter asked.

"Got a brother living near Wichita, but we haven't spoken in years. He didn't agree with my lifestyle."

"This might be the right time for the two of you to make connections," Parson Abel said as he came through the door. "I bought you a little gift as a going away present."

He handed Curly Bill a neatly tied package.

"What's this?" Curly Bill asked

"Open it and see," Parson Abel said. "It's something that's been saving lives for a long, long time now."

"No one gives me anything, so why should you start now?" said Curly Bill.

"This is a little something for a man who is looking for a new start," Abel said. "Open it and you'll see."

Curly Bill was like a little kid on Christmas morn. The wrapping gave way to his eager fingers and soon Curly Bill held a book with blank cover. He turned it over and saw the letters B-I-B-L-E stamped into the front.

"A Good Book?" he asked. "Yer givin' me a Good Book?"

Abel smiled. "I like to say, 'Open it up and you'll find your-self on the pages of this book.'"

Curly Bill reached out to hand the book back to Abel. "I can't take this," he said. "I'm no good and that's all I'll ever be, like my papa used ta tell me."

"Funny thing," Jones said. "Sometimes our papas say one thing, but the Bible has a different opinion all together."

"I am a sinner," Curly Bill said. He laid the Bible on the bed and pushed it away.

"Yes, you are a sinner," Abel pointed out. "But in God's eyes you are no more a sinner than I am. Or Potter here, or Jones."

Abel reached down and retrieved the Bible that Curly Bill had pushed away.He sat down beside him on the bed and thumbed through the pages until he found what he was looking for. "Let me read something to you," he said while Jones and Potter watched. When he found the place, he looked Curly Bill full in the face and read. "For God so loved the world, that He gave His only begotten Son, that whosoever believeth in Him should not perish, but have everlasting life. For God sent not His Son into the world to condemn the world; but that the world through Him might be saved.'"

"Are you sayin' that after all I've done that God does not condemn me?" Curly Bill asked.

"God does not like what you've done, but He does not condemn you because His Son Jesus died on the cross, taking all of your sins to the grave with Him.In God's eyes, Curly Bill, you are free. It's kinda like a school marm not liking the answer you wrote on yer slate. She takes a cloth to it and wipes yer slate clean and tells you to start over," Abel said.

"God would do that fer me?" said Curly Bill. He looked about the room.

Jones nodded. "God can and does," he said.

"What do I do now?" Curly Bill asked. His eyes welled up with tears.

"Let me ask you one more question," said Abel. "Have you been baptized?"

"Don't think so, no," said Curly Bill.

"Well, before you leave us, we're gonna see that you are baptized, so that you know for certain that God has washed you and made you clean," Abel said."Follow me downstairs and we'll get this done."

They all made their way to the back staircase.

"I just thought of somethin'," Potter said. "In my mind at least you will always been known as the man with two graves. One here in Sidney where we buried your old self today, and another grave that will hold the remains of the man you are about to become."

CHAPTER SIXTEEN

Bill Hickok dismounted in front of Swede's Mercantile and went inside.

"Mornin,' Bill," a familiar voice greeted him. Hickok recognized the voice as that of Adam Potter.

"Mornin', Adam," Hickok replied. "Is Jesse in this morning? Came in to say my goodbyes."

"You're leavin' us?" said Potter.

"Things have quieted down and I've taken enough money at faro in the saloons.Haven't tried the Last Chance, though. What do you think my odds would be?

"Of winning," Potter asked, "or simply of surviving? If it's surviving I'd say that the deck is stacked against ya."

"Me, too," Hickok said. "I like to sit facing the front door, but if I do that at the Last Chance, my back would be to Cincy's office door. Not the smartest thing to do 'cuz someone could sneak out of his office and shoot me in the back of the head."

"Oh, and by the way, no, Jones hasn't come in yet," said Potter. "He's over across the street havin' breakfast with Doc and the Parson. Probably gettin' an ear full, too. A lot of the merchants don't like Cincy trying to drive them out of business. Sheriff Blanton's in on the conversation, too."

Hickok bent down to tie the laces of his gun belt around his thighs. "Thought we might be done with gunplay for a while, but I guess I thought wrong," he said.

Jesse ambled across the street. "Potter, whose horse is that tied up out front?"

Hickok answered. "It's mine. Bought it at the livery stable a few minutes ago.I'm riding out."

"Can I ask where to?" Jones said.

"Got a telegram from an old friend of mine. We go back to the Pony Express days ahead of the war," Hickok said.

"You wouldn't be talkin' about Bill Cody, would you?" said Potter.

"You know him?" Hickok asked.

"Sure do. Helped us out of a jam or two a couple years back," Jones said.

Hickok continued, "Well, he sent me a telegram yesterday asking me to ride on over to North Platte. He said he wants to talk to me in person and get my opinion on somethin' Ned Buntline's cooked up."

"What would that be? Or are you allowed to answer that one?" Potter asked.

"Well, it seems Ned has written a little drama and he's thinkin' that there might be a part for me," Hickok said.

"Leave it to Buntline to come up with a harebrained, money-makin' idea like that," Potter announced.

Hickok turned on him. "Is that really a comment about Buntline or is it a comment on my acting ability?" Hickok noted the surprised look that registered on Potter's face and laughed. "Ha-ha-ha. That one caught you by surprise, didn't it?"

"It sure did," Potter announced. He was relieved that Hickok was only kidding with his remarks.

"So, what's the name of this little drama?" Jones asked.

"Cody told me that it was somethin' like 'The Scouts of the Prairie,' and that the idea was to have scouts like him and me share our adventures in person with audiences in big cities like New York and Chicago."

"Yep, big city folks ain't got any idea what things are really like out here on the plains," Potter said.

"And," Hickok added, "Buntline thinks there's good money in sharing our adventures in a setting where the audience can go home and sleep secure in their own beds."

"Does he really think that people will pay good money for all the B.S.?" Jones asked.

"He does," Hickok said. "Buntline says that if people are willing to shell out a dime for one of his novels, they will be willing to part with a whole lot more to hear the adventures of the men who lived them. I'm gonna hear him out at least and see where this leads me."

Jesse Jones was on his way to breakfast the next morning when a stranger rode by. Everything about the man said *hired gunman* from his bespoke black suit to the silver studs on his left-handed holster. Ammunition ringed his gun belt. Jones glimpsed his no-nonsense face with deep-set eyes, dark eye brows and a neatly trimmed moustache under a broad rimmed cowboy hat. The stranger sat tall in the saddle of a dark horse that held its head high and seemed to prance down the street.

"Did you see that?" Jones asked taking his seat in the Sidetrack Cafe where Potter and Doc sat eating.

"Did I see what?" Doc said without looking up from his steak and eggs.

"A professional gunman," Jones said. "He just rode by like he owned the place."

"Never saw him," said Doc, who was more interested in eating than making conversation.

"Neither did I," said Potter in a tone that sounded only half-believing.

"Go take a look for yerself if you don't believe me," said Jones. "He's heading east."

Potter went to the door and soon returned to his seat at the table.

"Well, I'll be," Potter said. "Whoever he is, he rode up to the Last Chance."

Doc looked up. "It looks to me that Cincinnati just raised the stakes in a winner-takes-all poker game." He poured himself some more coffee. "Can I warm anyone's coffee while I'm pouring?" he asked.

Potter put his cup under Doc's pour and Jones followed.

"This puts us in an awkward spot," Potter said. "Hickok rode out yesterday and a hired gunman rides in today. That changes our poker hand. Bill Hickok was the ace up our sleeve."

"I wouldn't be foldin' quite so soon," Jones said. "Not sure how all of this is gonna work out, but what I do know is that when it comes to poker, a flush always beats a four-flusher phony."

CINCY LIKED MONEY. He took pleasure in it. The feel and smell of money in his hands meant security; a security his upbringing never gave him. To Cincy, the poverty of his youth nettled him.

Long ago he promised himself never to return to that squalor. *Owning a tavern in a small town is a license to print money,* he often thought.

Lately, his thoughts had graduated to bigger things; like owning the town itself.

Cincy counted yesterday's take in his office while his principle body-guard, Jimbo, stood by.

Knock. Knock. Knock.

"Yeah, whadda ya want?" Cincy barked. His thoughts interrupted.

"Got someone out here who wants to see you," came Snider's voice from behind the door.

"Tell them to come back later. I'm busy right now," said Cincy.

"Boss, I think you're gonna want to open up. It's the man you sent for."

"In that case," Cincy replied, "wait just a moment and I'll have Jimbo let you in."

Cincy went to work to gather his money into two stacks; counted and uncounted. He shoved the uncounted stack into a desk drawer and carried the counted stack to his safe. When finished he gave a nod to Jimbo who turned the key and allowed two men to enter.

"Well, well," Cincy said. "I must say that you look every bit the gunfighter you're reported to be." He sat at his desk.

"You promised me five hundred for coming. I'm here to collect that five hundred," the gunman said in an all-business manner.

"Can I pour you a drink, Fitz?" Cincy asked. "You do want to be called Fitz, don't you?"

"You and I ain't drinkin' buddies," announced Fitz. "I came here on business.You promised me five hundred on arrival and five hundred when the job is done. Give me the five hundred you promised me or I'll take it out of yer hide."

Jimbo took umbrage at Cincy's mistreatment and went for his gun, but Fitz was faster. Much faster. Jimbo never cleared leather before he faced Fitz's .44.

"Don't ever try that again," Fitz said with complete calm. He turned to face Cincy. "Better tell yer friend here, he'd better not try that again or I'll blow a hole in him so wide you could drive a wagon through it."

"It's alright, Jimbo, Mr. Fitz has come on business." Cincy went to his safe and withdrew five one-hundred dollar bills. He walked over to Fitz and extended his hand with the money, only to withdraw that same hand when Fitz reached out to take the bills.

"Let me make myself very clear," Cincinnati began. "This is the down payment on a little job I want you to do for me."

He handed the money over to Fitz who deliberately counted out the bills, folded them, and put them in his vest pocket.

"So what is this *little job*?" Fitz asked.

Cincy eased back into his chair. "Have a seat," he said. "Make yourself comfortable."

Fitz neared Cincy's desk. "If you don't mind, I'll stand. Been in the saddle several days."

"The name is Jesse Jones," Cincinnati began. "He owns Swede's Mercantile and I want it. Jones keeps interferrin' in my plans."

"How do you want this done?" said Fitz.

"That's up to you; you're the professional."

"Do you have a deadline?" Fitz asked.

"I like that expression, I really do," Cincy said. "The *dead* line, as you put it, is as soon as possible. Does a month sound reasonable?" Cincy shrugged his shoulders. "I don't care. I guess you could say that the *dead* line is whenever you think you want your other five hundred dollars. Do whatever you think best to get me Swede's Mercantile."

Fitz thought for a moment. "However we do this thing, I don't want to spend time behind bars. That's just time away from me makin' more money. I'm gonna do whatever I can to provoke this Jones fella into makin' the first move."

"I like the way you think about money." Cincy turned to Jimbo and Snider who stood next to him. "We all like the way you think, don't we boys?"

They nodded their approval.

"And what if I need more money to make this happen?" Fitz asked.

"Don't come back here," Cincy said. "Just contact Jimbo or Snider and they'll come talk to me. I don't want anyone associating me with you. I'm a respectable businessman." Cincy looked back at Fitz. "You can go out the back door of my office," Cincy said. He pointed to the door.

"That ain't the way I work," Fitz fired back. "I came in by the front door and I'm going out the way I came in, as a respectable businessman myself." He turned and walked to Cincy's office door. When he reached the door he turned back into the room.

"By the way," Fitz said. "I used to have a sister living here named Sarah; Sarah Fitzpatrick. Same as my last name. Every heard of her?"

No one answered.

"They said she married a soldier from Ft. Sidney," Fitz continued.

"Do you have a name?" Cincy inquired.

"No. I'm afraid that's all I've got to go on," said Fitz.

"Don't think we can help you," said Cincy. "That's most likely before our time anyway. Haven't been here long."

"I'll do some nosin' around," said Fitz. "I'd like to find my sister."

Fitz stepped out of Cincy's office, closed the door, and was gone.

Cincy wasted no time resuming his life where he left it before Fitz arrived. He removed the cash he'd hurriedly stuffed in his desk and resumed counting.

He never looked up when he said, "Boys, I have half a mind to go down to the undertakers and order up a pine box for Jones. Right now Jones is just a dead man walking."

JONES WAS WALKING ALRIGHT, but he was far from dead. He entered Swede's with Potter and the two of them set to work in the back room in anticipation of Adeline's arrival to open the store.

"What are you planning to do now that Cincy's hired a professional?" Potter wondered aloud.

"I'm gonna sit tight for now," Jones replied. "The worst thing we can do is get all riled up. That's what Cincy wants us to do. Right now we don't know who this hired gunman is and what he's been hired to do. My guess is that we'll find that out soon enough. In the meantime we've got a business to run."

"Patience has never been my strong suit. I'm sorta like the vulture sitting on a telegraph line watchin' stuff walk by and sayin', 'Patience? Naw, I'm gonna kill somethin',' " Potter said.

"You're not a vulture and that kinda' thinkin' can get a man killed," Jones noted. He moved on to a different subject. "What are your thoughts about stacking these boxes over in the corner to make room for the supplies coming in today?"

"Sounds like a plan," said Potter.

The bell above the front door announced someone's entry.

Jones noted that the footfalls sounded heavier than usual. "I'd better go see who that is," he said. "It doesn't sound like Adeline."

Jones entered the store and found himself face to face with the gunslinger.

"Can I help you?" Jones asked.

"I've got a message for Jesse Jones," the gunslinger said. "I understand he owns this place."

"He does," said Jones, "and I'm the one you're lookin' for."

"The name's Fitz," he said. "And I've been hired to kill ya unless you turn ownership of this here store over to Cincy down the street. He's willing to give you a fair price."

Jones stood his ground. "Well, you can just walk back down the street and tell Cincy that I'm stayin'. He can keep his money."

"That's pretty bold talk. You just never know when somethin' might happen to yer friends or yer business," Fitz said.

"Let's just say that if somethin' does happen, then you'll be the one I'll be looking for," Jones replied. "I'm not lookin' for any trouble, but I'll tell ya right now, I won't walk away from it either."

"That's what Cincy thought you would say," said Fitz. "Guess we got no further business to transact."

Fitz turned and walked toward the door at the same time Martha entered. He touched the brim of his hat. "Ma'am," he said and was gone.

"Who was that man?" Martha asked.

"The latest installment of Cincy's plan to drive me out of business," came Jones' reply.

"You alright out here?" Potter stood in the doorway of the back room.

"Yeah, I'm fine," said Jones. "We were right about somethin'; Cincy did hire a gunman to kill me. He just stopped in to introduce himself."

"That man was a hired killer?" Martha said.

"He is. Cincy's raised the ante. He wants my store and he's willing to kill me for it," Jones said.

"Why don't you give Cincy what he wants?" she said.

"What would you have thought of me had I done that when he was holding your brother hostage?You can't give in to bullies. If you do they'll keep at it.You've got to stand up to them," Jones replied.

"But in the process you could get hurt or even killed," Martha said.

"So you're saying that you wouldn't like that very much?" Jones asked her.

Martha hugged Jones. "Of course, I wouldn't like that," she said.

Jones looked down into her deep blue eyes. "Nothing's going to happen to me," he said. "I've dealt with men who wanted to kill me all my life and I'm still standing."

"But it would only take one bullet," she said.

"Don't worry your pretty little head about me," Jones said. "I'll be alright."

She kissed him.

"I have to worry. I love you," she said.

CHAPTER SEVENTEEN

Jones maneuvered the buckboard into a spot in front of the Moore Hotel and tied off the horse. He felt the first rays of the morning sun warm his back as he did. He traversed the hotel lobby and bounded up the stairs two at a time. He arrived at the room with a metal "6" nailed to the door and knocked.

"Who is it?" a female voice from within asked.

Jones recognized the voice; it belonged to Martha Belt.

"It's Jesse," he answered. "You told me yesterday that you wanted to get to know me better, so I thought I'd take you on a little drive."

"You'll have to wait for me in the lobby, Jesse. I'll get dressed and come right down," Martha said.

Jones took a seat in the lobby and waited. The clerk behind the counter, a gentleman of later years with grey hair and substantial wrinkles, noticed him and motioned Jesse to his counter.

"I've been told by Cincinnati never to discuss what happens in this hotel," he began, "but there is a hired gunman staying in room twenty-five and he's been asking me a lot of questions."

"What kind of questions?" Jones inquired.

"Like where he might find his sister, for one."

"Did his sister have a name?" said Jones.

The clerk thought for a moment. "I'm sorry, Jesse, but my memory isn't what it used to be. I can't recall her name. Didn't mean anything to me anyway. I haven't lived in Sidney all that long."

"I'm sure he'll find the truth sooner or later, but for now I think you did just fine. If you think of the name sometime, just let me know."

The additional wait was not long and Martha came down the stairs.

"Hope I didn't keep you waiting too long," Martha said.

"Not long," Jones said while he escorted her through the front door and lifted her onto the buckboard.

"What's this all about?" she asked.

"I want you to understand what I'm dealing with, the memories that keep coming back," he said.

Jones steered the buckboard south until it met a trail near Lodgepole Creek.There he turned onto the trail and headed west, coming into a clearing an hour later. Here he pulled on the reins and drew the horse to a stop.

"Is this the place where you and your wife lived?" she asked espying the cabin in front of a windrow of trees.

"Yes," he said. "Here's where my dreams died."

"Oh, Jesse," Martha said, "I'm so sorry." She took him by the hand. "If you don't mind, would you take me around the place? This is such a lovely place for a home."

The tour, such as it was, did not cross the threshold of the cabin.

"This was where we planted our first garden," Jones

announced. "You talk about backbreaking labor; the sod along the creek had never been broken before. And right over there," he pointed out, "we put up a little chicken coop, but we couldn't keep the foxes out. One morning we woke up and found only feathers and broken egg shells. We were going to get a milk cow but we never got around to it before Sarah. . ." He stopped as tears filled his eyes. "Before Sarah was killed."

Martha wrapped him in her arms but said nothing. There was nothing to say.

Jesse looked down into Martha's eyes. Tears rolled down her checks, too.

"Someday I'll take you inside the cabin," he said, "but not today. I'm not ready for that today."

"It's alright Jesse. I'll wait," she said.

They rode back to Sidney in silence. There were times when Jesse held the reins in his left hand and rested his right hand on his thigh. It was then that he felt Martha's hand on his. The warmth of her touch brought a smile to his lips. Parson Abel's words in a recent sermon came to mind. 'It's not good for man to be alone.'

"Maybe someday," Jesse thought. *"Someday."*

JONES DROVE the buckboard to where the road intersected with the south edge of town with the sun setting over his shoulder. Turning north he saw the Abel's home at the top of the hill a mile away as the crow flies.

Martha nestled near him. "Jesse," she said, "would you look at that sunset."

Jesse looked left and watched the sun, like a bright orange ball sending fire rays heavenward while it sank beneath the Sandhills. He could not help but smile at Martha's *joie de vivre*.

They neared the town proper. Three gunshots interrupted their journey and spooked their horse, causing it to rear up on its hind legs. Jones held fast to the reins and regained control before the beast darted off.

"Those were gunshots," Jesse said with his full attention, wondering where the shots had been fired and by whom.

Citizens flooded the street asking themselves the same questions.

Jones steered his buckboard in the direction the crowd flowed. He saw Doc dart toward Sheriff Blanton's office.

"Stay here!" he commanded Martha. He left Martha in the buckboard after he tied off his horse and raced after Doc.

Doc shouted orders. "Get out of the way, will ya! Move aside!"

Jones entered Blanton's office right behind Doc. Blanton laid face down, slumped over his desk. There were blood splatters on the wall behind him with a hole about the size of Jesse's thumb in the midst of that splatter.

That's a good sign, he told himself, *it's a through and through.*

Doc pushed Sheriff Blanton back into his chair and drew out his stethoscope, applied it to the still man's chest and listened.

"He's got a heartbeat," Doc said to Jesse. "It's not very strong, but it's there.Grab a couple of men and get him over to my office. Hurry!"

Jones did as directed and with three other men hoisted Blanton from his chair and carted him up the back stairs of Swede's Mercantile and into Doc's office.They placed Sheriff Blanton onto Doc's operating table.

"Now you men, get outta here! I've got work to do!" Doc said.

All of the men left with the exception of Jones who

followed them and closed Doc's office door behind them once they'd exited.

"He's darn lucky, if you ask me," Doc said. "A couple of inches to the right and we'd be planning a funeral. A shot through the lungs is bad enough."

"Is he going to make it, Doc?" Jones asked.

"If we can stop the bleeding," Doc replied. "It's going to be touch-and-go through the night, but let me tell ya, I've seen a whole lot worse." Doc went to work to stop the bleeding.

A few minutes later Jones answered a knock on Doc's door to find Parson Abel with a woman Jones recognized as Sheriff Blanton's wife, Edith.

"How is he?" Parson Abel asked.

"Doc's working on him now," Jones replied. "He was hit once and the bullet went clean through."

Edith sobbed uncontrollably. "I told him that he needed to do something else now that we have children."

"There. There. It's alright, Edith," Parson Abel interjected. "He's doing what he feels God is calling him to do."

"But now he may be dying," she said.

Doc framed himself in the doorway separating his operating room from the waiting room. "He's not going to die," he said. "I got the bleeding stopped."

"Can I see him?" Edith said.

"I wouldn't just yet," said Doc. "He needs to stay calm. I've given him a sedative. He's lost a lot of blood. He should be a lot better in the morning."

"Who would want to do such a thing? He's never hurt anyone," she cried.

"I'm afraid we don't have an answer to that at the moment," said Jones. "I'm sure his deputies are at work on that."

"C'mon, Edith," Parson Abel said. "I'll walk you home and

stay with you while you tell your children what happened. I'm sure Doc has this situation well in hand, don't ya, Doc?"

"He'll be alright, Edith. It'll probably be a few weeks before he's fully recovered, but he'll be alright," Doc said. "Go on home now and see to your children."

Parson Abel led Edith out and Doc returned to his patient, but it wasn't long before Jones heard new footsteps on the stairs.

"How is he?" Potter asked.

"He's going to be alright," Jones said. "He's fortunate that whoever shot at him only hit him once. Any word on witnesses?"

"Nobody seems to know anything definitive," Potter said. "A couple of witnesses said they heard gunfire and saw a men dressed in black disappear down the alley behind the jail."

"No one saw his face?" Jones asked.

"Nope."

"Could it have been Cincy's hired gun?" said Jones.

"I can't say yes or no to that question," Potter said.

A FEW BLOCKS to the east in the Last Chance Saloon a figure dressed all in black stood before Cincinnati Culver.

"You did what?" Cincy's voice exploded.

"I thought I'd help you," came the excuse from the man in black.

"Snider, you stupid fool. All you've done is complicate things," Cincy replied. "What if anybody saw you?"

"They didn't, boss. I made sure of that. I killed him alright. I knocked on the door and when he said, 'Come in,' I came in, shot him and then hightailed it down the alley beside the jail," Snider offered.

Cincy was dumbfounded and stammered to reply. "You shot Sheriff Blanton. Just how in the dickens did you think that this would help?"

"It gets rid of a lawman, that's how," he said. "One less lawman to track us down."

"That's the bone-headedest answer I ever heard," Cincy said. "Now the whole town will come looking for whoever shot Sheriff Blanton."

"But they won't know it's me because I was in disguise," Snider said.

Jimbo burst through the door separating Cincy's office from the saloon.

"Hey, boss," Jimbo said. "Did you hear that someone tried to kill the sheriff this evening? Someone dressed all in black?" Jimbo noted Snider's clothing. "Was that you, Snider?"

Snider ignored Jimbo's second question, but answered the first. "Yeah, I've heard," he said.

"So, the report is getting around that someone tried to kill the sheriff, huh?" Cincy said. "That means that whoever it was didn't get the job done. Is that what you mean, Jimbo?"

"Yep. The sheriff's over at Doc's office. I heard tell that he's gonna live."

Cincinnati came around his desk and grabbed Snider by the collar. "Not only did you try to kill him, but you failed! I'm a bettin' man, and I'll bet Sheriff Blanton got a good look at you before you shot him. Wanna bet??? You said there were no witnesses and I'm tellin' ya now that there is a witness. And that witness is the very man you shot."

"That can't be true," Snider said, trying to escape Cincy's wrath. "I killed him fer sure. I saw the blood splatter all over the wall."

"You shot him alright, but you didn't kill him from what

Jimbo tells me," said Cincy. "And that makes you expendable. I can't have you around leading everyone back to me."

Cincy turned away from Snider. "I'm glad he came in the alley door and not the saloon door. That means that more than likely no one saw you. Jimbo," he said, "would you do me a big favor?"

"Sure, boss. What it is?" Jimbo asked.

"Would you take Snider here out the back door? We've got to tie up this loose end before my whole plan comes unraveled. If you know what I mean?" Cincy said.

Cincinnati saw fear crawl up Snider's face and stay there.

"No! You wouldn't do that would you, boss?" Snider cried out in a panic.

"I'm afraid I would," Cincinnati answered calmly. "I'm afraid I would."

Snider tried to scream, but before his scream could escape his lips, Jimbo's big left hand covered his mouth and the butt of his pistol dropped on his head with an audible thud. He dropped to the floor like a sack of feed.

"Leave him here and go around and get your horse," Cincy said. "Then take him out in the hills somewhere and let the buzzards have him."

Before Jimbo could carry out his assignment Fitz barged through Cincy's office door.

"Alright, Cincy. I want an explanation and I want it right now." Fitz slammed the door behind him. In an instant he was in front of Cincinnati and stood head and shoulders taller. "Did one of your men try and kill the sheriff or am I just hearing things?"

Cincy pointed at Snider's body crumpled on the floor. "He did," Cincy said but quickly added, "But without my permission. He said he thought he was *helping* me."

Fitz was nonplussed. "That puts my life in jeopardy and that's gonna cost ya another five hundred."

Cincy turned back to Jimbo. "Go on, get yer horse like I told ya. Jimbo left.

"Five hundred, did you say?" Cincinnati walked to his wall safe.

"Five hundred," Fitz answered him. "And if any one of yer men interferes in my business again, I'll be back. But I won't come gunnin' fer them, I'll come gunnin' fer you. Do I make myself clear?" Fitz sat in the chair in front of Cincy's desk and reflected. "I've always had a hankerin' to settle down and run a bar."

Fitz's remark rankled Cincy no matter how hard he tried to conceal it. He thought how easy it would be just to reach a little deeper into the safe and pull out the handgun he'd placed there and bring this conversation to an end. He thought better of it and left the gun there.

"Here's your money," he told Fitz. "Count it out for yourself, if you'd like. Do we still have an agreement?"

"We do," Fitz said as he stood up. "But just a moment ago I saw a hesitation as you stood at your safe. You hesitated and moved that black notebook. You wondered if you should reach for the gun at the back of your safe. Let me tell you that had you gone for it, it would have been the last thing you ever did."

Fitz left the same way he came in. Through the front door.

CHAPTER EIGHTEEN

Jesse Jones climbed the stairs to Doc's office and knocked. Doc answered the door.

"How's he doing, Doc?" Jones asked.

"He's starting to show signs of regaining consciousness. I'm glad I kept him sedated the last couple of days. His vital signs are much better," Doc replied.

"When will we have a chance to talk to him and ask what happened?"

"We can't rush things," said Doc. "We've got to slowly allow him to regain consciousness. His wife Edith was here for a while this morning. When she talked to him he started to move around a little like he was trying to wake up.That's a good sign."

Jones heard moaning.

"That's an even better sign. Let me look in on him. I'll be right back," said Doc.

After a few minutes Doc stood in the doorway to announce, "Blanton's awake. But give me a few minutes and I'll see if he feels well enough to answer questions."

Doc ducked back into the room and Jones heard conversation, however the volume was too low for him to understand any of the words. Again Doc appeared in the doorway.

"I've got him sitting up," he said. "Let's give it a try."

Jones followed after him. The smell of the room and the site of Doc's medical instruments brought back memories of a war that ended not yet a decade ago.He must have hesitated upon his entry for Doc asked, "Are you alright?"

"Yes," Jones said, "it's just that the smell of this room brought memories I'd like to forget."

Doc nodded in agreement. "Happens to me upon occasion. Old memories die hard, don't they?"

"They sure do," said Jones.

Doc stood near Blanton's bedside. "Jones wants to ask you a couple of questions. Still feel up to it?"

Blanton responded in a voice uncharacteristically soft. "I'll try," he said.

"Now, if you get tired. . ." Doc began.

"I'll let you know," Blanton cut him off.

"Can you tell me what happened?" asked Jones.

"All I remember is that someone knocked on the door to my office. I was at my desk cleaning my gun, so I said, 'Come in'. That's the last thing I remember."

"Did you see a gun, a hand, or maybe a face?" Jones continued.

Blanton paused a moment to consider that question then shook his head.

"Not that I can recall," he answered. "I'm getting sleepy, Doc. Is it okay if I rest now?"

Before Doc could respond, Blanton's eyes closed and he was asleep.

Doc turned to Jones. "It's not uncommon in cases of

trauma, like this one, where the mind blocks out the memory. We'll have to wait and see."

Jones knew that for the present there was nothing to be done. If Blanton could not identify his assailant they would have to take Doc's advice to wait and see.

Parson Abel met them in the outer room of Doc's office.

"When did you get here?" Doc asked. "I never heard you come up the stairs."

"That is entirely possible," Abel fired back. "I don't think your hearing is what it used to be."

"That may be," Doc said, "but I can still smell a rat." Doc smiled a *touché* smile.

"So, how's your patient doing? You haven't killed him or anything, have you?" Parson Abel said.

"Not planning to," Doc said. "He was sitting up a few minutes ago."

"And so far," Jones added, "he can't remember much about the shooting."

"It sounds like we'll have to wait and see if his memory returns or not," said Abel.

"Doc was just saying that," Jones noted.

"Really?" Abel asked.

"Yeah, it seems like you two think a lot alike," said Jones.

"Now that's a scary thought," added Doc.

ADELINE SAT a pot of soup on the table.

"Mmm," Parson Abel said as he filled his bowl. "There's nothing like your beef vegetable soup."

"That's for sure," Jones added.

"All three of us are in agreement," said Potter.

"Thank you, gentlemen," Adeline replied. "Cooler days are

soup days in my mind. A lunch like this should keep you warm inside the rest of the day."

Adeline helped herself to a bowl of soup and joined the men at the table.

"Any word on whether Doc will join us or not?" she asked.

"Don't think so," said Jones. "He's been watching over Sheriff Blanton's recovery like a hawk."

"You know, for all the grief I give him, he does a good job," said Abel.

"Have you told him that, sweetheart?" Adeline asked.

"No. I wouldn't want him to get a swelled head," Abel added.

"I would have to agree that Doc is doing a good job," Jones said. "My thoughts are that it won't be long and we'll know the identity of the man who tried to kill Blanton."

A knock at the Abel's front door interrupted the conversation. A few minutes later Parson Abel brought Martha Belt and her brother Brody into the kitchen.

"I didn't mean to interrupt your lunch," Brody announced.

"It seems that Brody's made a discovery out by his place," said Abel. "I'll let him tell you all about it."

"Maybe I should wait until everyone is done eating," Brody said.

"Or perhaps we men can join you in my study, if you think this is something the tender ears of women should not hear," said Abel.

"I'd feel better discussing this in private," Brody said. "Martha was with me and she has an inkling of what's going on, but I still think it's better not to talk about what I found in front of her."

"Gentlemen, if you'd join me, we'll go to my study," Abel announced and he led them down the hall. After the group reconstituted in his study, Abel invited Brody to begin.

"I came into town early this morning to pick up Martha so she could stay at our place for a few days," he said. "On the road home, about three miles from my place, I saw some vultures circling. They weren't there when I drove the wagon into town, but they were there now. This got my curiosity up, so I told Martha to stay behind while I drove over to take a look. That's when I found him."

"Who did you find?" Jones asked.

"I recognized him as one of the men who held us captive at the farm," said Brody. "The man they called Snider."

"That would be one of Cincy's men alright," Potter said.

"He was dead. I didn't have to ride all the way over to him to see that," said Brody. "From where I sat I could see a bullet hole in the middle of his forehead.The odd thing was that his hands were wired together behind his back and there was wire around his neck. Could have been barbed wire, but I didn't get that close."

"Sounds like whoever wanted Snider dead was serious about it," Jones said.

"Well, we can't just leave him out there for the buzzards," Parson Abel said."He needs a decent burial. Brody, do you think you can lead me to him? I'll take my wagon and bring him back to town."

"I'll ride out there with you, Parson," Jones said.

"Me, too," added Potter.

"I wonder if any of this has anything to do with the shooting of Sheriff Blanton.Seems too coincidental to me," said Jones.

"How is the Sheriff?" Brody Belt asked.

"Doc says he's gonna make it, but so far he hasn't been able to identify the one who shot him," said Jones. "Maybe I should pop over and let Doc know what's going on."

WHEN THE MEN left Parson Abel's study they split up. Jones and Potter went to visit Doc, while Parson Abel and Brody Belt made ready the wagon to retrieve Snider's body.

Doc had nothing new to report. Sheriff Blanton continued to cling to life with only occasional lucid moments.

"He comes in and out of consciousness," Doc reported. "I keep waiting for him to turn the corner, but it seems that whenever that corner appears, he moves in the opposite direction."

"So is he taking a turn for the worse, Doc?" Jones asked.

"Not really. He's just not making the progress I wish he'd make," Doc answered.

"I think Parson Abel would remind you that you are not God," said Jones.

"Now, don't you start talkin' like Parson Abel," Doc responded with a grin. "I'm already baptized, ya know." He sat in the swivel chair at his desk. "Doggone it but my feet are tired. Been standin' on 'em for quite a while."

Potter spoke up. "We're on the way to pick up a body," he announced.

"A what?" Doc asked.

"Brody Belt came across some buzzards out in the hills by his place and found a body under 'em," Potter noted.

"And by the sound of it, Brody thinks it's another of Cincy's men. The man named Snider.

"If it's true, Cincy's men are droppin' like flies," said Doc. "The man who wants to own the town can't keep his men from dyin' between the ones you shot up, the one Hickok killed, and now this one."

"Cincy's hired himself a professional and I'll bet he's got

money enough to hire a couple more men if he feels the need," Potter said.

Parson Abel and Brody Belt stood in the doorway.

"Are you about ready to go?" Parson Abel asked Jones. "We got the wagon."

"Just about. We were tellin' Doc that Brody discovered a body," Jones responded.

Brody said, "I think one of Cincy's men."

"So, what does that leave Cincy with if Snider's dead?" asked Doc.

"That leaves him with his hired gunman and Stevens," Jones said.

"Didn't Cincy have a mountain of a man working for him? A man named Jimbo?" said Doc.

"That's right," Brody recalled. "Jimbo."

Doc reminisced a bit. "Jimbo. That's the one I treated at the McNolte place."

"He seemed like he really liked you, Doc," Brody added. "Not sure what you did, but he really seemed to like you."

"I helped him once, that's all I did. That's what I do. I'm a doctor."

"Regardless, I'm not sure Cincy can count on Jimbo if the chips are down and Doc is involved," Brody announced.

"Now, I wouldn't go quite that far," Doc added.

"Well," Parson Abel interjected, "I think I've heard enough of Doc patting his own back, we've got a body to retrieve."

"I am not patting myself on the back," Doc bristled. "I'm just saying that I'm a doctor, that's all. How about you just stick to the buryin' and I'll stick to the healin'?"

"Alright, you two," Jones said with a laugh. "I think it's high time we saddled up and went out and brought Snider back."

Jones led the way down the stairs to the waiting wagon. Potter, Abel and Belt followed after.

Brody took the lead. "Let's make tracks," he said. "We have a long way to go and not a whole lotta time until sunset. Mount up!"

Doc opened his door to find the mayor and three members of the city council.

"Evening, gentlemen, what can I do for you?" Doc asked.

The mayor got right to the point. "We want to talk with Sheriff Blanton," he said.

"He's recovered enough that he can talk with you, mayor. But, I'd recommend you and I go back there. I don't want him getting too excited and slow down his recovery."

"I can respect that," the mayor replied.

Doc led the mayor into the inner office that served as Sheriff Blanton's recovery room. The other three men remained in the outer office.

"Sheriff," Doc said, "you've got a visitor. The mayor is here to see you."

The mayor stood over Sheriff Blanton who sat propped up in his bed with pillows behind his back.

"How ya feelin'?" the mayor asked.

"Tell ya the truth," Blanton responded, "I've felt better. But Doc seems to think I'm about three weeks from full recovery. Are my deputies doing a good job?"

"Fine. Fine. Your deputies are doing just fine." The mayor removed his hat and held it in front of him. "Well. It's just that in your absence I think. . ." He hurried to add. "The city council and I think that we need to appoint someone as sheriff. That is, until you are back on your feet."

"I see," Sheriff Blanton said.

"It's just that we heard that we got a murder to investigate and we got a hired gunman wandering about the town. In your absence someone's gotta stand up to Cincinnati or we'll lose the whole town," the mayor said.

A question flew out of Doc's mouth. "So, do you have someone in mind?" he asked.

"We. . ." the mayor began, "that is the city council and I . . . wondered if the sheriff might appoint Jesse Jones as acting Sheriff."

"I'm not so sure that Jones wants that responsibility," Doc interjected.

The mayor turned toward Doc. "That's why we were hopin' that between the two of you, you might convince him. I mean, he's kinda involved helping you anyway. That is when he's not busy runnin' Swede's Merchantile. We businessmen need to stick together."

Jones' voice was heard in the outer room. "Hey, Doc," he said. "We retrieved Snider's body. Do you wanna come and take a look at it?"

"Jesse, would you come in here a minute," Doc asked.

Jesse entered the room. He identified the mayor at once. "Hello, mayor, what are you doing here?"

"Jesse," Doc said, "the mayor has something he'd like to discuss with you."

Doc noticed that his words caught the mayor off-guard which is exactly what he had set out to do.

"We," the mayor began in awkward fashion. "That is the city council and I would like to ask you if you would step in as Sheriff until Blanton is fully recovered. Doc seems to think that he's about three weeks away from returning."

"Isn't that something you should get Sheriff Blanton's input on?" asked Jones. "He and I have been friends for years and I'm not about to do anything like that without having his approval."

"It's alright, Jesse," Blanton said. "It's gonna be temporary anyway. Do you think you could help me out for a little while?"

"Well, this ain't somethin' I bargained for," Jones said. "But, if you say you'd like me to step in for ya, I'll do it as a friend." Jones looked over at the mayor as he continued: "And not just because the mayor and city council want me to."

"Why don't you head over to my office, pick up a badge, come back and I'll swear you in," Sheriff Blanton said.

CHAPTER NINETEEN

Jones removed the tarp covering the body.

Doc examined it and found it entwined in wire. "Whoever did this wanted to make a statement," Doc said. "I can't be sure of the cause of death. It could be from strangulation from the wire around his neck or from the bullet in the forehead."

"There are powder burns around the wound," Jones noted. "I've seen that before. Am I correct in saying that this shot was fired at point blank range?"

"You're right about that," said Doc.

"This sure looks like Snider," Adam Potter said.

"Adam, would you do me a favor? Would you see if you can roust Cincy out of the Last Chance to come down here and identify the body?" Jones said.

A few minutes later Cincinnati Culver arrived accompanied by Jimbo. Jones noted that there was no sign of the hired killer and he wondered why that was the case.

"Cincy, is this man Snider?" Jones asked.

"Sure looks like him," Cincy said. "Where did you find him? I haven't seen him in days."

"Brody Belt found him a couple of miles from his place this morning," Potter said. "He must have been dead a while 'cuz buzzards were flying over him."

"Any idea why anyone would want to kill him?" asked Jones.

"Could be that Belt fella done it," Cincy replied. "You said it was out there near his place. Wasn't Snider one of the fellas Belt is accusing of holding him hostage?" Cincy looked around. "Where is Belt anyway? This seems awful suspicious to me."

"I sent him home," Jones said. He stood erect and Cincy couldn't help but notice the star pinned to his chest.

"When did they pin that star on you?" Cincy asked. "Did Sheriff Blanton die or somethin'?"

"Blanton is very much alive and I'm sending him home tomorrow," Doc interjected.

"With the Sheriff's approval, the mayor and city council appointed me Sheriff until Blanton returns," Jones said.

"That means ya better mind yer p's and q's," said Potter.

The look Cincy gave Potter did not faze him and he stood his ground as Cincy said, "Are you threatening me, Potter? 'Cuz if you are you'd better watch yer back."

"Nope," Potter said. "Just makin' a statement of fact with Jones in charge."

"What do you want me to do with the body?" Jones interrupted.

"Don't rightly care," Cincinnati snapped. "I say that you should have Belt bury him since he most likely killed him in the first place? Right, Jimbo?"

Jimbo stood emotionless and never uttered a sound.

"If ya don't have anything else to ask me, I got a saloon full of cowboys and I can't be a-waistin' any more of my time,"

Cincy said. With a nod to Jimbo, Cincy turned and walked away with Jimbo tagging along behind.

"There's just somethin' about that man that I can't stand," Potter said. "He's a liar from the get-go."

"Yeah," Doc added. "Cincy's one of the few men I know who has lied so often that he believes his own lies."

"You don't think for a minute that Belt killed Snider, do you, Doc?" Jones asked.

"Not for one minute. I don't think Belt could carry a grudge any longer than I can," Doc said. "I think we'd better get Snider here over to the undertakers. I gotta get back upstairs and see how my patient is doing."

With Doc out of sight, Jones turned to Potter.

"You sure got Cincy's attention when you told him to mind his p's and q's," said Jones.

"Sorry that I put you in a bad spot," said Potter.

"Nonsense," Jones replied. "I like it when someone is upset. People do stupid things when they're upset."

DOC PULLED his surrey up in front of Sheriff Blanton's home.

"Whoa, Becky," he said. After gathering his medical bag, Doc ambled to the front door and knocked. Blanton's wife Edith answered the door in a frock dress with an apron cinched at the waist.

"Mornin', Doc," she said, "I'm just fixin' breakfast, would you care to join us."

Doc stepped inside. "How's our patient doing this morning?" he asked.

"You can see for yourself. He's sitting at the table," she replied.

The Sheriff sat at the table in blue jeans and an undershirt, with suspenders looped over the top and fastened to his jeans.

"Other than a bit of paleness from the loss of blood, I'd say he looks pretty good after all the wear and tear," Doc said.

"Sit down, Doc. I'll get you some coffee and then throw a couple more eggs in the skillet. You do like eggs, don't ya, Doc?" Edith asked.

"Over easy," Doc said. "I like my yokes a bit runny so I can sop them up with some of that homemade bread I smell," he replied.

Edith returned to the stove and it was not long before the sound of eggs cracking was heard, followed by a sizzling sound as they hit the hot bacon grease already in the skillet.

"So, how are you feeling?" Doc plopped his medical bag on the table and pulled out his stethoscope.

"Still a little weak and light headed," Blanton replied. "But Edith is doing everything she can to make me stronger."

"Is the memory of your shooting coming back?" Doc asked, but before the sheriff could answer, Doc asked a second question. "Let me have a listen to your heart, will ya?" Doc applied the stethoscope to Blanton's chest and gave a listen. "Your heart sounds fine."

"My memory is getting clearer, Doc," Blanton replied. "It was a member of Cincy's gang alright. The one they call Snider."

"You can change the tense of yer sentence. Make it called instead of call," Doc interjected.

"Is he dead?" Edith asked setting a cup and saucer in front of Doc and pouring coffee.

"Thank you, Edith," Doc replied to the coffee pouring. "Yes, Snider is dead."

"When did this happen?" said Blanton.

"A couple of days ago, I'd say," said Doc. "Brody Belt was

returning home when he noticed buzzards. When he got closer he discovered Snider's body. The poor guy was wrapped up in fencing wire and shot in the forehead. Jones is investigating, but he's hitting lots of dead ends."

"By the Belt place, did you say?" Blanton asked.

"Yeah, and that's exactly who Cincy is blaming for killing Snider." Doc sipped his coffee. "He's all over Jones like stink on a skunk."

"Makes me think that Cincy's got somethin' to hide, if you ask me," Blanton added.

"That's what I'm thinking, too. Provin' it is another matter altogether," said Doc.

"It sure is," Blanton reflected, "but I'll about guarantee ya that Cincy's the weasel in the henhouse. When you get back to town tell Jones to keep his eye on Cincy and take everything Cincy's tells him with a grain of salt. What about the gunman Cincy's hired. Is he still in town?"

"Yeah. It's strange though, he seems like he's lookin' fer somethin'.He keeps nosing around," Doc said.

"Any idea what he might be lookin' for?" asked Sheriff Blanton.

"Nope," said Doc.

Edith returned to the table with a plate of food for Doc.

"Here ya go, Doc," Edith said. "Eggs just the way you like 'em, over easy and fried in bacon grease and a slice of my homemade bread and plenty of fresh churned butter."

SNIDER'S FUNERAL was nothing like Curly Bill's. For one thing Snider's body was really inside the casket, unlike the rocks placed inside of Curly Bill's casket to give the feel of a body inside. Try as they might, no one could remove the fence wire around Snider's body; so he went to his grave just as Brody Belt found him. That also meant that Snider was hurriedly buried without a church funeral service.

A small crowd gathered around the mouth of an open grave in Boot Hill Cemetery. Parson Abel stood over the grave and began his remarks over Snider's casket.

"Because Adam and Eve rebelled against God in the Garden of Eden and sin entered the world, life is now one-hundred percent fatal. That means that each one of us gathered here today will one day die. We don't know how. We don't know when. What led to Snider's death and the manner in which he was killed may not be known by those gathered around his grave, but someone knows; and certainly God knows. We know that for certain because Scripture tells us that God knows when even a sparrow falls to the ground. There may not have been any human witnesses to Snider's tragic end, but there was a Heavenly One."

Seeing Cincy, Jimbo, and the gunman Fitz in the crowd, Parson Abel aimed his closing remarks in their direction. "Whoever did this vicious murder will one day have to give an accounting of his actions before God's judgment seat. I call upon that person to come to me and make confession and receive from God's hand forgiveness for the sin of murder. Yes, there will be a civil accounting for this murder, however, the good news is that this person will not lose his soul and live forever in the fire and brimstone of hell."

Parson Abel noted that Jimbo's complexion turned ashen at these words.

"Oh, Lord," Abel continued, "we commit this body into your Almighty Hands. Ashes to ashes and dust to dust in the sure and certain hope of the resurrection of the dead. Amen."

Parson Abel bent down and grabbed a handful of dirt that

the grave diggers had removed from the grave and tossed it on top of the casket.

"Be at rest until God calls you forth," Abel said.

And those gathered at the grave answered him with their 'Amen'.

"Did you see the look on Jimbo's face?" Abel asked as the crowd dissipated and wandered back to town.

"I sure did," Potter said. "I think you scared the hell out of him."

"I hope so," Abel announced. "That was my intent."

"Does that invitation to dinner still stand?" said Jones.

"It does," Abel answered. "In fact, Adeline is counting on it."

"Then give me a few minutes and I'll head your direction. I want to stop for a few minutes at Sarah's grave," Jones said.

"I understand," Abel replied. "You do that. I will let Adeline know that you will be along in a minute."

Jones picked his way around the headstones until he found himself in front of a wooden marker with his wife's name on it. He removed his hat and bowed his head unaware he was being watched.

Jones walked to his horse at the bottom of Boot Hill and untied him. In the distance the bugler at Fort Sidney sounded *mess*, flooding his mind with memories of the late war and his service at the fort. In silence he slipped his left foot into the stirrup and mounted. In his mounting, his horse moved into a position where he could look back up the hill.

To his horror someone was stooped over in front of Sarah's grave. When the man rose again he recognized him at once.

It's Fitz! What's he doing there?

For reasons he did not fully understand, he turned his horse from his questions and rode to Parson Abel's to fulfill his invitation for the evening meal.

"It's about time you got here," said Abel opening the door to Jones. "We were about to give up and start eating without you."

"Was I that long?" asked Jones.

"You were," said Abel. "We were beginning to think you weren't coming."

Abel led Jones down the hall to the dining room where the others were gathered.

"Well, look who finally made it," Doc said.

"Sorry to keep everyone waiting," said Jones. "Sometimes when I'm at Sarah's grave time gets away from me."

"But you're here now and that's all that matters," Martha said. "I hope you don't mind, but I've saved a seat for you."

Jones seated himself in the chair Martha reserved for him.

"You'll never guess who I saw standing over Sarah's grave as I was leaving," said Jones. "It was Cincy's hired gunman."

"Fitz?" Parson Abel asked.

"Yeah, Fitz. I walked down the hill and mounted my horse and there he was stooped over her grave," Jones said.

Doc rubbed his neck and speculated out loud, "Is there some connection?"

"Between Fitz and Jones' wife Sarah?" Potter asked. "I would hardly think so."

"Wait a minute," Jones said. "Wait one cotton pickin' minute."

"What are you thinking?" said Martha.

"I'm thinkin' that there may be a connection between the two like Doc said. What if Sarah and Fitz are related? More specifically what if Sarah and Fitz are brother and sister?"

"How is that even possible?" Martha chimed in.

"Think about this for a moment," Jones told her. "Sarah's last name was Fitzpatrick and Cincy's hired gun is named Fitz. What if Fitz is a shortened version of his last name. . ."

"...and his last name is Fitzpatrick," Parson Abel finished Jones' sentence for him.

"Holy Cow!" Potter exclaimed. "Is that possible?"

"Sounds too coincidental not to be," said Jones.

"So Cincy hired a gunman named Fitz and brought him to Sidney to kill you," Doc said while he was looking at Jones. "And by coincidence Fitz came here and discovered that the man he was hired to kill was once married to his sister."

"I know this is going to sound preachy," Parson Abel said. "But I am not one to believe in coincidences. This sounds to me an awful lot like a God-incidence."

CHAPTER TWENTY

"Gentlemen, let me tell you why we are here," the man began. "Most of you know me already, but for the few of you who don't, I'm Mayor Truax. I've asked Jesse Jones and his business partner Adam Potter to host our little get together so that I might introduce you to Henry T. Clarke. Mister Clarke has the backing of the Union Pacific railroad and several business men in Omaha to survey and build a bridge across the North Platte River."

There was murmuring among the men seated in the back room of Swede's Mercantile. Jones cast his eyes to the far side of the room where Cincy and Jimbo sat. Cincy's arms were crossed and a scowl creased his brow. Jones read his lips as he spoke to Jimbo. "I told you this was comin'."

Mayor Truax continued, "Gentlemen, I give you Mr. Henry T. Clarke."

Clarke stood. He was all business from his suit to his closely cropped beard which was peppered with grey. His voice demanded attention.

"Thank you, Mr. Mayor. Gentlemen," he began, "I came

west several years ago and settled in Omaha during the war. Since that time I've made a good deal of money hauling freight and surveying routes for railroad expansion through Nebraska. There's something coming that could make this community very wealthy. I envision Sidney as the starting point for a route north to the gold fields in Dakota Territory. I'm sending surveying teams here in a month or two to gather supplies and plan out the route then begin site work for a bridge across the North Platte River. The Union Pacific Railroad has already invested in this project, as well as several prominent businessmen in Omaha. I'm inviting you to join them and me in making an investment in your future."

After speaking Clarke sat down again and Mayor Truax took over. "This changes everything, gentlemen. If others consider us the prime location for northward expansion into Dakota Territory, then I think it behooves us to invest in ourselves. Can you picture thousands of men, women and children stepping off trains and needing a place to sleep, a place to shop for supplies—"

"—And place to drink," Jimbo enthusiastically proclaimed to the laughter of everyone present.

"Yes, and a place to drink," Mayor Truax echoed back. "Mr. Clarke has an outstanding reputation for getting the things done he sets out to do. He platted the city of Bellevue and gave it its first school, and he's been freighting merchandise and mining supplies to Denver. So this is an opportunity for all of us to get in on the ground floor. Can I get a show of hands for all who are willing to support Mr. Clarke's latest venture?"

Jones watched as Cincinnati Culver rose to his feet. "Mr. Mayor before we give you a show of hands, I'd like to ask Mr. Clarke a question."

"Mr. Clarke," the mayor asked, "are you up to taking a question?" Henry Clarke nodded. As Clarke stood to take

Cincy's question, Mayor Truax said a few words as a way to introduce Cincy. "Mr. Clarke, this is Cincinnati Culver. He owns the Last Chance Bar down the street from here, as well as one of Sidney's two hotels."

"Go ahead, Mr. Culver," Henry Clarke said.

"Mr. Clarke," Cincy began, "what are we looking at for a time line? Look, I'm planning to invest, that's a certainty, and I'd just like to know what we're looking at?"

"Let me answer your question this way," Clarke said. "I'm thinking we only have a couple of years to get ready for the heavy migration north. Quite frankly, I'm planning to start construction on the bridge I'm calling Camp Clarke as soon as my surveyors return to Omaha. Does that answer your question?"

Cincy looked directly at Jones when he answered. "Yes, sir, it sure does."

THAT EVENING on the Abel's front porch, Martha listened as Jones recounted the meeting with Henry T. Clarke.

"There's a good deal of potential in Sidney," Jones said. "Clarke said we are in the perfect location. Trains will bring gold prospectors by the hundreds; fortune hunters ready to press northward into the Dakotas. What worries me is what this will mean to the Cheyenne and Sioux who view the Black Hills as sacred."

"Some say that its *manifest destiny*, that we have every right to occupy their land because we bought this land from the French," Martha said.

"I've heard of *manifest destiny* but what input did the natives who live on this land have in all of this?" Jones asked as they swung back-and-forth on the Abel's porch swing.

"None, really," she said.

"I'm conflicted right now," said Jones. "I'm the owner of a business that's on the verge of selling supplies to prospectors who may or may not have permission to swarm all over the Black Hills looking for gold."

"Sounds like this is inevitable. It's going to happen whether you agree with the idea or not," Martha said. "The only other alternative, it seems to me, is for you to sell out to Cincy."

"This badge I'm wearing prevents me from doing that," Jones said. "I can't run away from my obligation as Sheriff."

"Acting Sheriff," Martha corrected him.

"Even as *Acting Sheriff* in Blanton's absence. Cincy wants to own the whole town and right now I am the only thing standing in his way," said Jones. "All that Clarke did by showing up now is to turn up the heat on a pot already fixin' to boil."

On their right, over the Abel's porch railing, the sun shot its last rays into the autumn sky.

"What are you planning to do?" she asked.

"For right now I'm going to wait until Cincy makes his next move, but in the meantime I'm also going to look for an opportunity to talk one-on-one with Cincy's hired gun," Jones said.

"Isn't that dangerous?" Martha said. "After all he is a hired killer."

"But I have a strong suspicion that he's also my wife's brother," he said. "I saw him standing at Sarah's grave the day of Snider's funeral. He goes by Fitz and Sarah's maiden name was Fitzpatrick."

"Can I ask you what all of this means for you and me?" said Martha.

"It means that a resolution is coming sooner than later. It's kinda like what Doc says, 'When you got a boil on ya, it's better to sterilize yer knife and drain it than to let it sit there and continue to fester'," Jones noted.

Martha threw her arms around Jones and held him tight. "I don't want you to get hurt." Then she felt his strong arms surround her and his warm breath played upon her neck.

"I know this may sound foolish to you, but I have faced situations a lot more life-threatening than this one," he said.

He held her at arm's length and she looked up into his bright eyes and broad smile.

"I promise you that I will be careful. I won't go into any situation alone," he said.

"I don't want you to make a promise that you can't keep," she said. "Just do whatever you think is right and then return to me. I'll be waiting for you."

"That's reassuring," Jones said.

"And Jesse?" said Martha.

"Yes."

"I want you to know that I love you."

"Thanks for the reminder," he said. He held her close. "And I love you too."

JONES DID NOT HAVE to wait long before Cincy made his next move. He hadn't been in the sheriff's office more than twenty minutes when someone knocked on the door.

In the blink of an eye Jones remembered what happened to Sheriff Blanton and drew his LeMat. He aimed it at the door which burst open and in stepped Cincy, Jimbo and Fitz.

Cincy found himself staring at the point of a gun.

"Kinda jumpy, ain't ya, Sheriff?" Cincinnati said.

"A man can't be too careful these day," Jones replied.

"Ya can uncock that gun and put it away," Cincy said. "We

ain't gonna kill ya." He paused and then added, "Yet!" to the delight of Jimbo.

"My, that has to be the awfullest lookin' pistol I've ever seen. What the heck is that?" asked Cincy.

"It's a LeMat," said Jones.

"Heard of 'em, but never seen one before. Mind if I take a look at it?" Cincy said.

"Right now yer seein' it about as close as yer gonna get," said Jones. "Now, state yer business, cuz I got work to do." Jones uncocked the LeMat and laid in on his desk.

"I came here with a request, Sheriff," Cincinnati said. "I want you to arrest Brody Belt!"

Jones eased back in his chair. "And just why would you want me to do that?"

"Cuz he's the one who killed Snider and wrapped him in wire," Cincy said.

"And how do you know that?" Jones asked.

Cincy hovered over the front of Jones' desk. "Belt has wire out at his place. Jimbo's seen it. Ain't ya, Jimbo?"-

Jimbo nodded.

"So, I want ya to ride out to the Belt place and put Brody under arrest for murder."

"Now, that's a real bold accusation," Jones said. "Do you have any other evidence linking Belt to the killing, apart from knowing that there is wire out at his place?"

"Belt's got a reason to kill him," Cincy continued. "He knew that Snider was one of the men who held him and his wife hostage."

"With that kind of evidence you could just as well accuse Doc. Snider held Doc hostage, too. And you mentioned Belt's wife. Maybe she killed Snider," Jones said.

"Ain't no woman gonna wrap Snider up as tight as he was tied," Fitz said.

"Look," Jones responded. "I got no quarrel with you, so for the time being why don't you butt out?"

For a moment Jones thought that Fitz would throw down on him, but as he watched Fitz's eyes, he noticed Fitz thought better of it.

"There'll be another time," Fitz said.

"You can count on it," Jones replied. "Alright, Cincy. I'll ride out to the Brody place and have a talk with him. But in my mind yer leading me on a wild goose chase. I don't think Brody is our killer." Jones thought for a moment and then tossed out an accusation to gauge their reaction to it.

"I'm thinkin' that it would take a man more like your friend Jimbo here to kill Snider and to bind him up in fence wire," Jones said. He trained his eyes on Jimbo and thought he noticed Jimbo flinch.

"Of course, you got no way of proving that," Cincy came to Jimbo's defense.

"No, I don't, and that's for sure," Jones said. Again he stared directly at Jimbo. "But if there is one thing I've learned through the years, it's that someone can tell a lie only so long before that lie starts to unravel. Can't remember where I heard this sayin', but it goes like this, Two people can keep a secret if one of them is dead."

A SHORT TIME later in the back room of the Last Chance Saloon an argument was underway.

"I gotta get outta here," Jimbo said. He paced the floor like a caged animal. "Jones has got this whole thing figured out and I'm gonna hang for it."

"Calm down, Jimbo," Cincinnati said. "Jones ain't got

nothin' figured out. He's bluffing. He ain't got a good hand in this poker game, so he's bluffing."

"His bluff is scaring me," Jimbo said. "I ain't no good at playing poker. I have too many *tells*. You said so yerself. I have too many *tells*, you told me."

"Look, all ya gotta do is lay low for a while," said Cincy. "Jones doesn't have anything, but if you panic and run away, or something equally as stupid, Jones'll nail ya fer sure."

Jimbo stopped short and turned on Cincy. "Are you calling me stupid?"

"Jimbo, you know I'd never do that. We've been friends way too long for me to do that. You saved my life and I'm forever in your debt, but ya can't panic now or you'll get us all killed." Cincy walked over to his wall safe and pulled out a hundred dollar bill and handed it to Jimbo. "Why don't you buy yerself a bottle and then go down the street and have yerself a good time with the ladies.Come back in a day or two when yer feelin' more relaxed."

Jimbo crossed the room in three strides, snatched the money from Cincy's hand and bolted out the front door of Cincy's office and into the dark recesses of the Last Chance.

Fitz came out of the far corner where he had witnessed the entire conversation.

"I think you have a loose cannon," Fitz said.

Cincinnati sat at his desk. Who? Jimbo? Naw, he's alright. Give him a couple of days and we'll have nothing to worry about."

"I think that if someone lights his fuse, he'll erupt like *the mine* in front of Petersburg, only there won't be any survivors, you and me included," Fitz said.

"Look, I hired you to do just one thing and that's to get rid of Jones," Cincy fired back. "Do your job and I'll do mine!"

"I'm just concerned that if Jimbo starts shooting off his mouth and rats you out, I won't get paid," Fitz answered.

"You can stop being concerned. I know Jimbo. He'll stay loyal even if it kills him," Cincy said. He took a scrap of paper from his desk and scratched some words on it. He folded the paper and handed it to Fitz. "Take this to the telegraph office. I've got a friend in the Union Pacific office in Omaha. I'm going to see if we can get the railroad to declare a ban on Swede's Mercantile to keep them from supplying anything to Henry Clarke's bridge project. We're gonna tighten the screws a little bit and force the showdown you seem so reluctant to have."

"It seems that I may have underestimated you, Mr. Culver," Fitz said.

"Yeah, people do that all the time," Cincy replied. "And when that happens it usually comes around to bite them in the backside. Jones included."

CHAPTER TWENTY-ONE

Jesse Jones rode out to the Belt place first thing next morning. It was a somber ride spent thinking out the repercussions of arresting Martha's brother.Nearing his destination a thought occurred to him.

There is a way I can clear up this whole matter.

He held that thought to himself. At last he arrived in front of the Belt's home and he dismounted.

Martha peered from behind the curtains on the window nearest the door.Jones saw her smile and she soon greeted him with a kiss.

"Jesse," she said. "What a pleasant surprise. What are you doing riding out this way?"

"Is your brother at home?" Jones asked.

"What's wrong, Jesse?" she said. "I can tell by the tone of your voice that this is business and not pleasure."

"It is business, Martha. I've come to arrest your brother for Snider's murder."

"Jesse, my brother would never do a thing like that. He's never murdered anyone in his life."

"I know that, Martha. That's why I came in person, so your brother wouldn't be foolhardy and run off," said Jones. "I have an idea that will clear him of suspicion, but I need him to come with me voluntarily."

"He's in the barn getting ready to put a fence up," Martha said.

"I want you to stay in the house with your sister-in-law," said Jesse."Everything's gonna be alright, but you must stay out of the way. I have a job to do."

Martha went back inside. Jones felt her eyes watching him as he walked toward the barn.

Brody was exactly where Martha said he was, inside the barn and unrolling fence wire. Jones noted that the wire looked exactly like the wire that someone had wrapped around Snider's body after shooting him.

Brody looked up. "Jesse," he said. "What a pleasant surprise. Did you come all the way out here to see my sister?"

"Actually," Jones replied. "I rode all the way out here to see you."

"You did? What for?"

"I rode all the way out here to arrest you for Snider's murder."

"You what?" said Brody.

"I came out here to arrest you. Yer the one that found Snider's body, and the wire yer unwinding looks the same as the wire around his body," Jones said.

"Would it do any good to tell you that I didn't do it?" Brody said.

"The truth is," Jones said, "I already know that and I think I've got a way that we can prove your innocence if you'll ride out with me to the spot where you found Snider. Can you remember where that is?"

"Sure can," said Brody.

"Get your horse and let's ride out there together," Jones said.

The ride to the site of Snider's murder was not a long one and the two men, with Brody Belt in the lead, were soon there.

Jones recalled seeing the place for the first time. There were signs of a struggle in the sand, and foot prints—lots and lots of foot prints. The men lit off their horses at a distance of fifty feet from where the sand was disturbed and walked the rest of the way.

"So, how is this going to prove my innocence?" Brody said.

"We're going to compare your foot prints to those here in the sand," Jones said. "Any place where your boot fits into the prints in the sand will show where you were. Any other prints were made by somebody else. If we find your prints near where Snider's body was then I gotta arrest you. If we don't find your prints there then I'm gonna let you go free."

"That makes sense," said Brody.

Brody stepped in several footprints that were obviously his, but around the murder scene they found several prints made by a much larger boot, with a distinctive tread pattern.

"Go on back home," Jones said. "You're not the murderer, but I know who is."

ADAM POTTER and Parson Abel were busy stocking shelves when Henry T. Clarke arrived at Swede's.

"Gentleman," Clarke said brandishing a telegram, "I'd like a word with you."

"Parson, why don't you head into the back room and I'll stay out front to tend the store," Potter said.

Parson Abel escorted Clarke into the back room where just

a few days before several of Sidney's merchants had made Clarke's acquaintance.

"I don't understand the communiqué I received a few minutes ago," Clarke said.

"How can I help you?" Parson Abel asked.

"Well, I have a telegram from Union Pacific headquarters in Omaha instructing me not to do business with you," Clarke said. "Never had anything like this happen before and I can say that I don't know quite how to handle this."

"Does your telegraph give a specific reason why you should not do business with us?" Parson Abel asked.

"No. No it doesn't. And frankly it is signed by a railroad Vice President who I know very little about. I've only met him once," Clarke replied. "I don't feel any need to hold anything back from you, you can read the telegram for yourself."

Abel took the telegram from Clarke and read.

"Pursuant to a claim made against Swede's Mercantile, I am instructing you not to do business with this firm until the matter is resolved.' Rodney Silverton, Vice President Union Pacific Railroad."

"Do you have any idea what this claim might be?" Clarke asked.

"I'm as confused by this as you are. What I do know is that Cincinnati Culver has been employing whatever means at his disposal to get his hands on our business," Abel said.

"Doesn't he own the Last Chance Saloon and the Moore Hotel?" Clarke said.

"Yes, and Cincinnati wants Swede's for some reason," said Abel.

"I can give you a reason if he somehow has connections back east and knows about the expected land route into

Dakota Territory. Owning a mercantile store of your quality, along with a hotel and a bar, would be like giving someone permission to print money if the gold fields to the north pan out like we think they will." Clarke paused and then added, "Sorry about the pun there with the *pan out* regarding the gold fields."

"That would explain it alright," Abel announced. "That's got to be the reason, but how do we put a halt to Cincy's plans? It's certainly not something I'm qualified to determine. You see, I'm just a minority stockholder in a family run business."

"And who might be the majority stockholder? Jesse Jones, I presume?" said Clarke.

"That's exactly right," said Parson Abel, "and he's out of town right now arresting a murderer, one that Cincy put him on to."

"Seems to me that Cincy has his fingers in a lot of pies around here," said Clarke. "I sure hope that Jones knows what he's up against."

"I'd say that he does, but he is spread a bit thin with running this place and serving as the city's temporary sheriff," Abel said.

"Well, I've heard it said that if you want to get something done, give the job to someone who is already busy."

"That fits you as well, doesn't it," Abel said. "You seem to have taken on a lot of responsibilities from founding Bellevue and building its first school house, to building bridges for the railroad."

"That's very true," Clarke said. "The truth is that it takes a lot of people to make this all work. And you don't get places without knowing people in high places. Let me send a telegram to Horace Clark, President of the Union Pacific and we'll see if we can get to the bottom of all this."

"Are you two related?" Abel asked. "You have the same last name."

"In a way, yes," Clarke replied. He chuckled. "But, my family had the good sense to keep the *e* on the end of our last name. Horace's side never did that."

Jones rode into town. He reined his horse in front of the Last Chance and went inside. Although bright sunshine shone outside the inside was dank, dusty and dark. It took Jones a few minutes for his eyes to adjust. When they did he saw a doorway at the opposite side of the room and made his way toward it. He had to weave his way between the chairs and tables of gamblers, hustlers, and those there merely to drink. The sights and smells of the place was an insult to his senses, chewing tobacco spit that had missed its spittoon, and the smell of cigarettes, cigars, and warm beer. He spotted Jimbo, sitting with his back to him, at the faro table.

Jones ignored the laughter, the shouts, and the catcalls of the ladies hoping to make a quick buck and knocked on Cincy's door.

"What do ya want?" came a shout from inside the closed room.

"It's Jones. I want to talk to ya, Cincy." Jones replied.

"Come back later, I'm busy," Cincy said. "Say, in about an hour?"

Jones grabbed the doorknob, turned it, and burst into the room with gun drawn. A saloon girl leaped from Cincy's lap and raced by Jones and out of the room.

"What is it that is so all-fired important that you couldn't wait?" Cincy asked.He adjusted his clothing. "Did ya arrest Brody like I asked ya to do?"

Jones strode into the room and sat opposite Cincy. He pushed back his hat.

"No, I didn't," Jones responded.

"Then we're through here," Cincy said. "You've got work to do and so do I."Cincy stood to accent the point that the conversation was over.

"I didn't arrest Brody because Brody isn't Snider's killer," Jones said calmly.

"Oh? Then who is it?" said Cincy.

"It's yer man Jimbo," said Jones.

"I hardly think so. Jimbo would never do a thing like that," Cincy said.

"Not unless you ordered him to," Jones responded. "Bring him in here and I'll know for sure."

Cincy went to the door and called out to Jimbo. "Jimbo, would you step into my office for a minute?"

"In a minute, boss. I'm right in the middle of a hand," Jimbo said over his shoulder.

Cincy returned to his seat behind his desk. Jones kept a wary eye on him.

"I wouldn't go for that gun in your desk if I was you. You do and I'll blow yer head clean off," Jones said matter-of-factly when he saw Cincy's right hand drop off the table.

It wasn't too long before Jimbo barged through the door and lumbered into the room.

"What's he doing here?" Jimbo asked. He gave Jones a stare.

"He's been out lookin' for Snider's murderer and he thinks he's found him," Cincy answered.

"Really?" Jimbo now towered over Jones who remained calm in his chair."And who might that be?" he said.

"Jimbo, I hate to tell you this," Cincy began, "but he says that *you* are the one."

Jimbo went for his revolver, but Jones sprang into action and in one continuous motion stripped away Jimbo's revolver and smashed it into the side of Jimbo's head, sending him to the floor with a loud thud. Just as quickly he turned on Cincinnati, LeMat in hand.

"One move and yer a dead man!" he snapped.

Jones positioned himself in such a way that he could get a full view of Jimbo's boots. *Sure enough. Jimbo's boots are a dead ringer for the boots in the sand where Snider was found.* Jones walked over to the dresser, grabbed a pitcher of water and doused Jimbo with it.

Jimbo stirred in response.

"On yer feet," Jones commanded. Then with his LeMat placed in the middle of Jimbo's back, he marched him off to jail.

Not long after Jimbo's jail cell door clanked closed and Jones had placed the key in his desk for safe-keeping, Parson Abel, Doc and Adam Potter burst in.

"We heard you arrested Jimbo Livingston," Potter said. "That you marched right in to Cincy's office and brought Jimbo out at gunpoint."

"Yeah, it was somethin' like that," Jones said. "Doc, I've got him in the far cell. You might want to give him a quick once over. I hit him pretty hard with his gun butt." Jones retrieved the key. "Here's the key." He tossed it to Doc who caught it.

Doc left the others and made his way to Jimbo's cell.

"I thought you went out to the Belt place to arrest Brody. How in the world did you end up arresting Jimbo instead?" said Abel.

Jones sat down on the corner of his desk.

"On the ride out there I did some thinking, Jones said. "Whoever killed Snider would have left evidence at the scene. So I took Brody out to where he discovered the body. We found three sets of footprints. One set of foot prints matched the bottom of the boots we took off Snider. The other matched Brody's boots, but the third set was too large to be Brody's, and besides they had a unique tread. After I walloped Jimbo I gave his boots a quick looky-see and sure enough they matched the tread near where Snider was murdered."

Doc returned.

"I'm gonna have to go over to my office and get my medical bag," Doc said."Jones, not only did you give Jimbo a big goose egg on the side of his head, but you split his head open. It's gonna take a few stitches. He'll have a headache for several days, but he should be alright. What did you say you hit with?"

"He said that he hit him with a gun butt," Parson Abel chimed in.

"That's what I thought he said, but with the size of the wound I would have thought he hit him with a lead pipe or somethin'," Doc said.

"I didn't think that I hit him that hard, Doc," Jones responded.

"It's ok. I can sew him up," Doc said. He looked over at Parson Abel. "I've gotten pretty good at sewing wounds shut as I recall."

"You mean what you did to my cheek a couple years back?" said Abel.

"Yea, that's precisely what I mean. I did a pretty good job of it, too, didn't I?" Doc said.

"Sounds to me like yer fishing for a compliment," Abel replied.

"I'll take all the compliments I can get, whenever and however I can get them," said Doc.

"Well, this is about as close to a compliment as you're gonna get from me," Abel said egging him on.

Doc waited. When nothing further came out of Parson Abel's mouth he said, "Well, what's the *as close as a compliment* that I'm gonna get out of you?"

"You really don't know?" Abel asked.

"Humor me," said Doc.

"Well, for one thing I've never criticized your work stitching up my face," Parson Abel said.

"That's true," said Doc.

"And the other is this," Abel paused for effect. "I paid my bill. Those two things are as close as you'll get to a compliment from me."

"Why you old coot," Doc said with a smile. "I should have known."

CHAPTER TWENTY-TWO

Doc returned to Jimbo Livingston who was sprawled out on his jail cell cot with his feet dangling over one edge and his head barely on the other. Doc took notice that Jimbo had bled through the preliminary bandages he'd hurriedly wrapped around his head.

Removing these bandages won't be easy. It looks like the coagulated blood has matted the gauze to his hair and scalp. He decided instead to wrap more gauze around Jimbo's head to staunch the blood and woke Jimbo in the process.

"Mmmmmmm," Jimbo moaned. His eyes opened only a slit.

"Now, you just lay still for a moment," Doc said. "I don't want you trying to get up. You got clobbered pretty good."

"Where am I?" Jimbo asked in a volume barely above a whisper.

"You're in a jail cell. Don't you remember?" Doc put a hand on Jimbo's chest preventing him from rising. "I know you want to sit up, but its best you lay still. Now that you're awake I gotta put a couple of stitches in that head of yours."

Instinctively Jimbo's beefy left hand went to the wounded area. He brought it in front of his face and saw the blood on it.

"Jones," Doc shouted, "can you come back here and give me a hand? Bring Potter with you."

In moments Doc had the help he needed and he began ordering the two about.

"Potter, boil up some water, will ya?" Doc ordered. "And Jones, I'm gonna need you to hold Jimbo down so that I can put in a couple of stitches. But first I've gotta remove these bandages."

"Jimbo," Doc said. "Yer gonna have to trust me. What I am about to do is gonna hurt like mad, but I've got to remove these bandages so I can stop the bleeding. Do you understand? We'll start as soon as Potter gets back in here with my hot water."

Jimbo winced.

Doc smiled down at him. "It's gonna feel better once it stops hurting," he said.

That remark brought a smile to Jimbo's face.

When Potter returned Doc went into action.

"Alright," he said. "Jones I want you to hold Jimbo's legs down. And Potter.Potter, you hold his arms down to keep him from interferin'."

With both men in place, Doc began to remove the gauze. It was a painful process for Jimbo and he struggled mightily to free himself.

"Hold him down," Doc ordered. Once the old bandages were removed Doc took a good look at the wound. "Jimbo, I want you to hold as still as you can. This is gonna take five stitches to close." Doc took a cloth from his bag, dipped it into the hot water Potter had brought in a basin and wrung the excess water from it. With deft hand Doc cleaned the wound and applied iodine.

Jimbo screamed and tried to free himself, but Jones and Potter kept him from doing so.

"I know, Jimbo," Doc intoned. "I know. But be patient with me and it will all be over soon."

Doc threaded the needle and wove five stitches into Jimbo's flesh.

"Just about done," Doc told Jimbo. "Can you hang on for another three minutes?"

Jimbo nodded through the pain.

Doc tied off the stitches and cut the thread. He daubed the wound and wiped away the remaining blood before another liberal application of iodine. This he followed with clean gauze over the wound and more gauze wrapped about Jimbo's head.

"How are you doing, Jimbo?" said Doc. "I'm all done. I want you to lie still today. Can you do that?"

Jimbo mouthed the words, "Thank you."

"You're welcome," Doc answered. "I'll be back this afternoon to take a look at it. Does that sound ok to you?"

Jimbo nodded.

In the outer office of the jail, where Parson Abel kept watch, Adam Potter asked Jones to sit for a minute.

"I'd rather stand," Jones said.

"I think you might want to sit down for this," Parson Abel said.

Both men waited until Jones had seated himself behind Sheriff Blanton's desk. Potter began, "Henry Clarke came into the store earlier today. He brought some bad news."

"What kind of news?" Jones asked.

Potter removed a folded up piece of paper from his pocket and handed it to Jones. "He brought this," he said.

Jones read the words:

Pursuant to a claim made against Swede's Mercantile, I am instructing you not to do business with this firm until the matter is resolved. Rodney Silverton, Vice President Union Pacific Railroad.

"What is this all about? Did he explain?" asked Jones.

"He doesn't know any more about this than we do," Potter said.

"We're both thinking that Cincy is pulling some strings because we won't sell Swede's to him," Abel said.

Jones stood. "I think I'll just amble down the street and ask Cincy in person."

"You don't need to do that," Potter said.

"Clarke knows the President of the railroad personally, so he said he'd send a telegram asking for an explanation. He's gonna by-pass this Rodney Silverton fella altogether," Abel said.

"I still think I should pay Cincy a call," said Jones.

"I'm in favor of waiting this out," Abel said. "Remember what you told me before, 'Sometimes desperate men make mistakes'. Cincy's gotta be half outta his mind by now. Everything he's tried has fizzled like a misplaced fuse on the Fourth of July. Money drives men to do stupid things."

"Yeah," Potter said. "And like Parson Abel always says, 'money is the root of all evil.'"

"That's not quite what Scripture says," Abel jumped in. "What it says is that 'the love of money is the root of all kinds of evil'. Money, in and of itself, is not evil. It's when we *love* money above all else that it can lead to evil things. Such as in the case of Cincy with attempted murder, stealing, and hiring a gunslinger so he can get his way."

"I stand corrected," said Potter apologetically.

"It's alright, Adam. That's a common mistake," said Abel.

"So, what are you suggesting?" Jones asked.

"I'm suggesting that as the man of God that you are, you let God handle this.Sounds preachy, I know, but you'll just have to accept that as an occupational hazard of mine," Abel said. "You let God have his way with you a couple of years ago after the murder of your wife and he kept you from strangling the killer to death. He's not gonna abandon you."

"I know that, but it feels weird to let Cincy play out his hand and not do anything about it," Jones said.

Abel walked over to where Jones sat and put his hand upon Jones' shoulder."I don't doubt that for a minute, but let's give Henry Clarke an opportunity to get to the bottom of the railroad's decision. If what I think is going on, is actually going on, Cincy's about to have the rug pulled out from under him--"

"--and that's when he'll start making mistakes," Potter interrupted.

"What I'd like to know," said Jones, "is the role that Cincy's gunfighter is going to play in all of this."

"Have you told Fitz that you think he is your brother-in-law?" Abel asked.

"Not yet," said Jones. "I haven't seen him around town very much lately.There's another somethin' goin' on there that I'd like to get to the bottom of."

CINCY WASN'T AT ALL happy when Fitz knocked at his office door and then entered without so much as a *come in* on Cincy's part.

"Where have you been hidin'?" Cincy asked.

"I've been around," Fitz replied. "Been checkin' out the lay of the land."

Cincy stood in Fitz's path.

"I needed you here when Jones arrested Jimbo and you were nowhere to be found," Cincy barked up at him. "Jones just sauntered in here, whacked Jimbo upside the head and marched him off to jail. I needed you here and you weren't here."

"I didn't know that you needed me to babysit ya," Fitz answered back.

"I hired you for one thing and one thing only. I hired you to get rid of Jones.And as best as I can tell, you ain't done that yet," Cincy said.

"So now you are all alone. Is that what yer tellin' me?" Fitz said. "I'm supposed to be in two places at once. Is that it? I'm supposed to be here protectin' yer hide while at the same time checking out the town and pickin' out where and when to kill Jones."

Cincy turned his back to Fitz; walked to his desk and sat. "Let me tell you the *lay of the land* from my point of view," he said. "I'm expecting Jones to barge in here at any minute. By now I'm sure word has gotten to him that the railroad won't be doing any business with him. I've secured an embargo against Jones and Swede's Mercantile so they won't be gettin' any money to supply Henry Clarke and the bridge he'll be buildin' across the Platte River."

"How did you pull that off?" Fitz asked.

"I got my way of doin' stuff," Cincy said with pride. "I know what levers to pull and what buttons to press. Let's just say that I know people in high places.Let's also say that I've grown used to gettin' my own way. Let's also say..." He paused as a point of emphasis. "That I've given you an assignment. I've paid you well, and I expect results and not excuses."

Fitz rubbed his chin. "Alright," he said. "I'll goad Jones into a gunfight and kill him like you want it. It will be nice and legal-like. But after I do I want what's comin' to me. Then I'm ridin' clean away from this place. There's too much goin' on here that I don't like."

"Don't go all self-righteous on me," Cincy said. "Once you've done yer job, I don't much care where you go. Cuz with Jones dead there won't be nothin' stoppin' me from taking over the town."

"But how are you gonna do that by yerself?"

"That's the easy part," Cincy replied. "All I gotta do is step into my bar and put a hundred dollars down for any man who helps me. There's nothin' that a hundred bucks can't buy. A hundred bucks would be like wavin' a red cloth in front of a bull. The men would come chargin' in." Cincy stopped and looked Fitz directly in the eyes. "That's why I'm tellin' ya not to cross me. I'm willin' to bet a hundred dollars that yer life won't be worth a plug nickel if ya do. Do I make myself very clear?"

"I don't like threats," Fitz said. "From you or from anyone else."

"Mister," Cincy spat out with contempt. "This ain't no threat. This ain't no threat at all. This is fact." Again he paused for emphasis. "Nothin' personal.This is business. I'm tellin' ya that if you don't do yer job and kill Jones within the week, you are a dead man. I don't know how I can make this any plainer.Now get out."

JESSE JONES STOOD ALONE at his wife Sarah's grave. It was hot day with no breeze, unusual for late autumn. So hot and humid one could sweat without any exertion whatsoever. Jesse's clothing clung to him.

"Sarah," he said under his breath. "I think I'm falling in love." He paused seemingly waiting for a reply that never came. "This is hard for me to say," he resumed, "but I just wanted you to know that I never intended this to happen."

Again he listened and nothingness responded.

All was silent save for the distant commotion of city life blocks away.

CRACK.

What was that? Jones listened more intently.

Nothing answered.

CRACK.

Behind you! Jones spun around, drawing his LeMat as he faced Fitz, Cincy's hired gunman.

Fitz held his hands up in front of him.

"Whoa," he shouted. "I didn't come out here to kill you."

"Then don't come sneaking around like that," Jones said. "What do you want?"

Fitz pushed his hat back on his head. "I came out here to talk to you. Put yer gun away."

Jones holstered his gun.

"That's better," Fitz said. "I think a whole lot better when I'm not lookin' down the barrel of someone's gun. Let me explain somethin' to you. The reason I came to Sidney in the first place was to find my sister."

"You didn't come because Cincy is paying you?" Jones responded.

"That was part of it. But that just gave me a good excuse to come and the travelin' money to do it. Call it a five-hundred dollar incentive."

"Cincy offered you five-hundred dollars to kill me?" Jones said.

"Yeah. Rive hundred to get here and five hundred to kill ya. You must be a real thorn in Cincy's backside."

"Must be," Jones said. "So, is yer sister who I think she is?" Jones pointed to Sarah's grave. "Her last name was Fitzpatrick. I'm assuming that Fitz is yer nickname, a shortening of Fitz-patrick."

Fitz nodded. "And I'm assuming that she was yer wife."

"She was murdered a couple of years ago," Jones said. "Killed by a man named Custus Leaverette. In case yer wondering, he lies in an unmarked grave over there." Jones pointed to the southeast corner of Boot Hill.

"Did you kill him?" Fitz asked.

"Tried to," said Jones.

"What does that mean?"

"Yer sister kept me from doing it from the grave," said Jones.

"From the grave?"

Jones nodded. "From the grave. I wasn't there when Custus killed her and with her dying breath she circled the words, *'Vengeance is mine,' saith the Lord* in her Bible with her own blood. Those words came back to me when I was choking Custus to death. I let him go, turned my back on him and walked away."

"So, how did he die?"

"Custus found his Bowie knife and was about to throw it at my back when a Cheyenne brave named Red Hand skewed him with an arrow," said Jones.

The questioning expression on Fitz's face told Jones that he was confused."It's a long story," Jones said. "God did take out his vengeance on Custus, but that's a story for another time. What's more important is what you're going to do now that you know that the man you're hired to kill was your sister's husband."

"Did you love her?" Fitz asked.

"More than you'll ever know," Jones answered. "She was carrying our baby when Custus killed her."

Fitz looked down at Sarah's grave and then, a moment or two later, back up at Jones. "You loved my sister and she loved you, too." Jones nodded. "That does present a problem, doesn't it?"

CHAPTER TWENTY-THREE

Martha's mind could not comprehend what her eyes were seeing. Fitz stood in the doorway with Jones one step behind him.

"Would you mind letting us in?" Jones asked. "We've come to see Parson Abel."

She led the two men into the entryway.

"What's he doing here?" she asked.

"I guess I could ask the same of you," Jones replied.

"The Abels invited me to stay with them a few days. I'm interviewing to teach school," she said.

"Martha, this is Fitz," Jones said.

"I know who he is," she said. "But, I thought he was hired to kill you."

"That's all changed," Jones said. "That's why I wanted him to meet Parson Abel."

"He's in his study, praying," she said. "He's asked not to be disturbed."

Jones knocked on the door to the study. "I think he'll want to see this," Jones replied. He knocked again.

"Alright. Alright," Abel said. "What's all the commotion out there?"

"I told them you didn't want to be disturbed," Martha said.

"Parson Abel," Jones said. "I have someone out here that I want you to meet."

Abel opened the door and like Martha was dumbfounded by what he saw.

"What's he doing here?" Abel asked.

"Those were my exact words, too," Martha said.

"Fitz and I had a little conversation at the cemetery this morning," Jones said, "and I thought you might be interested in what we discovered."

"Well, don't just stand there in the hallway," Parson Abel said. "Come on in."

When Jones, Fitz and Martha had entered his study, Abel shouted up the hallway, "Adeline, would you be a dear and bring five servings of tea into the study and join me there?"

"Five servings?" Adeline responded.

"Yes, dear. We have guests and I'd like you to join us." He turned back into the room and smiled at Jones. "Now, what's so all-fired important that you disturbed my prayers?"

"Parson Abel, I'd like to introduce you to Fitz," Jones said.

Abel extended his right hand and Fitz took it.

"Fitz is exactly who I thought he was. He's the brother of my wife, Sarah. Fitz is short for Fitzpatrick, her last name and his," said Jones.

Martha pondered this revelation.

"I had no idea that I was coming to Sidney to kill the very man that my sister had married," Fitz said. "All I knew was that the last letter I got from her said that she was in Sidney and that she was falling in love. She never told me the man's name or anything else. That was the last letter I received from her, so when I heard Cincy needed a gunman, I took the job."

"It took him a while to put two and two together. He scared the dickens out of me this morning on Boot Hill," Jones said. "I was standing over Sarah's grave and he sneaked up on me. I heard a twig snap behind me and I wheeled around to find him standing there."

"You left out the part that you had yer gun drawn when you wheeled around," Fitz said. "I thought there for a minute that you would drop me dead in my tracks."

"You should have seen the look in your eyes when I wheeled around," Jones said.

"Now that I've discovered your true identity as my sister's husband, I have a big problem. I can't kill ya and I've five hundred dollars from Cincy that says I gotta," Fitz said. "As the old sayin' goes, I find myself between a rock and a hard place."

"You may not believe me when I tell you, this is what I was praying for before you got here today," Abel said.

"That I'd be in this situation?" Fitz asked.

"No, not that," Abel answered. "I prayed that there wouldn't be a gunfight between you two."

"That gunfight won't happen," Fitz said. "But, I can only imagine how angry Cincy's gonna be when I give him his money back. Less expenses, of course."

"CAN you give me a hand with the dishes?" Adeline asked.

"I'd be glad too," Martha replied. "It's the least I can do in return for my room and board."

Adeline removed a pan of hot water from the stove and poured it into an enamel wash pan on the counter. With a butcher knife she shaved off lye soap and added it to the water.

Martha gathered the dishes and brought them to Adeline.

"So, tell me again when you start teaching school. Is it Monday?" said Adeline.

"Monday," Martha said. "I'll have ten children."

"That's quite a lot to manage," Adeline said. She placed the dishes into the hot, soapy water. "Ouch. I'm going to have to let the water cool down a bit. These plates are too hot to handle. Let's sit at the table a minute."

"The oldest student is twenty-one and the youngest is eight," Martha said as she sat. Adeline joined her.

"The sad part is that I only have them for a few weeks," Martha continued, "Then they all are needed around the house or in the field for harvest."

"So the saying goes in our household, 'for some students the best five years of their lives was spent in the third grade'," Adeline added.

Martha giggled.

"What does Jones think of your new venture?" said Adeline.

"We haven't discussed it. He's been too busy," Martha said. "I've got to be doing something and apart from having an offer to work in the Last Chance, this is the best I can do."

"You were offered a job at the Last Chance?"

"Not really," Martha replied. "A drunk came through the door as I was walking by the other day. He said that I looked pretty enough to work in the Last Chance. I just nodded and kept walking not knowing whether to feel insulted or complimented."

They shared a laugh.

"May I ask you something?" said Martha, interrupting the laughter.

"Oh, my, this sounds serious," said Adeline.

"It is," said Martha. "Would you tell me more about Jesse? She continued never waiting for Adeline's reply. "What kind of man is Jesse Jones? I mean, I've only known him for a short time, but already I'm in love with him.And I'm sure he's in love with me." She hesitated. "Before I go any further I'd like to know more about him."

"Let me start by saying that he is a man of convictions," Adeline said. "He knows what he believes and is willing to stand up for them. He's always had a firm conviction to stand up for the underdog. He doesn't like it when someone takes advantage of anyone. Oh, and the parson baptized him a while back." Adeline waited a moment. "But, that's not what you're really asking me, is it?You're asking me if I think he will make a good husband and father for your children."

"I guess that is what I'm asking."

"I'll answer that question this way, I base it on what I witnessed firsthand with his relationship with his first wife. You will never find a more loving, caring man to marry than Jesse Jones. Except for my husband, of course."

IN THE JAIL all was quiet as the sun began its downward arc on a clear Nebraska day. Potter occupied the front desk, giving Jones the afternoon to put together an order to restock the shelves at Swede's. Doc tended to Jimbo in his jail cell.

"How are you feeling?" Doc asked.

"My head still hurts and I'm still dizzy," Jimbo answered.

"Understandable," said Doc. "Jones put a big ol' knot on yer head. Yer gonna be dizzy for another day or two."

"Any word on when the judge'll get to town?"

"It'll be another week or two according to Jones," Doc said.

"I'm gonna hang, ain't I?" said Jimbo.

"That looks like a real possibility," said Doc. "Jones has got a lot of evidence against you."

"Didn't think I'd ever be scared of dyin', but I am, Doc. Real scared."

"You know, as much as he's a pain in the rear to me, I think maybe you should have a little chat with Parson Abel," Doc said.

Doc heard a clamor in the alley outside then a face looked in through the barred window of Jimbo's cell. "Don't worry Jimbo, Cincy sent a bunch of us to get you out," a voice said.

"Is that you, Ethan Cole?" Doc asked.

"Howdy, Doc," the man in the window answered back. "Didn't know you was in here a tendin' to Jimbo."

"It's alright, Cole," Doc said. "I just finished puttin' new bandages on Jimbo's head."

"I hope I ain't interruptin' nothin,' Doc," Cole said. "I was just lettin' Jimbo know that we was a bustin' him out of jail."

"Cole, ya big dummie," a voice shouted from the alley. "Ya done let the cat outta the bag. Now, get down from there. You weren't supposed to tell no one what we was up to."

Cole turned his attention to the voice below the window. "Hush up, Travis. Ain't no one heard me but ol' Doc and he ain't gonna tell no one," he said.

All the commotion outside the jail brought Potter to Jimbo's cell. "Doc," Potter said, "I think you better scramble out the back way and get Jones while I secure the front door."

Doc watched as Potter went to the front window and looked into the street. "There's at least a dozen armed men in the street. Looks like they're fixin' to storm the place and set Jimbo free," Potter said. "If I bolt the door I should be able to hold them off until Jones gets here."

"I'm scared, Doc. Don't leave me. What if Cincy's tryin' to free me, so he can kill me?" Jimbo pleaded.

"You'll be safe in here. Potter's got everything under control," Doc said.

"Cole could shoot me through the window bars," Jimbo said.

"I don't think Cole is smart enough to know one end of the gun from the other," Doc replied.

In moments Doc was out the back door and into the alley. He heard Potter bolt the door behind him. He breathed a sigh of relieve.

"Hands in the air, ya varmint!" a voice shouted from behind. Doc turned and came face-to-face with the business end of Cole's revolver.

"Not smart enough to know one end of the gun from the other, huh?" Cole repeated Doc words. "Bet, you didn't think I was listenin,' did ya? Well, I was."

"You tell him, Cole." Doc recognized the voice. It belonged to Travis Hostetler.

"You stay out of this, Travis," Cole said. "This here's between me and Doc."

Doc heard the distinctive click as the hammer of Cole's pistol locked into place, but he never anticipated what came next. Cole began to laugh. Uncontrollably.The gun barrel pointed away from Doc. "Go on, Doc. Get outta here," Cole said between laughs. "I was just funnin' with ya."

Doc ARRIVED out of breath at the Abel's front door, knocked twice, and waited.He did not wait long.

"Doc, what are you doing here?" said Abel.

"Took you long enough to answer the door," Doc said, bursting into the hallway.

"The door was unlocked you could have come right in," Abel responded.

"Why would you leave your door unlocked?" asked Doc.

"It's usually unlocked during the day," Abel answered. "The only ones who would come in are family. From now on knock twice and come on in."

"Why didn't you tell me that before?" said Doc.

"I did. You just didn't remember," Abel said.

"You didn't tell me that," Doc said. "And my memory is as sharp as ever."

"It is, huh," Abel replied. "Then tell me why you're here?"

The question caught Doc by surprise and hesitated momentarily.

"That's what I thought," Abel said. "You can't remember."

"I came to find Jones. Assuming you remember where he is," Doc fired back.

"He's in my study," Abel replied. "Why the panic?"

"There's a bunch of rowdies at the jail threatening to break Jimbo out," said Doc.

Abel led the way into his study.

Doc went at once to Jones. "Potter's got a problem at the jail. There's a bunch of rowdies outside and they're going to break Jimbo out if we don't hurry," Doc said.

Jones' response was immediate. He raced out the door with Fitz and Abel right behind, and Doc bringing up the rear. When Doc arrived a standoff was underway in front of the jail. Jones looked at Fitz. "Stay out of this. It ain't yer fight. Let me handle it," he said.

"I didn't come all this way to stand by and watch you get killed," Fitz said.

"But you're in enough trouble with Cincy without getting in the way of this mob. Let me handle it," Jones said.

Jones pushed himself between the crowd and the door.

"Step away from the jail," Jones commanded. "No one's bustin' Jimbo out.Now, go on home."

The mob held its ground.

"I said, go home," Jones said. His voice was as steeled as his resolve to keep Jimbo captive. "Most of you men got families. Go on home before someone gets hurt."

"You can't kill us all, Sheriff. There are too many of us," a man in the crowd said.

"But I can kill you and that's all that matters to me right now," Jones replied.There was no wavering or panic in his voice.

No one moved for what seemed to Doc an eternity.

The door of the jail opened and Adam Potter emerged, shotgun in hand.

"This evens the odds a bit," Potter said to Jones as he took his place at Jones' right hand.

A murmur went through the crowd, but no one moved.

"Go on home, I said," Jones repeated.

"You heard the man," Fitz said, brushing the crowd out of his way and standing next to Jones.

Jones looked at Fitz. "You shouldn't be here," Jones whispered.

"I've chosen my side," Fitz replied. "My sister faced death without fear, so will I."

"So, you've chosen sides, have ya, Fitz?" a voice sounded from the back of the mob. In response the crowd parted like the Red Sea. The man in the back moved to his left and soon stood directly in front of Fitz at a distance of thirty feet.

"I got no quarrel with you," Fitz said.

"But I got one with you," the man replied. He widened his stance and flipped his coattails away from his holster.

"Who are you, friend?" Fitz asked.

"For one thing," the man answered, "I ain't yer friend. The name's Babbit. Stone Cold Bruce Babbit."

"Yer name means nothin' to me," Fitz said. "Clear out before I drag you out feet first."

"Prove it," Babbit said. He made a play for his gun.

Bam.

The bullet from Fitz's Navy Colt made its mark in the middle of Babbit's chest.His face registered disbelief. For a moment his body stood still, then, without warning, his legs collapsed and he pitched forward, and fell face-first into the street.

The crowd evaporated.

Three blocks away and in front of the Last Chance, Doc saw a lone man standing.

Watching.

Cincinnati Culver.

CHAPTER TWENTY-FOUR

Cincy stormed through the swinging doors of the Last Chance like a tornado.Anyone in his path stepped aside for fear of becoming the object of his wrath.He slammed his office door closed and sent a picture of President Grant crashing to the floor.

"Jones!" He pounded his fist on his desk. "I hate that man! He ruins all my plans. No matter what I do or where I turn, there he is and I hate him for it."

A knock at the back door.

In his anger, Cincy ignored it.

A second knock.

"Go away," Cincy bellowed in anger.

The door opened a smidge, just wide enough for Ethan Cole's head to appear in the opening.

"Can we come in?" Cole asked.

"What do you want?" Cincy fired back.

"Me and Travis came to collect our hundred dollars," Cole said. He entered Cincy's office and Travis followed.

Cincy spit out the words, "Oh, you did, did you?"

"Yep," Cole said. He made his way to the chair in front of Cincy's desk and sat.Travis followed but found nowhere to sit. He nervously stood behind Cole."You owe us each a hundred dollars. That's how we figure it, don't we, Travis?" Cole said.

"And just what makes you think I owe you each a hundred dollars?" Cincy asked.

"For attacking the jail like ya told us to," Travis said. He looked down at Cole to seek his support. Cole nodded.

"I'll give ya each fifty dollars," Cincy announced.

"Fifty?" Cole replied.

"Ya, fifty," said Cincy. "Because ya only did half the job I sent ya to do."

"Wadda ya mean?" said Cole.

"I said that I would pay ya a hundred bucks to attack the jail *and* spring Jimbo," Cincy said.

"I don't remember that part, Cole. Do you?" asked Travis.

Cole looked up at Travis.

"Nope," said Cole.

"You two need to go back to school so you can remember what the word *and* means. In this case it means *in addition to*. I wanted you to do two things. Attack the jail *and in addition to* get Jimbo out." Cincy stood. He walked to his wall safe and withdrew two fifty dollar bills. He held them up so that Cole and Travis could see them. "I'll give each of you fifty dollars now and another fifty dollars when you bring Jimbo to me. Is that clear? *And* be careful Jones doesn't kill you in a gunfight like he did tonight."

"Jones never kilt no one tonight," Cole announced.

"Ya, he did," said Cincy. "I saw the whole thing from the door of my saloon."

"We may not know what the word *and* means," Travis replied. "But the two of us know what we seen. It weren't Jones who killed that young fella." He paused and looked down at Cole for help. "What's the young fella's name again?" he asked.

"For cryin' out loud, Travis. I can't remember stuff like that," Cole said.

"Anyway," Travis resumed. "It weren't that Jones fella who did the shootin.' It was that gunman from outta town who done it."

"Fitz?" Cincy asked.

"If that's his name, then that's his name," Travis replied.

"The gunman I hired is the one who did the killin' tonight. Is that what yer sayin'?" asked Cincy.

"That's what we're sayin,'" Cole said.

"Well, I'd say that this little bit of information has earned ya each an extra fifty bucks." Cincy went back to his safe.

Cole and Travis watched with eager eyes as Cincy took out a wad of bills and peeled off two fifties and handed it to them.

"Let's just say that you earned yer hundred bucks for tonight," Cincy said.

TRUE TO HIS WORD, Doc brought Parson Abel to visit with Jimbo. Jones unlocked Jimbo's cell, brought up a stool and sat outside it to keep an eye on things as the two men visited.

"Doc said you wanted to talk with me," Abel began.

"I do," Jimbo said. "I'm scared of hanging."

"Who said you were going to hang?" Abel said. "You haven't even had a trial yet."

"I can't lie to you, Parson," Jimbo said. "I done some bad things in my life and I'm gonna pay for 'em."

"Did you kill Snider and wrap him in wire?" Abel asked. It was the question that Jones wanted answered although he already had the evidence of Jimbo's footprints in the sand.

"I did," Jimbo said. "Ain't no use lyin' about it. Jones has the evidence."

"Maybe a better question for me to ask is *why?*" said Abel.

"I was just followin' orders. Cincy's orders," Jimbo responded.

"Tell me what that was all about," Abel said.

"Cincy's got a hankerin' to own the town. Said somethin' about gettin' in on the ground floor of makin' all kinds of money when the road goes north of here into Dakota Territory," said Jimbo.

Parson Abel turned to Jones. "This is just what I was saying the other day, 'the love of money is the root of all kinds of evil'."

Jimbo corrected Abel. "Parson, it's money that is the root of all evil."

"Money isn't the root of all evil, Jimbo. Money is an inanimate object. It can do nothing on its own. But, when someone *loves* money so much that it turns one's attention away from God, all kind of evil follows," Abel noted. "It sounds to me like Cincy *loves* money far too much. So much so that he is willing to have others kill and lie for him."

"I thought Cincy was my friend. We've been through a lot together," said Jimbo.

"Right now I'd be willing to say that Cincy is your friend as long as you help him get what he wants," Jones added.

"And because of that I'm gonna hang," Jimbo said.

"We won't know that until the judge gets here, but right now I'd say that the odds are not in your favor," Abel said.

"Ain't there nothin' I can do about it?" said Jimbo.

"The only thing I can think of Jimbo, is that you testify to what Cincinnati is doing when you make your defense," said Jones.

"Can I do that?" asked Jimbo.

"You can tell the judge everything you just told us. Can't make any promises, but the judge might think kindly on what you say and that might keep you from hanging," Jones said.

"But, Parson, won't God know what I done to Snider?" said Jimbo.

"He'll know," Abel said.

"Ain't there nothin' I can do about that?" said Jimbo. "I remember hearing about hell as a young boy. Ain't that where I'll go when I die 'cuz of what I done did?"

"Well, there is some good news I can share with you today," Parson Abel began. "In John's Gospel Jesus tells Nicodemus 'God so loved the world that He gave His only Son that whoever believes in Him should not perish but have eternal life. For God did not send His Son into the world to condemn the world, but in order that the world might be saved through Him.' Do you believe these words of Jesus?"

"I do," Jimbo said.

"Then eternal life is yours this day. Jimbo? May I ask if you've been baptized?" Parson Abel asked.

"No, I ain't," said Jimbo.

"Would you like to *be* baptized?" Abel said.

"Yes!"

"Jones would you bring me the water pitcher?" said Abel.

A few minutes later Parson Abel applied water to Jimbo's head with the words, "I baptize you in the Name of the Father, and of the Son, and of the Holy Spirit.Amen."

THE TOWN WAS STILL for a few days. But, it was an uneasy stillness like the stillness ahead of a range fire. Everyone knew that something was coming, the tinderbox was stoked. What they didn't know was what would provide the spark to set everything ablaze.

Sheriff Blanton made slow progress in his recovery. His wife saw to that as she meticulously followed Doc's wound protocol. Blanton was growing tired of the continuous liquid diet Doc prescribed and was craving a medium rare steak, something not yet on his diet.

Doc nursed Jimbo back to physical health and Parson Abel attended to Jimbo's spiritual health.

Jones kept his relationship with Martha at arm's length, unwilling to commit to anything more until he was sure he could provide for her safety.

"When will this be over and we can settle down?" Martha asked.

"I wish I had an answer for you. All I can say is that right now my life is in danger and I don't want yours to be in danger, too," Jones said.

"But Jesse, my life is intertwined with yours, so I am already in danger. Why don't we head to California and get away from all this?"

"And leave this town without hope?" Jones said. "I can't do that. I gotta stay until this is settled."

The sun started its daily journey further south now. Tumbleweeds rode the plains like so many miniature horses, pushed along by cool breezes off the Rockies. Those who planted gardens in the spring knew it was time for the fall clean-up. Plants not harvested had long ago withered and died, producing no more this year. Old timers said the effects of this year's drought made it seem as if the whole Nebraska panhandle was a tinderbox waiting to be set on fire.

One week after the showdown outside the jail, a telegraph addressed to Henry T. Clarke arrived that put a match to the tinderbox. Not the prairie, thankfully, but the hopeless situation in Sidney.

Henry T. Clarke read the telegraph, folded it, stuffed it inside his jacket pocket and walked at once to the Sheriff's office.

Jones greeted him from behind his desk. "Mr. Clarke, what can I do for you?"

Clarke walked to where Jones sat, retrieved the telegraph, and handed it to him. "I knew something was fishy back in Omaha and this proves it," Clarke announced.

Jones read.

Silverton not authorized to negotiate contracts.
Fired him immediately.
Arriving in two weeks with U.S. Marshals
to clear matters up.
Horace Clark,
President Union Pacific Railroad.

"Well, this certainly changes things around here," Jones replied.

"It certainly does," Clarke answered. "I figured there had to be some shenanigans going on. I'd never experienced anything like this before and this telegraph explains it all. Cincinnati's been using his contacts back east to pull some strings."

"And now that his string is all played out, it's time to reel him in, as Doc would say," Jones said. "How do you want to play this?"

"I want to wait until President Clark arrives," Henry Clarke announced.

"WELL, well, Mr. Fitz. Or should I say Fitzpatrick? Do have a seat." Cincy walked from behind his desk and sat on the desk's corner.

Cole pushed the bound Fitz forward to the chair in front of Cincy's desk. Here Travis caught him.

"I said, *have a seat.*" Cincy's words were no longer a request, but a command.

Fitz refused.

Cole slid the chair up against the back of Fitz's knees and he collapsed into it.

"Boys," Cincinnati continued. "Untie Mr. Fitz here. He and I are going to have a civilized conversation before you kill him."

Cole and Travis did as they were told. They stood Fitz up and removed the lariat that held him fast.

By instinct Fitz reached for his holster only to find it empty.

"Lookin' for this?" Cole asked. He cocked the gun and stuck the barrel against the back of Fitz's head. Cole and Travis shared a laugh then shoved Fitz back down in his chair. Cole un-cocked the pistol and slid it into his belt.

Cincy remained untouched by their humor.

"I hear tell, that you turned against me." Cincy stood. He raised his right hand and administered a heavy slap to Fitz's right cheek. "No one does that and gets away with it."

A thin red line of blood crept down from the corner of Fitz's lip.

Cole and Travis laughed.

"I gave you an ultimatum. I told you to kill Jones or else," Cincinnati continued. "You deliberately disobeyed my order and nobody, absolutely nobody gets away with that." A second time Cincinnati struck Fitz. This time blood splattered from Fitz's nose.

"How could I kill my sister's husband?" Fitz tried to plead his case.

"You're a hired killer, ain't ya?" Cincy fired back. "That means you do as yer told for money. What you do isn't personal. It's business."

Cincy raised his hand a third time, but before he could strike, Fitz rose to his feet and grabbed Cincy's hand.

Fitz stared into Cincy's eyes. "I'd be a bit more careful about who I slapped around, if I were you."

There was a matter-of-factness to Fitz's voice that made Cincy's blood run cold.He didn't like that feeling.

Fitz reached for his vest pocket. Behind him, two gun hammers clicked into firing position.

"Unless you wanna die," Cincy began. "Ease that hog leg out slowly."

Fitz withdrew his hand. Between his thumb and forefinger he held his wallet."I'm giving you back your five hundred dollars. Less expenses, of course."

Cincy shook his head. "No, yer not getting' off that easy. I got a reputation to uphold. Ain't no one takes money from me to do a job and not complete it.Boys, I want you to ride out into the prairie with Mr. Fitz here and teach him a lesson he won't forget. Now, don't kill him. I want him to remember me the rest of his miserable life."

These were the last words Fitz heard before his world went dark.

FITZ WOKE to Cole using his face as a punching bag while someone held him secure. Fitz heard laughter, an almost demonic laughter behind him and attributed that laughter to Travis. He saw Cole's fists flash back and forth through slits in swollen eyelids. He felt the sting of each blow.

With all his remaining strength, Fitz willed his right arm to break free and countered Cole's right hand. He willed his left hand into a fist and smashed it into Cole's belly. Cole crumpled like an accordion complete with a high pitched squeal as breath escaped his lips.

Travis shielded his face in anticipation of Fitz's blow, but his body met the same fate that Cole's had. Down he went headlong into the sand.

Fitz retrieved his revolver from Travis' belt and crammed it back into his holster. He untied a saddled horse from the wagon he found nearby. Wincing in pain, he forced one foot into the stirrup and slung his right leg over the saddle to mount. He looked skyward. By the position of the sun, he gauged it was late afternoon.

Fitz glanced once over his shoulder. Cole and Travis lay prostrate before him.He removed a canteen secured to the saddle horn and tossed it between them and rode away.

CHAPTER TWENTY-FIVE

That evening, in the backroom of Swede's Mercantile, Jones brought together Parson Abel, Adam Potter, and Doc for a meeting.

"Gentlemen," he began, "Mr. Clarke received a telegram today in answer to his inquiry to the railroad. He shared it with me earlier today."

Henry T. Clarke held the communiqué in his hand. "I don't need to remind all of you here this evening, that what you are about to read is confidential. I'd even go so far as the say that the fewer the number of those who know about this, the better." Clarke paused for effect. "Do I make myself clear, gentlemen?"

"Does the mayor know about this telegraph?" Potter asked.

"No," Jones said. "Mr. Clarke wants this kept among us."

Clarke passed the telegram to Parson Abel who quickly read the missive.

"Looks to me," said Abel, "that Cincy's love of money is about to catch up with him. When you build your house of sand, any rain that comes along washes your house away."

Abel passed the message to Doc who read it. "Was that one of yer Bible analogies?" Doc asked.

"Yep," Parson Abel said with a grin.

Doc passed the telegraph to Potter who read it and passed it to Jones.

Jones read the message a second time before passing it back to Clarke, who folded it up and placed it back in his vest pocket for safety.

"Here's what I was thinkin' about doing," Jones said. "I was thinking about taking Potter with me and rounding up Fitz.Then the three of us would make our way to the Last Chance and present this telegraph to Cincy."

"I'll give you two reasons why I think that's a bad idea," Potter said. "First, Cincy's got a couple of thugs around him these days."

"You aren't talking about Ethan Cole and Travis Hostetler, are you?" Doc said.

"That's right," said Potter.

"Those two don't have half a brain between the two of them," said Doc."They're as libel to shoot you as look at you."

"You said you had two reasons. What's the second?" asked Jones.

"The second is that I haven't seen Fitz in town since this morning. It seems he just up and vanished," said Potter. "Saw Cole and Travis leave town in a wagon earlier today, too. Haven't seen them since."

"You been keepin' an eye on them, have you?" Doc said.

"Jones asked me to, that's all," Potter replied.

"I don't mean to put the kibosh on all your good intentions," Henry T. Clarke said. "But, what I'd like to do is to get some preliminary quotes for the material I need to supply my men. I want to get back up north where the surveying is taking place. I'm asking you not to tell anyone about this telegraph or do anything until President Clark gets here with the U.S. Marshals. We don't want Cincinnati to run before we get our hands on him. I believe this matter goes up all the way to Washington. Keep your eyes on Cincy, but don't let him escape.He's trying to make himself rich on the backs of the American people."

"Won't we tip Cincy off if we start sending supplies north for your bridge?After all Cincy has the telegraph saying that Swede's is banned from doing business with you," Jones asked.

"Good point." Clarke thought the matter through for a moment. "We'll just tell him that I authorized the purchase before I got Silverton's telegraph and being a man of my word, I'm honoring this purchase. We'll leave it at that."

THAT EVENING the sun set splashing the sky with crimson and gold before the massive fireball disappeared and day gave way to night in the sandhills.Temperatures dropped and two creatures huddled together for warmth as their wagon inched slowly back to Sidney.

"When we get to town, let me do all the talkin'," Cole said while steering.

"You always get to do the talkin'. Why is it that I never get to say nothing?" Travis said.

"'Cuz every time you open yer big mouth you put yer foot in it, that's why."

For the next ten minutes the men rode on in silence, before Travis opened the conversation with a single word question: "So?"

Cole pulled the horse to a stop and stared at Travis. "Soooo, what?" Cole said."Don't just leave me a hangin'. Soooo, what?"

"So what are you a-gonna say happened?" Travis asked.

"Why do you wanna know?" Cole responded.

"I kinda thought that we was a team. So I wanna make sure that I...well, you know...that we are both sayin' the same thing when we go see Cincy." He waited for a reply, but got none, so he continued. "That is what we're a-gonna do, isn't it? Report to Cincy?"

"Yeah, that's what I was figurin' we was gonna do," Cole said.

"Okay, then. What is it yer a-gonna say to him?" Travis asked again.

Cole thought for a moment, flicked the reins to start the wagon rolling down the dirt path to town. "I was thinkin' I would tell him when we arrived at the spot where we decided to stop, we was met by five men." Cole stopped because Travis was shaking his head. "What?" Cole asked. "Is there somethin' wrong with my thinkin'?"

"I like the plan up until you said that we was met by five men," Travis said.

"What is it that you don't like about it, if I may be so rude as to ask ya?" Cole said.

"Ten. I think ten would be a better number of men who surrounded us."Travis drew his six-gun. "There ain't five men around who could have stopped us in the middle of nowhere and taken that Fitz fella from us. We're too good a shots for that ta happen. I say it was ten men and we kilt five of 'em before the other five escaped while we was reloadin'."

"I like it. I like it a lot," Cole chimed in.

"Just goes to show that I didn't make it all the way through third grade fer nothing,'" Travis added.

"Do you think Cincy'll buy it?" Cole said.

"Of course, he will," Travis said. "After all we've been known to exaggerate a bit, but we never lie."

"That's fer sure. That's the one thing my pa never tolerated," Cole said.

Cole and Travis rode the rest of the way into town without speaking and pulled their wagon into the alley behind the Last Chance. They knocked twice at the back door, tried the latch and found it locked.

"Cincy must be workin' the saloon tonight," said Travis. "We can always go around the front."

"You can do that if'n you wanna," Cole said. "But to tell ya the truth, I'm thinkin' about callin' it a day. Got me a bottle of whiskey in my room at the Moore Hotel. So I'll say good night to you. 'Sides my face hurts from where Fitz slugged me."

"Mind if I join ya?" asked Travis. "I ain't got nowhere else to go."

"That's for sure," Cole said. "After all, we're roommates. But, if you think that I'm sharin' my booze with ya, ya got another think a coming'. I'm only invitin' ya because I don't like drinkin' alone."

JONES AND POTTER welcomed the dawn with two hours hard labor already behind them. Muleskinners met them at the alley door behind Swede's at four a.m. and commenced loading supplies destined for Camp Clarke along the North Platte River. Surveyors only days before had selected a spot along the river where a bridge would cross, shortening the distance to supply Fort Robinson, and then on into Dakota Territory.

As Henry T. Clarke suspected, the early morning activity up the street from the Last Chance awakened Cincinnati Culver.

Cincy splashed water on his face, noted his early morning stubble reflected back to him by his mirror but chose to ignore it. He pulled on his trousers and boots, threw on a shirt and hustled into the street. He followed the noise to the alley where Jones and Potter oversaw things. Cincy ignored them. Instead he made a beeline for Henry T. Clarke.

"What's the meaning of all of this?" Cincy began.

"Why, Mr. Culver, good morning to you," Clarke responded with all the politeness he could muster.

"Would you mind explaining what you think you are doing?" Cincy bellowed.

"As you can see, we are loading these wagons with supplies. We're getting ready to build a bridge," Clarke answered.

"I can see that you are loading supplies. I'm not blind, you know," Cincy said. "I just want to know why you are doing business with Swede's when you have a telegram forbidding you to do so."

"Mr. Culver. If anything, you should know by now that I am a man of my word. I placed this order with Swede's before I received that telegram. I am keeping my word." Clarke looked Cincy eyeball to eyeball. "And I'm sure that if I had given you my word instead of Jones and Potter, you'd want me to keep my word, wouldn't you?"

"I'll have you know, Mr. Clarke," Cincy spit out the words in anger, "I'll be telegraphing your superiors the minute the telegraph office opens this morning. Do I make myself clear?"

"You do what you think best, Mr. Culver. But, what I think you will find is that my relationship with the railroad is not that easily shaken. I have a record of delivering on my promises and because of that the railroad has given me a lot of latitude," Clarke said.

"We'll see about that. I'd put my contacts ahead of yours anytime," Cincy responded in a huff. He turned, walked back up the alley and passed the wagon where Jones worked.

"You may have won this skirmish," Cincy announced to

Jesse as he strode by. "But you have not won the war. I'm going to see to it that I put you six feet under before I'm through."

"Why, Mr. Culver, that has all the earmarks of a threat," Jones answered calmly.

"No, sir," Culver responded. "That was not a threat. That was a promise. You just keep meddling in my affairs. I've told you to stop. I've even offered to buy you out, but you just keep meddlin'." Culver kept walking and soon exited the alley.

"Wow," Potter exclaimed. "I've seen Cincy hot under the collar before, but never this hot."

"Remember what I told you. When people get angry they lose their ability to think straight and they are more apt to do stupid things," Jones said.

"I remember," said Potter.

"That's why I agreed to let Clarke do what he's doing. It's kinda like puttin' a frog in a pan of cool water and turning up the heat. The frog will just sit in the pan and not notice the water is getting hotter until it's too late," Jones said.

"You really think that's what's gonna happen with Cincy?" Potter asked.

"I'd bet my life on it," Jones replied.

SHERIFF BLANTON FELT WELL ENOUGH to return to work without Doc's permission. The thought of spending another day away from the office bothered him. It was his sense of duty and obligation to the office to which the citizen's of Sidney had elected him.

After tying off his horse, he strode to the front door and found it locked. He knocked. There was no reply from within so he took out his keys and let himself in.

"Hello," he said.

"Is that you, Sheriff?" the reply came from the direction of the jail cells.

"Yes," Blanton said. He stood in the doorway between his office proper and the cells. "Is that you, Jimbo?"

"Yep," Jimbo responded.

"So, where is everyone this morning?" Blanton asked.

"Jones was here earlier, but left again to fetch my breakfast," said Jimbo. "I'm guessin' he should be back any minute now."

"How about I make us a little coffee?" said Blanton.

"Not gonna hear no objection from me about that," Jimbo responded.

Blanton opened the front of the potbelly stove and shoved in a couple of pieces of wood. He found that someone had prepared the coffee pot already.

"Shouldn't take too long and we'll have us a cup," Blanton said.

With that the front door opened and Jones entered with Jimbo's breakfast plate.

"So, how ya feelin' this morning, Sheriff?" Jones said as he walked through the room to deliver Jimbo's breakfast.

"I'm probably gonna catch it from Doc for being here, but I'm just so tired of bein' sick and tired," Blanton said.

"Yer just darn lucky to be alive," Jones said.

Blanton took a seat behind his desk. "I know that full well," he said. "Doc reminds me of that fact every time he comes by."

Jones pulled the door closed that separated the two rooms in Blanton's office.

"I know I've been out of it for a while, so tell me again why Jimbo's locked up," Blanton said.

"Brody Belt found a body all wrapped up in wire with a slug in his forehead near his place and the footprints out there matched the boots Jimbo's wearin'.The body was one of

Cincy's men, a man named Snider. The way I figure it, Snider shot you and Cincy had Jimbo get rid of him in an attempt to pin the murder on Brody Belt. But, now I've gone and spoiled it all for Cincy by arrestin' Jimbo," said Jones. "Jimbo's confessed as much."

"Help yerself to some of the coffee," Blanton said. "It should be ready. Pour me one while you're at it."

Jones did and handed a cup to Blanton and kept a cup for himself.

"There's something else you need to know," Jones said. "Cincy's running a little scam. He got someone at the railroad to say that Clarke shouldn't do business with me. But Clarke knows the head of the Union Pacific and he has a telegraph from him saying he's headed this way soon with a couple of U.S. Marshals to investigate Cincy."

"Does Cincy know all this?" Blanton asked.

"Not yet," Jones said.

"Sounds like you're going to need an extra gun when all this happens," Blanton said. "I'm just glad I'm feeling better."

"I am, too," Jones said. "When Cincy finds out, he's gonna be madder than a wet hen. Who knows what he'll try. I'm just glad you're back in the saddle and available to give us a hand."

CHAPTER TWENTY-SIX

Cole and Travis shared a bottle of hooch in their hotel room. It was their crude attempt to steel themselves for their inevitable conversation with Cincy.

"So, are we agreed then?" Cole asked.

"I don't think it's a good idea to lie to Cincy," Travis answered. "My pa always said that the truth always comes out. Somehow, some way, the truth has a way of comin' out. And when it does it can be like a mean old hound dog and bite ya right in the tail feathers."

Cole poured himself another drink as he sat on the edge of the unmade bed. "There ain't no way that Cincy's gonna know what went on out there in the Sandhills" he said. "We're the only two that was there. Besides that Fitz fella, of course. And he's done run off somewhere."

Travis fired back, "I know that, but tellin' Cincy we was bushwhacked when we wasn't just doesn't sit right with me."

Cole made his way to the window. In the darkness of the evening he couldn't see much, but he could hear a lot of activity just up the street. "Take another swig and let's head on over to the Last Chance and see if we can get ourselves in a card game. Maybe Cincy's forgotten the whole thing and we won't have to lie about nothing," Cole said.

"Now, that there is the best thing I've heard all day," Travis responded. He grabbed the bottle by the neck and took a large gulp then used his ratty shirt sleeve to wipe the evidence from his lips.

It was not long before they found themselves sitting side-by-by at a Blackjack table, laughing and drinking their lives away. They may have forgotten the mission Cincy sent them out to do earlier in the day, but for sure, Cincy hadn't.

"Cole, get yer backside in here!" Cincy thundered. "You, too, Travis."

"Cash us in, will ya, Burt," Travis said to the dealer. "We'll be back."

"Wouldn't count on that," Burt replied. "Cincy's got his dander up. He's been waiting in his office all afternoon."

Travis followed Cole toward the open office door.

"Let me do all the talkin'," Cole said. He ignored Travis' eye roll.

Once inside the office, Cincy closed the door behind them.

"So, I heard from Burt that you've been lookin' for us," Cole started.

Cincy held his hand up to command silence.

"I sent you boys to do a job, but ya never reported back," Cincy said. "Do you mind tellin' me what took you all day to do?"

Travis jumped in with an answer much to Cole's chagrin. "We done the job, boss. We really did."

"Not sure who yer trying to convince, but it ain't workin' on me," Cincinnati said. "I gave you a simple assignment. Get rid of Fitz."

"We did," Travis followed up. "We did get rid of Fitz."

If looks could kill, certainly Cole's look would have dropped Travis dead in his tracks.

"If you did as I instructed, then tell me why you've got a black eye, Travis. And how'd you get bruises, Cole," Cincy said. "Look, you two might think that you can get away with stuff, but you can't get away with stuff with me."

"I told you to let me do all the talkin'," Cole snapped.

Cincy sat behind his desk. He reached down and withdrew a Navy Colt from the top drawer and placed in on the desk.

"Now," Cincy said, "I want you to start at the beginning and tell me what happened. I want you to tell me a convincing story and give me a very good reason why I shouldn't kill ya where you stand."

A FEW DAYS later the morning sun delivered a warm feel to the autumn air. In the jail, Jones sat a plate down on the table.

"How are things around town?" Sheriff Blanton inquired.

"They seem a bit uneasy this morning, with the Circuit Judge set to arrive in a couple of days. What do you think Jimbo's chances are with Judge Thomsen?"

"I'd think a snowball has a better chance of surviving on a hot day than Jimbo has of not hanging," Blanton answered. He made his way to the cell block and brought Jimbo to the table. He removed Jimbo's handcuffs and took away the fork and knife from his plate, leaving him with a spoon.

"The widow Salak sends her best wishes," Jones said. He found the chair opposite Jimbo to his liking and sat down.

"Tell her thank you for me," Jimbo said. "It's mighty nice of her to fry up these eggs. Over easy, too, just the way I like 'em."

"Heard from Judge Thomsen this morning," Sheriff Blanton began.

Jimbo's face turned as white as a sheet. "The Hangin' Judge?" he asked.

"We don't know that he'll hang ya. Besides, we're gonna do everything we can to tell the judge your side of the story," Jones said. "What I can't understand is why Cincy hasn't made another attempt to break you out."

Jimbo stared forward.

"You better eat, Jimbo. You need to keep up your strength," said Blanton.

"I just lost my appetite," Jimbo said.

Potter came rushing in off the street. "Sheriff, I got a telegraph from Judge Thomsen."

"I already know that much. He'll be here in a couple of days, right?" Blanton said.

"Well, now he's ordering the construction of a gallows. He wants it ready in time for his arrival," Potter said.

Jimbo stood spilling the contents from the table as he did. "I ain't hangin," he screamed. "I ain't taken the fall for something that Cincy ordered."

It took all three men to subdue Jimbo and return him to his cell.

"This ain't right, I tell ya. Cincinnati ordered me to kill him and he's getting' off scot-free," he said.

"Calm down, Jimbo," Blanton said.

"I ain't calming down," Jimbo bellowed. "It ain't right, I tell ya. It just ain't right."

"Run and get Doc, will ya, Potter? Tell him that Jimbo's all riled up. He's about the only one I know who can calm Jimbo down when he gets like this," Jones said.

It wasn't long before Doc appeared in the doorway of the jail.

"I brought Parson Abel along with me, Jimbo," Doc said. Both men stood outside Jimbo's cell.

"Don't let them hang me, Doc," Jimbo pleaded.

"I'm going to do everything in my power to help you, Jimbo. That's why I brought Parson Abel along," Doc said. "Not sure exactly what we're gonna do, but the two of us will think of something."

"I don't want to die, Parson," Jimbo said, grabbing a hold of the cell bars.

Parson Abel tenderly took Jimbo's huge hands in his and began to pray so softly that everyone in the room strained to hear.

"O, Lord, I come before you with your servant, Jimbo. Bring comfort and peace to this man. He knows he has disobeyed your command not to kill and he is most heartily sorry," Abel prayed.

Tears rolled down Jimbo's cheeks. "Yes, Lord," he said. "I have done wrong by you."

"For the sake of your son, Jesus, forgive this man, Lord," Abel continued. "Bring peace into Jimbo's heart. Bring that peace that passes all human understanding."

At that moment Jimbo exhaled and his body went suddenly calm.

"I pray all this in the precious name of Jesus, my Lord and Savior, Amen," Abel said.

AROUND THE NOON meal in the Abel's house the discussion turned to Jimbo.

"I don't think there is a thing we can do to save Jimbo's life," Jones said. "Not when Judge Thomsen has reviewed his case and ordered a gallows built before he arrives."

"The poor man," Martha said.

"He's not as poor as you might think he is," Doc added.

"After all, he has admitted to killing Snider and making it look like your brother did the killing."

"I just feel sorry for him, that's all," Martha said. "From what Jesse has told me it sounds like he regrets doing that he did."

"He does," Abel said. "And I have offered him forgiveness for what he's done.And the Good News is that God has forgiven him. However, society still has a right to extract punishment for what Jimbo has done. God specifically gives society that right when he tells Noah in Genesis chapter nine, 'Whoso sheddeth man's blood, by man shall his blood be shed: for in the image of God made he man'."

"But that don't mean that we can't try to plead for a lesser charge. One that doesn't mean the death penalty, does it?" Doc said. "I've kinda taken a liking to Jimbo."

"And he's taken a shine to you as well, Doc, "Jones added.

"Ever since I took the time to help him out when he wasn't feeling well," Doc added.

"Your act of kindness is being rewarded," Parson Abel noted. "Would someone pass the potatoes back this direction?"

"What can we do to help Jimbo?" Adeline Abel asked.

Jones handed the potatoes to Abel. "I asked Sheriff Blanton that very question this morning. He suggested the three of us ask Jimbo's attorney if we can provide a character witness on Jimbo's behalf. He said sometimes that makes a difference in cases like this when God has worked a change in a man's life."

"We've got to try something," Doc said.

After the noon meal, the men returned to work, but Jones stayed behind.

"I'll be along in a minute," he told Potter. "I have something I want to talk over with Martha."

Jones took Martha by the hand and they stood side-by-side on the Abel's front porch.

"I've done some thinkin'," Jones began.

"About what?" she asked.

"About us," he said.

"I like when you think about us," Martha said. "I do that a lot you know."She turned to face him."What have you been thinking about us?"

"I was thinking that this might be a good time to ask you to marry me," Jones said.

"Why, Jesse, this comes as a big surprise," said Martha. "I thought you had it in mind to wait until this whole thing with Cincinnati and all blows over."

"I just decided I'd let you know what my intentions are," Jones said. "I still think we should wait to get married after this is over, but I want you to know that I love you and want to spend the rest of my life with you."

"Oh, Jesse, I don't know what to say," Martha said.

He smiled. "Well, then that is a first. You not knowing what to say?"

She returned his smile. "You know what I mean, Jesse." She thought for a moment. "You just caught me off-guard a little. I wasn't expecting this today."

"And?" he asked.

"And," she said. "I would be happy to marry you. And, yes, I will wait for you.You are worth waiting for."

They kissed.

From a half block away, two pairs of eyes watched. Cole and Travis.

EARLY THE NEXT morning Martha returned to the one room school. She tugged hard at the bell rope and rang the bell calling the children back to class. The younger children fairly skipped into the classroom while those a bit older still wiped the sleepy dust from their eyes. Once each child found their assigned desk, Martha opened the primer on her desk.

"Good morning, students," Martha began without looking up from her desk.

"Good morning, Miss Martha," they responded.

In the cacophony of young people's voices, Martha heard the deeper tones of more mature male voices and the jingling of spurs.

Martha looked up to find two men standing midway in the aisle.

"May I help you?" Martha asked.

"We come to get some book learnin', didn't we, Travis?" Cole began.

"Yep. We's here fer educatin'," Travis replied. "Mr. Cincinnati Culver said we wasn't very smart, but the new school marm could ed-u-cate us."

Cole and Travis restarted their walk to the front of the classroom. Travis learned over the desk to within inches of Martha's face. "Well, what do ya say?Can you ed-u-cate us?" He laughed a sinister laugh.

"OR perhaps we can ed-u-cate you? What do you say to that?" Cole said. He folded his arms across his chest and glared across the desk at Martha.

Martha felt the color bleach from her face.

"Children," she said, mustering as much courage as she could in the face of danger. "I'm going to ask you to return to your homes. School will resume tomorrow morning."

A loud cheer arose in the classroom and chaos broke out as

elated students fled the building like hornets whose nest had been struck with a stick. It was but moments later that the one room school was empty except for Martha and Cincy's henchmen.

"Now, what should we talk about?" Travis said. "How about starting with the fear that I see perched on yer face? C'mon now, I ain't about to hurt ya. I just want to get to know you a little better, that's all."

Martha stood erect and braced herself with her left hand. She sent her right hand flying curled slightly to expose her fingernails. She raked his face and espied four trails of blood where her nails made contact.

Travis screamed in pain. His hand flew to his face. When he withdrew it, his hand was full of blood.

"You little minx," Travis shouted. "You shouldn't have done that." He dove at her over the desk but missed grabbing Martha when she sidestepped away.

Cole chased after Martha who placed herself in position to dodge his moves by keeping school desks between them.

"C'mon now, missy," Cole said. "Ya know you've always wanted a man like me."

Travis tried to weave between the desks, only to stumble and fall. When he stood again, he shoved the chairs out of his way.

Soon only one desk stood between Cole and Martha. He grabbed it and tossed it aside, the wood splintering as it slammed against the wall.

"I seen her first," Travis protested. "Yer gonna have to wait until I get done with her, Cole."

"Not hardly," Cole said. He spun around and faced Travis.

A loud crash drew everyone's attention to the front door. Martha sighed in relief.

Jones stood in the doorway.

"Would you mind telling me what you boys are doin' here?" Jones asked.

"We come to get an ed-u-ca-tion," Travis said.

Jones drew his LeMat.

Two sharp clicks followed to give warning to Cole and Travis that the gun was cocked and ready for action.

"I have yer education waiting for you," Jones announced. "It's at the point of a gun."

Cole stood erect. Travis did likewise.

They faced Jones.

Suddenly, they bolted and dove headlong through a pair of school house windows and were gone.

CHAPTER TWENTY-SEVEN

Martha sat at the table in Sheriff Blanton's office. Blanton sat on the other side of the table. Jones, Potter and Parson Abel stood.

"And then what happened?" Blanton asked. He took notes as Martha spoke.

"I looked up at the sound of jingling spurs and two men were coming down the center aisle," Martha said.

"Did you recognize these men?" said Blanton.

"Never saw them before in my life," she said.

"I recognized them. Two of Cincy's henchmen, Cole and Travis," Jones said.

"We've had trouble with them before," Potter said.

"They said that Cincy sent them. That they needed more education," Martha said. "But, I could tell they had something else on their mind. They were animals."

"It was quick thinking on your part to send the children home," Jones said. "I knew something was up when I saw the kids pouring into the streets."

"It was a good thing you got there when you did." Martha put her head in her hands and sobbed. "They tried to attack me. Why would anyone want to hurt me?"

Potter jumped into the conversation. "I can answer that one. Cincy sent them to get back at all of us for not selling out to him."

"Now you know why I don't want to get married until the dust has settled over Cincinnati," Jones said.

"That's an interesting way of saying that," Parson Abel said.

"Do you want to swear out a warrant for the arrest of Cole and Travis, Martha?" Blanton asked. "That might put a little heat on them."

She deferred to Jones. "What do you think? I just don't want to live like this, always wondering where the next attack is going to come from and when."

"Until this part of the country gets civilized, this is what's going to happen," Parson Abel said. "Someone is always gonna be taking advantage of someone else. It's gonna take men, like these three, to make sure that does not happen. And to drive out men like Cincinnati. Until the love of money is replaced by the love of God, this is what happens."

"Well, Parson, I guess that leaves us with one option, doesn't it?" said Jones.

"Martha, if you'll swear out a warrant for the arrest of Cole and Travis, I'll take it down the street and we'll put those two in jail."

"Do you have room for them in the jail with Jimbo already in there?" Parson Abel wondered aloud.

"My jail is a bit like your table at mealtime, Parson. There's always room for one more," Sheriff Blanton said.

DOWN THE STREET at the Last Chance, Cole and Travis were giving Cincy their version of their encounter with Jones.

"Then Jones pulled the ugliest pistol I've even seen," Travis said.

Cole agreed. "Yeah, what kinda gun was that? Ain't seen anything like it before."

"It's a LeMat," Cincy said. "The story is that Jones took it off a dead rebel during the war." Cincy paused thinking that Travis would continue his story.When he didn't, Cincy continued, "You don't want to be on the business end of that gun. Nine chambers and a scattergun."

"So, when Jones drew his gun, we decided it was best to skedaddle outta there," Travis said.

"What do you want us to do now, boss?" Cole asked.

Cincinnati walked to his wall safe and took out a wad of money. "Here," he said. "Take this money and get lost for a couple of days. If I know Jones, he'll be comin' after ya and I don't want you anywhere around when he does."

"We're not afraid of him, boss," Travis said.

Cincinnati could not believe what he was hearing. "If you aren't afraid of him, why did you run away when it was two against one in the schoolhouse?"

"That was different. He had the drop on us. His revolver was out and cocked before we had a chance to pull on him. It wasn't a fair fight, so we dove out the window."

"Well, I got somethin' in mind for Jones, somethin' that will put the odds in yer favor instead of his. But fer now I don't want the two of you around until I have everything in place. Do we understand each other?"

Cole and Travis took the money and ran out the back door.

Once Cole and Travis cleared the back door and heard it close and lock behind them, Cole stopped and turned around to face Travis.

He took out the money he had hurriedly thrust into his trouser pocket and waved it in front of Travis. "Did you see the wad of bills Cincinnati had in his safe?"

"Yeah. What about it?" Travis said.

"Cincinnati peeled off just a few hundred bucks for me and you and kept the rest for himself," Cole said. "I don't think that's fair. We do all the work. Put our lives on the line, and we get a few lousy bucks between us and Cincy's got so much more."

"I don't think I ever thought of it that way," Travis said. He nodded in agreement with Cole. "Yer right, we do all the hard work and Cincy gets all the money."

"Keep yer voice down or ol' Cincy'll hear us," said Cole. "I got me an idea that'll give us everything Cincy's got in the safe."

"You do?" Travis said.

"Yep, and Cincy will never know who done it. And by the time he does figure it out, we'll be long gone. Have you ever wanted to go to Mexico?" Cole asked.

"Don't think I've ever thought about it," Travis said.

"I heard tell there are some lovely senoritas there. Beautiful Mexican girls who know how to treat men like you and me right," Cole said.

"So, just how are we gonna get Cincy's money? He ain't a gonna hand it over to us simply because we say *please.*"

"No, he ain't, that's fer sure, but he's gonna hand it to us none the same," said Cole. "All we gotta do is use our heads. Think about it."

"I tried thinkin' once, Cole, but it hurt too much to make me wanna do that again," Travis said.

"Alright, just let me do the thinkin' fer the both of us," Cole said.

"You got it. I'll be the brawns if you'll be the brains," said Travis.

"Deal, partner. Let's shake on it," said Cole.

THE EXIT of Cole and Travis out the back door marked the entrance of Jones, Potter and Blanton through the front door. There was no time for Cincinnati to close his safe. The money he had within was visible for the three men to see.

"What's the idea of barging in unannounced," Cincy bellowed. "Didn't you read the sign on the door that said *private?*"

"We ignored it," Sheriff Blanton said. "Any man that's got a notion to hire two scoundrels like Cole and Travis needs ta be barged in on."

"Come on in then," Cincy said. "They ain't here." Cincy calmly walked over to his wall safe and shut it. "As you plainly see, I ain't got nothin' to hide." He sat behind his desk.

"Keep yer hands on top of your desk where I can see 'em," Blanton ordered. "I don't want you to so much as move. Keep him covered will ya, Jones? I don't want that pretty white shirt yer wearin' to have a bullet hole in it."

Jones took out his LeMat and drew a bead on Cincy's chest. He moved to his left until he was even with the back end of Cincy's desk. Cincy laid both hands on his desk.

"What's the meaning of this?" Cincy asked. "I told ya that

Cole and Travis ain't here and you can see fer yerselves that they ain't."

Sheriff Blanton reached into his vest pocket and withdrew a piece of paper folded in quarters. He tossed in front of Cincinnati.

"That's a warrant for the arrest of Cole and Travis for an incident that took place at the school house. Your two men attacked Martha Belt and she said that they told her you put them up to it," Blanton said.

"That's her word against mine. And I say whatever they did they did on their own," Cincy fired back. Cincy looked at Jones. "Why would she accuse me of anything like that? You need to teach that woman of yours some manners.She shouldn't go around accusing people of doin' stuff they didn't do."

Jones drove an angry right hand into Cincinnati's face. Cincy glared back at him, removed a pocket handkerchief and wiped the blood from the corner of his mouth.

"That's enough, Jones," Blanton said.

A smile crossed Cincinnati's lips and his eyes remained on Jones. "I should file charges of assault against you," Cincy said.

"But you won't," Jones responded. "You won't because there's no one in town who would believe you didn't provoke me."

"Shoot," Cincy answered. "Give me a couple of months and I'll own this town.And when I do, the three of you won't be welcome here no more. You'll have ta find another little stink hole to settle into." Cincy made sure that he looked into the eyes of all three of his adversaries.

"C'mon," Blanton said. "Let's get out of here." He turned his back on Cincinnati and headed toward the door.

Jones bent down to Cincy's eye level. "You will let us know if Cole and Travis come back, won't ya?"

Cincy smiled. "Sure," he said. "The way I got it planned,

you'll be the first to know. In fact, you may not even know what hit ya."

"Dɪᴅ you see all that money in Cincy's safe?" Potter asked once the three men were outside Cincy's establishment. "He's got enough money in there to buy the city three and four times over."

"Not enough for us to sell out to him though," Jones joined in. "It's gonna take more money than Cincy can find to buy me out. I'm not selling. It's the principle of the thing."

"Ya, but, think of all the principle his money could buy," Potter said.

"When a man sacrifices his principles on a pile of money, that's when a man ain't fit fer livin," Jones said.

"I once heard it put this way," Sheriff Blanton joined in. "If you don't stand fer something, you'll fall for anything. That's the way my pa put it anyway."

"Your pa sounds like a very wise man," Jones said.

"He was," Blanton said. "We never had much when I was growing up, but the one thing I could count on was that my pa always told the truth and he always stood up for the little guy."

"My pa was a lot like that, too. He was as honest as the day was long," Jones said. "Worked from before sun up and didn't take a rest all day until his head hit the pillow long after the sun went down."

"And my pa had me helping him by the time I was three or four," Potter noted. "He told me that the best thing I could do was to work with my hands. He said it built character."

"Yer dad is correct," Jones said. "Hard work does build character. And I can prove it."

"You can?" Potter said.

"Yes, I can. You must have worked hard because you are quite the character." Jones laughed at Potter's expense, and so did Blanton.

"Alright, you two," Potter fired at them. "I was just trying to be serious."

"Oh, we realize that," Blanton added. "But, we don't want you to be too serious."

Parson Abel and Doc made it their mission to keep Jimbo from the business end of the hangman's rope. They met with Jimbo daily even though construction noise reminded them that the gallows was nearing completion only two blocks away.

As usual Jimbo sat at the table in Sheriff Blanton's office. Parson Abel sat with his Bible in front of him at the opposite end of the table. Doc hovered over the two of them.

"I'm not sure who Judge Thomsen will appoint as your attorney, Jimbo, or who the prosecuting attorney will be," Parson Abel said.

"But regardless of who they are, Parson Abel and I want you to be prepared to defend yourself," Doc said. "It's obvious that Judge Thomsen believes you are guilty of murder and deserve the death penalty."

"You don't need to tell me. The pounding just up street reminds me," Jimbo said.

"And I don't know if Doc and I have any chance at all in saving you, but we're going to try our best," Abel said. "I'm thinking your best hope is to admit what you did and fall on the mercy of the court."

"I'm thinkin' if Parson Abel and I are allowed to serve as character witnesses to the change in you and how you'd like a chance to start over, that might just work," Doc said.

"Can you remember what we taught you to say to Judge Thomsen?" Abel asked.

Jimbo cleared his throat and paused before he began. "Yer, honor, sir." He hesitated.

"Go ahead and stand up, Jimbo, and try it again," Doc insisted.

Jimbo stood with head bowed. "Yer, honor, sir," he began anew. "May I please have a moment to speak on my own be---" he fumbled for the correct word.

"Behalf," Doc coaxed.

"I'm sorry Doc," Jimbo said, "but I don't use that word. What does it even mean?"

"Behalf means for your own benefit," Parson Abel said.

"Can't I say that instead of tryin' to remember some big fancy word and all?" said Jimbo.

"Sure you can," Doc said. He turned to Parson Abel. "There's no need for all the fancy talk yer given him. Let him put his defense in his own words."

"I just thought--" Abel said.

Doc interrupted at once. "There's your biggest problem, right there. You thought. Go ahead, Jimbo. Try it again."

"Yer honor, sir, may I please have a moment to speak for myself," Jimbo began. "I'm sure this is something that ain't done very often, but I need to admit to you right now that I am guilty. What I want to do is to throw myself at to the mercy of this court, your honor."

"*On* instead of *at*, Jimbo," Parson Abel urged. "Throw myself *on* the mercy of this court."

"*On* the mercy of this court," Jimbo corrected himself and then continued. "Since my arrest I've been in the care of two of the most respected men in Sidney, Doc Hardesty and Parson Abel. Doc has always shown me the greatest kindness, and Parson Abel has led me to confess Jesus Christ as my Lord and

Savior. I've even been baptized. If you are willing, judge, I'd like these two men to speak on my be--" Jimbo stopped short again, but finished with these words, "—speak for my benefit."

CHAPTER TWENTY-EIGHT

The Cheyenne County Courthouse served as the site for Jimbo Livingston's murder trial. Only a few years old, the building still smelled of newly hewn wood and fresh paint.

Jesse Jones and Martha Belt sat directly behind Jimbo and his attorney. Doc Hardesty and his wife, and Parson Abel and Adeline completed the row. Although Sheriff Blanton was in total agreement with Jimbo's planned confession, he sat behind the prosecution team on the other side of the room. Jimbo was, after all, his prisoner.

The bailiff checked his watch and called out, "Order in the court. Please rise. This court is now in session. The Honorable Judge Amos Thomsen, presiding."

Judge Thomsen entered. Jones noted the fixed scowl on the judge's face. He turned to Martha and whispered, "Right now I don't like Jimbo's chances."

Martha put a finger to her lips silencing any further comment.

Judge Thomsen sat.

"You may be seated," the bailiff said. The packed courtroom did as instructed.

Judge Thomsen looked at the sheet of paper before him and read, "The State of Nebraska verses Jimbo Livingston on a charge of premeditated murder. Is the prosecution ready?"

"Yes, your honor," the lead attorney said.

"Is the defense ready?"

"We are, your honor," Jimbo's attorney said.

"Is the jury ready?"

"We are, your honor," the jury foreman replied.

"You may precede, Mr. Prosecutor," Judge Thomsen commanded.

The prosecuting attorney stood. "Your honor, the state intends to prove that the defendant, Jimbo Livingston, deliberately and with intent did murder Ambrose Snider and wrap his body in wire and dump it in the sandhills. This we intend to prove beyond a shadow of a doubt and in so doing will seek the death penalty, asking your honor, to declare the life of Jimbo Livingston forfeit and that he be hung by the neck until dead." He sat down.

Without looking up, Judge Thomsen said, "Mr. Defense Attorney?"

Jimbo's attorney rose to his feet. "Thank you, your honor. At this time, your honor, I would ask that you allow my client to make a statement."

Judge Thomsen's eyes shot forward to meet Jimbo's attorney's gaze. "This is highly irregular, sir," Judge Thomsen announced.

Jimbo's attorney stood his ground and replied, "Indeed, it is, your honor. But, if it please the court, your honor, my client has an opening statement to make before we proceed any further."

Judge Thomsen's eyes quickly moved to meet Jimbo's. "Is this your wish, sir? Because if your attorney is stalling, I will find him in contempt," he said.

Jimbo stood. As he spoke, Jones noticed calm in his voice and demeanor.

"It is, your honor," he said.

Judge Thomsen looked at the prosecution table. "Does the prosecution have any objection to allowing the defendant to address the bench?"

"No, your honor," the prosecutor replied.

"You may proceed, Mr. Livingston," Judge Thomsen said.

Jimbo began, "Yer honor, I've come here today to plead guilty to the charges against me. I did murder Ambrose Snider, wrap him in wire and leave him in the sandhills. I did this at Cincinnati Culver's request."

Jones heard a gasp among those in the courtroom.

"The wire was added to frame Brody Belt and make it look like he done the killing," Jimbo continued. "Cincinnati paid me twenty-five hundred dollars to complete the job, which I freely admit I done."

"You do know," Judge Thomsen interrupted, "that by admitting to this crime I could sentence you to death?"

"I do yer honor. But I had to get this off my mind. All I can do at this point is to fall upon the mercy of this court," Jimbo said. "I would ask that before you pass sentence that you hear a couple of character witnesses I brung with me to talk about the change they've seen in my life."

JUDGE THOMSEN RETIRED to his chambers where he met with the two attorneys.

"Gentlemen," the judge said. "This is highly unusual. I don't recall having anyone serve as a character witness for a murderer. Let alone two character witnesses. Mr. Defense Attorney, did you have any idea that the accused was going to do what he did today?"

"Your honor, I was aware that he was going to plead guilty and that Mr. Livingston had something else to say, but he never shared what that something else was," he said.

"Your honor, there's been a lot of shenanigans going on in town and Mr. Culver seems to always be at the bottom of it," the prosecutor joined in. "I'd really like to hear what the character witnesses have to say and I can say with some degree of certainty that Sheriff Blanton does as well."

"If we are all agreed, gentlemen," Judge Thomsen said, "then let's hear out the two character witnesses and see where this leads us. I'd hate to hang someone and leave the instigator run free. It's kinda like my oldest son. He stirs up his younger brother to do something and then stands by with a grin on his face when he gets punished. I don't want that smudge on my reputation as a judge."

THE BAILIFF CALLED the courtroom back into session and Judge Thomsen gaveled the room to quiet down.

"Mr. Livingston," he said, "I have discussed your request with both attorneys in this trial and we all agree that we would like to hear from your character witnesses. We all believe that there is something going on in this city that we need to get to the bottom of. Perhaps your character witnesses can shine a light on what's going on."

Jimbo Livingston stood. "Yer honor," he said, "my first character witness is Dr. Hardesty." Jimbo sat back down.

Doc stood. "Your honor," he began. "I first met Mr. Livingston here several months ago. He had a cough and I gave him some medicine to give him some relief. Your honor, what I have since learned about Mr. Livingston is that he is easily influenced by the men around him. In particular by his boss, Cincinnati Culver. It seems there is a bond between these two men that dates back to the War Between the States. Not sure what that bond is, but whatever Cincinnati asks Jimbo to do, he does it. There doesn't seem to be much discernment in this man's head—no offense, Jimbo..."

"None taken," Jimbo replied.

"So, yer honor, I feel that it would be a grave mistake to sentence Jimbo to death for something he was manipulated into doing. 'Sides," Doc said, "I've grown kinda fond of him over the last several weeks. I don't want him to die and watch the one who put him up to it continue to do what he's been doing."

"Can you explain that, Doctor Hardesty?" the judge asked.

"If you don't mind, your honor," Doc replied, "I had in mind that Parson Abel might answer that question."

"You may proceed, Parson Abel," Judge Thomsen said.

Doc sat and Parson Abel rose.

"Your honor," Parson Abel said, "I'd really like to begin by addressing Mr. Livingston's spiritual health. Over the past several weeks he and I have talked about some of the things he has done. And although I cannot and will not reveal anything about his past, I can tell you that he has confessed to the killing of Ambrose Snider. For this murder, and the other sins he has confessed before me, by the authority given my office as a pastor, I have forgiven him in the name of Jesus Christ. I can tell you that he is now a baptized member of the family of God and is growing in his faith. I would say to you, that I have every reason to believe that if you set him free into society, he would take his place and give glory and honor to God for setting him free. Your honor, there are some things going on in this town that are causing us all to live in fear. I would be happy to talk more about these things in your private chambers. But here in public, I don't think that it's a good idea."

THE JURY CONSIDERED the charges against Jimbo throughout the afternoon, spent the evening sequestered in the Moore Hotel and met again the next day. On the second day about five o'clock they announced that they were deadlocked.

Judge Thomsen ordered them back to the jury room.

Two hours later the jury foreman sent a message to Judge Thomsen that the deadlock continued and a conviction was not possible. Thomsen brought the jury into the courtroom at seven-thirty.

Jesse Jones joined Parson Abel and Doc Hardesty in seats behind Jimbo and his attorney.

"Mr. Foreman," Judge Thomsen said, "would you please share the results of your deliberation?"

The jury foreman stood. "Yes, your honor. We the jury find that we cannot agree on what to do in this case. Six of us have voted to convict the defendant and six have asked that the defendant be released based on the testimony of Doc and Parson Abel. We find ourselves a hung jury, your honor."

"Better a hung jury than a hung man," Jones whispered to Parson Abel.

"Agreed," Abel responded.

Judge Thomsen gaveled the courtroom into silence.

"Order in the court," the judge shouted. "Order in the court."

With order restored Judge Thomsen said, "It is the decision

of this court that the charges against Mr. Jimbo Livingston be dropped and that he immediately be set free."

Parson Abel hosted a celebration. Adeline served refreshments including two home-made cherry pies taken from her oven about the time the hung jury declaration had been made.

"I still can't believe that Judge Thomsen turned me loose," Jimbo said. "I mean the scaffold was finished it just needed someone to hang. I'm just glad it wasn't me."

Doc laughed out loud. "That's fer sure how I thought it would be."

"A hangin' judge turning someone loose," Jones said. "I've never heard of such a thing."

"All I can say is God be praised," Parson Abel said. "The judge took pity on you and set you free."

"I'd say that's quite a coincidence," Doc said.

"You know the older I get the less I believe that things are a coincidence," Parson Abel said before he took a sip of his coffee.

Everyone waited quietly for Parson Abel to finish his sips and complete his thought, which he did. "No, I believe this is an example of a God-incidence."

"How can I ever thank you all for helping me?" Jimbo said.

"You can start," Sheriff Blanton began, "by telling us anything you know to bring Cincinnati to justice."

"I'm afraid I don't know nothin'. I've been in jail for quite a while and I'm sure that by now Cincy has changed his plans at least two or three times. I've never seen someone change his mind so often, but Cincy changes his mind as often as the wind changes directions in the sandhills."

"Do you think he's still after our store?" Jones asked.

"I doubt that has changed," Jimbo said. "What no doubt has changed is how he is going to go about getting it. Is that hired gunman still around? What's his name—Fitz?"

"We haven't seen him around for a few days," Potter announced.

"What we have seen though is that Cincy's hired a couple of new men named Cole and Travis. And I think they're about as desperate as they come. In fact, I'd be willing to say that if their brains were dynamite they wouldn't have enough fire-power to blow their noses," Potter added.

"They attacked Martha in the school house a couple of days ago," Jones added.

"And if it hadn't been for Jesse," Martha said, "I am scared to think of what might have happened."

"Sounds to me like Cincy is getting desperate," Jimbo said.

"And as I've always said," Jones added, "desperate men make desperate decisions. Jimbo, I'd suggest you stay out of sight for a few days. Cincy may be desperate enough to want you dead."

"You know, I think I'll just do that," Jimbo replied. "I can't see any future in being dead."

INDEED, Cincinnati was a desperate man. With Jimbo now running free instead of dangling from a noose, he saw his plans unraveling. He sent out spies in search of Cole and Travis and they soon found them in the Moore Hotel.

"Change of plans," Cincinnati announced. "I want you two men to track down and kill Jimbo. I want you to do the job Judge Thomsen was supposed to do for me."

"Any idea where we can find him?" Cole asked.

"No, I don't," Cincy said. "And from now on that's your job. I don't care what you do to find him. Turn the town upside down if you have to but find him and get rid of him."

Cole stuck his hand out. "That's gonna cost ya," Cole said.

Cincinnati made a play for the gun in his desk and got there before Cole could draw.

"Get outta here, before I kill ya both," Cincy said. "We'll talk money after you've done your job and not a minute sooner. Do I make myself clear? I've given you all the money I'm gonna give ya until you rid me of Jimbo Livington. I promise ya I'll make it worth yer while."

"Alright," Cole said. "If that's the way it's gotta be, then that's the way it's gotta be. Let's get outta here Travis. Looks like we got us a job to do."

"And boys," Cincy said. "I want you to make it look like Jimbo took his own life.I don't want no one pullin' on loose ends that might lead them back to me. Do you understand me?"

"We understand, don't we Travis?" said Cole.

Once outside the conversation turned from Jimbo Livingston to the plan Cole devised to rid himself of Cincinnati and gain the cash stuffed in his safe.

"We'll look around for Jimbo alright, but we put my plan into effect tonight," Cole said.

"Are you sure we can pull this off?" Travis asked.

"It'll be just like shootin' fish in a rain barrel," Cole said.

"You sure?"

"Sure I'm sure," said Cole. "Cincinnati's so worked up he'll be a perfect target for us to waltz right in and steal his money. All we gotta do is lay low through the rest of the day."

"What about Jimbo? You promised Cincy we'd get rid of Jimbo," Travis said.

"Look, we ain't gonna worry our pretty little heads about Jimbo," Cole said."Not when we got ourselves bigger fish to fry."

A puzzled look came upon Travis' face. "What do you mean?" he asked. "We don't really got no fish to fry, do we? Well, do we?"

CHAPTER TWENTY-NINE

Sheriff Blanton released Jimbo from jail. He laid Jimbo's holster and six-gun on his desk.

"You're free to go Jimbo," Sheriff Blanton said.

Jimbo scooped up his holster and put it on. "Just where do I go now that I'm free?" he asked.

"Wherever you put a mind to," replied Jesse who was seated at the table in the center of the room.

"I got nowhere to go," Jimbo replied. "I can't show my face in the street for fear that Cincy's hired someone to gun me down."

Sheriff Blanton announced, "Maybe it's best for you to ride up north. Perhaps you can catch a break and get hired on with the crew building the bridge across the Platte River." Blanton turned to Jones and asked, "What's the name of the bridge, do you remember?"

"Henry T. Clarke's bridge. Is that the one?" Jones asked.

"Yeah," Blanton replied, "but I don't think that's the name of the bridge."

"No, it ain't," Jones replied. "Let me think. Oh, yeah, now I remember, he's calling it Camp Clarke Bridge."

"That's it. Camp Clarke Bridge," Blanton said. "They're building a settlement nearby. Maybe you can get on there. I think they're calling the settlement Bridgeport."

"Never tried my hand at buildin' nothin'," Jimbo said. "Fact is the only thing I'm good at is dealin' Faro and Black Jack."

"Well, you can bet if a settlement's going up, there's gotta be a bar nearby," Jones said.

"Or two or three," said Sheriff Blanton. "Ain't no harm in you riding on up there and takin' a look around, is there? I hear this new settlement is right along the Mormon Trail. Ride north 'til you hit the trail and head west a little ways.Either that or you can hang out around town until Mr. Clarke returns and ask him if there's some way you can help him. He might need someone to ride shotgun takin' supplies up there."

"I wouldn't feel safe stayin' in Sidney another day," Jimbo said. "The sooner I can ride out of town the better I'll feel about it."

"Where's your horse?" Blanton asked.

"At the livery stable," said Jimbo. "Hope 'ol man Schultz has taken good care of him."

"You don't have a thing to worry about. Schultz is a good man, and a fair one, too," Jones said. "Why don't I walk with you?"

Jimbo reached his hands into the front pocket of his trousers. "That's gonna be an awkward conversation. I don't have any money," he said.

"I'll give ya a little grubstake until you get back on yer feet," Jones said. "Had a pretty good month at the store with all the supplies Mr. Clarke needed."

"I'll take you up on that grubstake and I'll pay you back next time I come into town. How does that sound?" Jimbo said.

"It sounds good to me," Jones replied.

Jimbo tipped his hat to Sheriff Blanton. "See ya next time, Sheriff," he said. "And thanks for the room and board."

It wasn't long and everything was squared away with 'ol man Schultz at the livery stable and the two men stepped into the street, Jimbo leading his horse saddled and ready to ride.

"Hold it right there," someone shouted. Jones recognized Cole's voice. "Goin' somewhere, Jimbo?"

"Leavin' town," Jimbo replied.

"Well, Cincy wouldn't like it if you left without sayin' good-bye," Travis said.

Jones turned to Jimbo. "I'm gonna count to five and draw their fire. When I do, I want you to mount up and ride like the wind."

"You'd do that fer me?" said Jimbo.

Jones ignored the question and began counting slowly and deliberately: "One. Two. Three. Four. Five! Go! Go!" he yelled.

Jones drew quickly and fired.

The round stuck near Cole's boot. Both men glared at Jones, spun around, and raced up the street like the Devil himself was after them.

Jones turned to see Jimbo's horse kickin' up dust as it sprinted out of town.

PARSON ABEL WASTED no time in assembling his little congregation that evening. He set aside time for them to meet and to pray.

"Something is happening," he told Jones. "I don't know what it is for sure, but something is happening and the best way to prepare for it is in prayer."

About a hundred and fifty citizens packed the pews, a mix

of Sidney's leading citizens, businessmen and women, and a few who had obviously recently exited one of the city's twenty saloons.

Parson Abel stood before the congregation. He removed the jacket he always wore regardless of the season, unbuttoned the cuffs of his shirt and rolled up the sleeves. Sweat already streamed down his face.

"The Lord has called us together tonight," he began. "There is a reason He has called us here, and that is so that we might pray over our city. We have lost our way and God is calling us to repent and return to him. We have become lovers of money. We have coveted what does not belong to us. We have committed murder or sent others to do the murdering for us. We have gotten drunk on liquor and lost our inhibitions. We have gambled away the money God intended us to use in support of our families."

"You preach it, Parson!" someone yelled.

"Now is the time to repent and ask God to forgive us," Abel said. "A time to be on our knees before a loving God who sent His Son to take away our sins.

"Amen!" came a shout from the congregation.

"Stay as long as you like, come and go as you please, but for the next hour this place is a house of prayer," said Parson Abel.

A WEEK later a wagon arrived in town and attracted a lot of attention especially after it was noted that Jimbo Livingston was at the reins of the wagon carrying Henry T. Clarke. Cincinnati Culver watched from a window in the Last Chance as they rode by. Jimbo brought the wagon to a stop in from of Swede's Mercantile and tied off the horses. He and Henry T. Clarke went inside.

Jesse Jones greeted the two men as they came in. "You made the round trip in record time, Mr. Clarke," he said.

"Jones, I'd like you to meet my new associate, Jimbo Livingston," Clarke said.

"We know Jimbo quite well," Jones said. "In fact, I watched him ride out of town yesterday."

"He rode into my camp last night and we had a wonderful chat, so I put him to work for me immediately," said Clarke. "I've never been in the military, but if I had been, I'd call Mr. Livingston my aide de camp."

Adam Potter entered from the back room. "Well, well," he said. "Good to see you again Mr. Clarke."

"Look, gentlemen," Clarke said. "I believe we know each other well enough that you can just call me Henry."

"Are you here to stock up on supplies?" Jones asked.

"Yes, I'm going to do that, but before I do, I wonder if you can invite the mayor and Sheriff Blanton over for another little chat," Clarke said. "I had a trooper from Fort Sidney ride out to me yesterday with a message I want to share."

"Right away, Mr. Clarke," Potter said. He caught himself and corrected his mistake in the next sentence. "Right away, Henry."

Potter walked by Jones on the way out of the store and under his breath muttered, "That don't seem right to me calling a man of Mr. Clarke's status by his first name."

"I know what you mean," Jones replied.

It was not long and Potter returned with Mayor Truax and Sheriff Blanton. After they arrived, Jones led them into the back room and away from prying eyes.

"Gentlemen," Clarke began. "I received this urgent telegraph by courier from Fort Sidney yesterday. I won't read it in its entirety, but the gist of it is that President Clark of the Union Pacific Railroad is arriving tomorrow at noon on a special train. He will be accompanied by two U.S. Marshals. He wants to get to the bottom of Cincinnati Culver's telegram to one of his Vice Presidents requesting that we conduct no business whatsoever with Swede's Mercantile in our preparations to build a bridge over the North Platte River. Our little meeting here today must be kept completely confidential. Any word of President Clark's arrival may cause Mr. Culver to flee, and would spoil any chance we have on finding who is leaking information from the Grant administration in Washington. Yes, gentlemen, we do believe information is coming down to Cincinnati Culver from among the White House staff."

THE NEXT DAY the noon train chugged into Sidney and came to a standstill. Steam vented from under the skirts of the locomotive to wrap it in a wispy shroud.

Henry T. Clarke stood waiting on the platform with Jones, Potter, and Sheriff Blanton at his side.

The last car in tow belonged to Horace Clark, President of the Union Pacific Railroad. Jones could tell that this car was once a box car, but those days were gone. It appeared to be twice the length of a caboose and was decorated with red, white, and blue buntings on the side. It was obvious that this car carried a man of importance.

It was Clark's personal assistant and not Clark himself who emerged from the rail car. He recognized Henry T. Clarke and shook his hand.

"Good afternoon, Henry," he said. "Good to see you again. How's our latest project coming along?"

"Good to see you as well, Robert," Henry Clarke responded. "All is going as expected, except for our one little supply glitch."

"I'm thinking between you and Horace, and the two men he brought with him, we should be able to get to the bottom of things," Robert answered.

"Robert," Henry Clarke said, "I'd like you to meet Jesse Jones and his associate Adam Potter."

"Gentlemen," Robert said to acknowledge the introductions.

"And the gentleman with the bright shiny star is Sheriff Blanton," Clarke said.

"My pleasure, sir," Robert said. "Well, gentlemen, now that the pleasantries are finished, I'll take you on board so you can meet President Clark." Robert led the way.

Horace F. Clark remained working behind his desk. When he looked up, Jones noticed a firmness to his bewhiskered face, an almost stoic appearance. He was dressed in a dark suit, white shirt with dark bow tie. Two men stood at his sides; one on the left and one on the right. Jones surmised that these two were the U.S. Marshals.

"Mr. Clark, I would like you to meet the entourage from Sidney," Robert began, "Sheriff Blanton, Adam Potter, and Jesse Jones. Of course, you already know Mr. Henry T. Clarke."

"I certainly do know Mr. Clarke," Horace Clark said, "It was his family that thought themselves so important that they added an 'e' to their last name." He laughed a hearty laugh in which Henry T. Clarke joined in. "Gentlemen, I cannot tell you how important it is to get to the bottom of this incident. The reputation of the Union Pacific is at stake. I've already fired one of my vice presidents over this matter. I've had these two marshals working on the case and they have learned Cincinnati Culver of your fair city has a contact back east. What they haven't discovered is who that contact is and who is giving Culver information about the planned expansion into Dakota Territory. Someone is trying to jump the gun and cheat all the businessmen in town out of a whole lot of money."

Parson Abel's words came into Jesse's mind. *The love of money is the root of all evil.*

CINCINNATI CULVER WATCHED the special train arrive and detected something was amiss with his plans, but like a man caught in the path of a tornado, he couldn't get out of the way fast enough.

He watched as his nemesis, Jesse Jones marched toward the Last Chance with Sheriff Blanton, Adam Potter and two men he did not recognize. Cincy thought about barricading himself in his office but reconsidered.

They'll only break down the door. Doggone it. I should have kept Cole and Travis around to run interference for me.

Instead of barricading his door from inside his office, he closed the door, sat behind his desk, and waited for the knock he knew was coming.

He didn't have long to wait.

Three knocks on his door were followed by the voice of Sheriff Blanton, "Cincy, we know you're in there. This is Sheriff Blanton. Open up!"

"It ain't locked, Sheriff," Cincy said.

Blanton entered followed by the entourage Cincy had seen earlier.

"What can I do for you, gentlemen?" Cincy said.

"We've got a written order saying that you are to produce the name of your contact in Washington, D.C., signed by a Judge in Omaha," Blanton said. He removed the order from his vest pocket and tossed it in front of Cincy.

"I don't have any idea of what you are talking about," said Cincy.

"Let me refresh your memory. A while back you produced a telegraph signed by a Vice President of the Union Pacific, banning Mr. Clarke from purchasing any goods from Jesse Jones," Blanton said. "Well, Mr. Clarke sent a telegraph to the President of the Union Pacific asking for a clarification only to find out that you and one of his Vice Presidents were in cahoots to take over as many businesses in town as you could. Then when the route north began you would sell supplies and make a killing."

"Prove it," Cincinnati replied. "It's his word against mine."

"Read the order from Judge Spencer in Omaha," Blanton said. "He gives you twenty-four hours to produce the name of your source in Washington."

"Or what?" asked Cincy.

"Or these two marshals will take your office apart looking for the name," Blanton said.

"You actually think that I would write the name down? What kind of idiot do you expect me to be?" Cincy said. He leaned back in his chair and put his feet on his desk.

"I'm not sure what kind of an idiot you are," Blanton said. "That's for a judge to decide. All I'm telling you is that you have twenty-four hours to turn over the name of your source in Washington or you will be riding back to Omaha under guard."

Cincy glared at his adversaries.

"And," Blanton continued, "As you have a habit of saying, *Do I make myself clear?*"

After Blanton and the others cleared the room, Cincy went to his safe. He removed a black notebook, looked inside, and then returned it to his safe.

Nearly an hour later Cincy arrived at the telegraph office with a coded message for his contact in Washington, D.C. An hour and a half later he received a return telegraph similarly encoded. Using his black notebook, he deciphered the message: "Too hot. Lay low!" was all it said.

The marshals obtained copies of both missives using their badges as their authority. They carried the copies to Horace Clark who shook his head and handed them to Blanton and Jones.

"It's coded. We know it went to Washington, but to whom?" Clark said.

"I wonder what Cincy's up to?" said Jones.

Horace Clark was still shaking his head when he replied, "It's all Greek to me."

CHAPTER THIRTY

Cole chose this day to put his plan into effect. He and Travis spent the daylight hours in their room fortifying themselves. It was early evening now.

"Have another shot," Cole insisted.

"I think I've had enough," Travis responded.

"You ain't had nearly enough," said Cole. "This here is liquid courage. And for what we're about to do in a couple hours, we're going to need all the courage we can get."

"Right now my courage is making me sleepy," Travis said.

"Let's go over the plan one more time," said Cole.

"Can't I just lie down and snooze for a while?" asked Travis. "You review the plan and I'll read the inside of my eyelids fer a bit. How does that sound?" Travis plopped himself on one of the two beds in the room.

"This plan ain't a gonna work unless we rehearse it," Cole said.

"I already got my part down. I'm rehearsed out," said Travis. He was asleep. Cole knew it. He could tell by Travis' deep breathing and heavy snoring.

"Dadgummit," Cole mumbled to himself. "I gotta do all the plannin' and he's still gonna want a fifty-fifty share of the loot. Don't seem right, but a deal is a deal."

Cole walked to the lone table in the room and pulled up a rickety chair. He struck a match and lit the kerosene lantern sitting in the middle of the table bathing the room in light as darkness fell outside. Cole's filthy hand removed a piece of paper from his shirt. He unfolded the paper and spread it out on the table before him and read the timeline he'd set for the evening's events.

"Ten p.m.—I'm in the alley behind the Last Chance when Travis goes in the front door. Cincy'll be in his office counting some of the day's receipts. Safe'll be open," Travis read.

"Then, at ten-fifteen Travis will start a fight. Get the whole place involved in the ruckus. Travis ducks outside in the middle of the fight and brings our horses 'round to the alley.

"I'll listen at the back door for Cincy to leave his office to stop the fight. When I hear his office door close, I'll bust the back door in and clean out his safe.

"The whole thing will be over before Cincy knows what hit him and Travis and me will be long gone by the time he does." Cole poured himself another shot of whiskey and swallowed it. He grimaced at the taste, but he liked how the booze warmed him from the inside out. Cole folded up his plan and pushed it back into his shirt pocket, confident everything would go as desired.

Cole let Travis sleep a couple of hours and then woke him.

"Wake up, Travis," Cole said. "It's time to make our fortune."

"What?" Travis replied. "What time is it?"

"Eight o'clock," Cole answered. "We got a couple of hours to sober you up. You know, I was thinkin'. Ain't it too bad that our good fortune has come at the expense of Cincy?" Cole scratched his head. "I always liked the guy, ya know.But, as Cincy always says 'This ain't nothin' personal, it's business.'"

Cole plied Travis with coffee and by nine-thirty they were ready to take their places, Cole at the back door and Travis at the front door of the Last Chance.

At precisely ten o'clock Travis entered the bar. He had a few drinks while he selected someone to pick a fight with. Travis chose someone smaller than himself, imagining that the return blows would be lighter.

When ten-fifteen arrived, he walked across the room and landed a haymaker to the face of a man he did not know. Instantly the bar erupted in chaos with hats and fists flying everywhere. Travis ducked out of the bar the moment he heard Cincy's loud voice.

"What in the sam-hill is going on out here?" Cincy shouted.

Travis grabbed the reins of their two horses and led them to the alley where Cole stood grinning from ear to ear.

"Stuff this in yer saddle bag," Cole said. "You got half the loot and I got the other half. There's a black notebook in yer half. Not sure what it's for, but it's in there. Mount up. Let's ride."

It took Cincinnati less than five minutes to bring the fight under control.

"Who started this fracas?" Cincy asked.

"It was Travis," someone shouted from the front of the bar. "I watched him deliberately walk over, rear back and wallop this stranger. Then just as deliberately he walked out the front door.But by then the place was a barroom brawl.”

“And the one who started it didn’t get so much as a black eye?” Cincy asked.

“That ain’t so,” said the stranger who had taken Travis’ haymaker. “I pasted him one. He’s gonna have a black eye alright.”

Everyone in the bar laughed, except for Cincy. He spun around, went back into his office and slammed the door behind him.

Cincy stood there mouth agape. His safe was open and empty.

He shouted at the top of his lungs. “Cole and Travis! You little weasels! Steal my attention, will ya, and then steal from my safe. I’ll get the two of you if it’s the last thing I ever do!

Cincy followed the path of fallen twenty dollar bills to the back door. He opened it and saw Travis’ horse spring from the alley and into the street.

“Travis, you’ll never get away with this.” Cincy’s voice echoed through the streets of Sidney. “Do you hear me? Never.”

Cole rode about two horse lengths in front of Travis. They galloped east, putting ten miles distance between themselves and Cincinnati Culver. A blood moon hung overhead washing their path in an eerie red.

“Whoa!” Cole ordered and pulled his reins taunt. His horse stopped a few feet later.

Travis pulled alongside.

“Well, what do you think of my plan now, huh?” Cole offered with a smile.

"There's only one part about it that I don't like," Travis said.

"Whatta ya mean?" said Cole.

"There's a part of yer plan that I don't like," said Travis.

"We got all of Cincy's money. What's not to like about it?"

"Ya never told me that I'd get a black eye outta all this," Travis said. "I took a punch to the face that I never counted on. Was that in yer plan? Because if it was, I'd never have agreed to it."

"With every reward there comes a risk," Cole said. "Didn't yer pa ever teach ya that?"

"Nope. My pa taught me that if at first you don't succeed, give up because to continue will only make a fool out of ya," Travis said.

"Well, anyway, we got Cincy's money, don't we?" said Cole.

"How much do ya think we got?"

"Don't know. But I'll tell ya what. We're gonna ride a few miles more and take a break," Cole said. "We're not gonna build a campfire and attract a lot of attention. You can be sure Cincy will send some men after us first thing in the morning. I want to put as much distance between them and us as we can."

"Did you put any vittles in yer saddlebag, 'cuz I forgot to in mine," Travis said.

"I guess I never really thought about bringing any vittles along," Cole said."Tell ya what, tomorrow morning we'll be on the lookout for a place to stop.How about that?"

"That'd be great. Especially a farm house. I could go fer a whole mess of eggs, some bacon, and home-made biscuits," Travis said. "Are you sure I gotta wait until morning?

"Do you see any farm houses around? Any light?" Cole said. "I mean it's gotta be after midnight. Ain't nobody gonna be up this late when they have to get up with the chickens."

Cole spurred his horse into action.

Travis followed.

An hour went by before he halted a second time and dismounted.

"I reckon we've gone far enough," Cole said. "Climb down and give yer horse a rest. We can put our heads on our saddles and use them fer pillows."

"Don't think I'm gonna do that. Every time I've tried it, I waked up with a stiff neck outta the deal," Travis said.

"Do it or not, it don't make me no never mind," Cole said. "A few hours of sleep and we'll count the loot we got. How about that? Does that sound okay to you?

"It does. It seems good to me to know how much money I once had before they hung me," Travis said.

"They ain't gonna hang you," Cole said. "They ain't gonna catch you. You're gonna live like a king for the rest of your life, thanks to old Cincy and me—yer old buddy Cole."

CINCY WAS fit to be tied. He felt alone for the first time in a long time. Worst of all he felt betrayed. First by his contact back east, and now by the two men he'd hired to get rid of Jones.

"I'll pay a hundred dollars cash to anyone who will bring me Cole and Travis," he yelled as he entered the barroom. Six men volunteered at once.

"I got the beginning of a posse," Cincy said. "Anyone else willing to ride out tonight?"

"Hey, Cincy," someone called to him from the end of the bar. "Have you been outside? Ain't no way I'd be askin' anyone to ride out tonight. It's a blood moon and to me that ain't a very good moon to be ridin' out in."

"If you wait until morning, I'll go," someone else said.

"Can't wait until morning," Cincy said. "Cole and Travis cleaned me out."

"Then, how can you afford to pay us, if you ain't got any money?" came a reply.

"Yeah," came the reply from the other men in the bar.

"There should be plenty of money in the till to pay whoever wants to ride out tonight," Cincy said. He shoved the bartender out of the way and opened the cash drawer. Cincinnati stood dumbfounded over the open drawer. There was very little money there.

"Don't you remember, boss?" the bartender said. "You cleaned out the til a little before ten o'clock like you usually do."

Cincy slammed the drawer closed in disgust. "Look fellas," he said. "I'll give each of you a hundred bucks if you'll ride out tonight, but I can't pay you until you ride back with my money."

"You can count me out," said the man closest to Cincy. He pushed his hat back and rubbed his brow. "I ain't goin' after no man unless I get half down and half when I get back."

"Right now I don't have that kinda' money." There was panic in Cincy's voice.

"Then right now, ya ain't got no posse, neither," someone yelled at Cincy.

Cincy yelled right back. "The longer you sit here the further away my money rides. Can't you see? I got plans for this money. I'm gonna own this stinkin' town," he yelled.

One by one the men in the bar finished their drinks and left the Last Chance, leaving Cincy alone with his bartender.

Jones was sitting behind the desk in Sheriff Blanton's office when Cincy burst in. Jones could tell that Cincy was disappointed to see him.

"What are you doing here?" Cincy asked.

"Sheriff Blanton has the night off. He's asked me to watch over things for the night," Jones said.

"You gotta help me," Cincy pleaded. "Cole and Travis robbed me. You've got to go after them."

"I'll be pleased to do that first thing in the morning, but I can't tonight. I gotta stay here and watch over the town," Jones said.

"You don't understand," pleaded Cincy. "I need my money back and I need it back tonight."

"Why don't you put some of your money to work by buying yourself a posse?" Jones tried very hard not come across as sarcastic, but he felt he hadn't succeeded.

"Can't you get it through your thick skull that I can't. I don't have any money. Cole and Travis stole it all," Cincy yelled.

"Then I guess you have only one option left to ya," Jones said.

"And what's that, Deputy Jones?" Cincy snarled.

"You're just gonna have to wait until Sheriff Blanton gets back in the office after breakfast tomorrow. Because then I will be free to round up a few men and go after your money. And not before."

"What about Potter? Is he available to help me?" Cincy said.

"Not anymore tonight. It's late. He and I will ride out tomorrow morning as soon as Sheriff Blanton gets in. I'm afraid that's the best I can do for you tonight."

"That's not good enough," Cincy bellowed. "I'm going to file a report with the mayor and have yer badge."

"I will be glad to have you file the report with the mayor, but you'll have to wait until morning," Jones said with a grin.

Cincy slammed the door on his way out.

EAST OF SIDNEY some ten miles or so, Cole woke from his sleep to the smell of freshly brewed coffee.

"What are you doing? Are you crazy, Travis? I told you not to build a fire," Cole said in anger.

No one answered as the morning sun peaked over the sandhills.

Cole forced himself to sit up. Not too far away a man sat with his back to Cole, hunched over what Cole imagined was the fire.

"I didn't make no fire," came a voice on Cole's right. Cole recognized the voice as that of Travis.

"If that's Travis, then who the sam-scratch are you?" Cole asked the man at the fire.

"Don't tell me that you have forgotten me already?" said the man. He rose to his feet and turned to face them.

"Fitz!" Cole and Travis exclaimed at the same time.

"In the flesh," Fitz said. "What are you two boys doing so far from town?"

Travis took pride in announcing, "We robbed Cincy last night. Took every penny."

"Travis you shouldn't have told him about that. Now, he'll want a cut and we ain't got a cut to give him," Cole said.

"Well, I'm a guessin', boys," Fitz said. "I'm a guessin' Sheriff Blanton will be on your tail come morning. Why don't we just ride on back to meet him?Whatta ya say?" Fitz took a sip of his freshly brew coffee.

Cole motioned to Travis to stand up. After he did so, the two men widened their stances.

"We ain't going anywhere with you. Ain't that right, Travis?" said Cole.

Fitz took a slow sip of his coffee before casting it aside, cup and all.

"Are you sure that's the way you boys want it?" Fitz asked.

"That's the way we want it. Ain't that right, Travis?" Cole asked.

Travis nodded.

Fitz's six-gun made that the last question Cole ever asked.

CHAPTER THIRTY-ONE

Fitz returned to Sidney with two men draped over their saddles. Jones was leaving the Sheriff's office on his way to breakfast when Fitz rode up.

"Well, if this isn't a surprise," Jones said. "Where have you been?"

Fitz dismounted. "Had a little run in with these two a while back and left town.After thinking about, I decided to come back and help you clean up the place. If fer no other reason than to honor the memory of my sister," Fitz said.

"She would have been so proud of you," Jones said. "So, tell me why these two came into town draped over their saddles and not sittin' upright in 'em?"

"I was headin' back to town when I ran into these two ten miles out," Fitz began. "They said that they'd robbed Cincy of every last cent. When I said we needed to return the money, they went for their guns."

"They robbed Cincy alright. He came into the office about eleven all bent out of shape wanting me to form a posse and ride out after these two," Jones said. "I told him that I'd ride out this morning when Sheriff Blanton got back to the office, but that wasn't good enough."

"Well, now you don't have to ride out at all," Fitz said. He reached up and removed two saddlebags from behind of his saddle. "Got all of Cincy's money here in Cole's saddlebags." He handed the saddlebags to Jones.

"Let's not do this in the street," Jones said. He led the way back into Sheriff Blanton's office.

Once inside, Fitz unbuckled the strap on one side of the saddlebags and dumped out the contents.

"Wow, would you look at that," Jones said as the pile grew on the table.

Potter came in.

"Are those two men the ones who robbed Cincy last night?" Potter asked.

"They are," Jones said. "And you could do me a big favor and take them down to the undertaker."

"I'm sure their horses would appreciate it, too," Fitz said.

"And so would anybody walking by," Potter said. "Did you bring 'em in Fitz?"

"I did. They didn't like my idea that they should give the money back to Cincy.There was some gunplay and they were too slow," Fitz said.

"I'll be back in a few minutes," Potter said while going out the door.

"Any idea how much money is in this stack?" Jones asked.

"No idea, but there is more money in the other pouch," Fitz said. He unstrapped the second saddlebag and dumped its contents, creating a money pile equal to the first. "You know," Fitz said, "I thought there was a lot of money to be had being a gun for hire. I'd go from town to town and put my life on the line. What I should have done instead is to settle down in a town like Sidney and run a bar. Running a bar is the right business for me, low risk and high return."

"There's always the occasional shootist or card sharp riding into town. No job is perfect," said Jones.

"Maybe not, but I'd have enough money I could hire someone like me to take care of life's little problems," Fitz said.

"The biggest disadvantage, at least in Cincy's case, is he has let money become his everything," Jones said.

"I heard it said once that money isn't everything, but it is well ahead of anything in second place," Fitz said.

"When money becomes so important it controls your relationships, and your only desire is to have more money, then a lot of people are gonna get hurt. Whatever Cincy does, his goal at the end of the day is to have more money than he had at the start of the day," Jones said. "I think Cole and Travis followed Cincy's lead and look what it got them, a visit to the undertaker and a one-way trip to Boot Hill.

For the second time Jones moved for the door. "Let's lock up the place and grab some breakfast. I'm so hungry that my stomach thinks my throat has been cut," he said. "We'll talk about this again when Sheriff Blanton gets here."

He opened the door to find Blanton standing there.

"I heard you talking about me," Blanton said coming inside. "Where did all this money come from? That's quite a stack." He walked over to the table.

"It came from Cincy's office last night," Jones said. "Cole and Travis took it from him."

"So, how did it wind up here?" Blanton asked.

"I took it back from them," Fitz said stepping from behind Jones.

"When did you get back into town, Fitz?" said Blanton.

"I rode in this morning," Fitz said. "I brought in Cole and Travis draped over their saddles. Ran into them a fewmiles out. Told them they needed to bring Cincy's money back, but they refused. They drew on me, so I shot 'em."

"All this happened last night while I was at home? Why didn't anyone come out to my place and get me?" Blanton said.

"Wasn't anything I couldn't handle," Jones said. "Besides last night was the first night in a while that you got to sleep in yer own bed."

"Has Cincy been here?" asked Blanton.

"He was here last night," said Jones. "He wanted me to form a posse and take off after Cole and Travis. Cincy was so angry when I told I wouldn't form a posse without your say-so, he could have bit a square nail in two. I told him you'd be here after breakfast."

"So, he hasn't been here yet?" Blanton asked in an effort to get caught up on all the details.

"Not yet, but I expect him at any moment," Jones said.

Blanton pulled up a chair by the money. "It looks like I'm in the wrong business," he said.

"I was just sayin' that," Fitz said. "There appears to be plenty of money in the bar business."

"You know I've heard that some lawmen have given up their careers to become bar owners, or faro dealers. Even gamblers upon occasion. Wyatt Earp comes to mind," Blanton said.

"There are just as many lawmen who put in an honest day's work for an honest day's pay," said Jones.

"We could always skim a little off the top of this stack and Cincy would never know," Blanton said.

"We could, but we're not going to," Jones said. "This whole stack belongs to Cincy and like him or not, we're not taking something that rightfully belongs to him. It wouldn't be right."

"I know. I know," said Blanton. "But it sure would be nice not to have to rely on my wife's milk and egg money to make ends meet. I mean, after all, you did give up the army to go into the mercantile business, didn't you?" This last question he addressed to Jones.

"Yes, but I have to tell you sometimes there is very little money in retail. After you pay the suppliers, and your help, there are times when the boss is the last one to be paid," Jones said. "To be honest with you, there are times when the boss doesn't get paid."

"But it sure does look like Cincy gets paid. And often," Fitz said. "Not that I want to steal any of Cincy's money, but it doesn't look like he's missed a payday for a very long time."

"I have to agree," said Jones. "Maybe he's got outside help."

CINCINNATI'S BOOTS thudded on the boardwalk as he made his way to Sheriff Blanton's office. His gait told everyone to step aside because he was all business and no bull.

Cincy was drawn to the window of the undertaker's parlor where two men were laid out for the town to see. He recognized them at once as Cole and Travis.

Did Jones go out after them despite telling me that he wouldn't? The more he wondered, the madder he got for having been lied to. *It's too good for these two thieves to be shot to death. I'd have preferred to have them squirm before Judge Thomson and then hang by the neck until dead for robbing me. Poor fellas probably had no chance at all against Jones' LeMat.*

At the end of his thinking, Cincy arrived at Sheriff Blanton's door and stepped inside.

"Nice to see you in yer office this morning, Sheriff," Cincy said. He saw the bundle of money on the table as was drawn to it like a magnet. "Is this my money?" he asked.

"It is," Blanton said. He arose from his desk chair and made his way to the table where Cincy had already started counting.

"Had someone you know bring in a saddlebag full of money this morning," Blanton began.

"Shh," Cincy hissed at him. "Don't interrupt me."

At last Cincy finished counting and a scowl crossed his face. "Who did you say brought in this money?" demanded Cincy.

"I didn't," Jones replied.

"I want the name and I want it right now. There's a whole lot of money unaccounted for. Whoever brought it in stole at least half of it. I want a name," Cincy said.

"Jones told me Fitz brought the money in this morning," Blanton said.

"I should have known Jones was at the bottom of this. He wouldn't form a posse and go after Cole and Travis as I asked him to. Oh, but he'd set out with Fitz alright." Cincinnati was angry and he didn't care who knew it.

Blanton took a defensive tone: "This is all the money they recovered," he said.

"So they said," Cincinnati said. "But what if they took half my money? Were you here when Fitz came in? Did you see Jones put the money on the table?"Cincinnati did not wait for Blanton's reply. "No. No, you weren't. You were tucked warm and cozy in yer bed. You can't trust Jones any further than you can throw him and Fitz cheated me. Which is worse in your mind? Someone who steals in front of yer face or behind yer back? It's all the same, ain't it?It's called stealing either way."

"I trust Jones," Blanton said.

"Of course you do," Cincinnati said. "That's because you

are in cahoots with him. You probably looked at a big stack of my money and said to yerselves that you'd like to have a part of the money Cincy made running a bar, didn't ya?—Well, didn't ya?"

"We agreed it was a lot of money, but we didn't take any of it," said Blanton.

"Then how do you explain that at least half of my money is missing if you didn't steal it and split it among the three of you?" Cincinnati barked. "I had close to ten thousand dollars in my safe and there ain't but fifty-five hundred in this stack. And where is my black notebook? I'm missing a black notebook. The three of you have a lot of explaining to do."

CINCY SPENT the remainder of the morning and early afternoon in a foul mood.He tried unsuccessfully to use the money returned to him to hire men to do his bidding. Not many were polite in their reply. At last he slammed the door on them and sulked in his office. His plans were evaporating like a rain cloud on a sunny day.

Cincy had worked himself into a lather by the time Horace Clark and his marshals arrived, accompanied by Blanton, Jones, Potter, and Fitz.

"Go away," Cincy shouted in response to the knock at the door.

"Mr. Culver, this is Horace Clark of the Union Pacific," Clark said. "You're twenty-four hours has expired. We're here to get the name of your contact back east."

Clark did not hesitate. He turned the door handle and stepped into Cincy's office. The others followed.

"You had the audacity to bring a thief with you?" Cincy began at the sight of Jones.

"Mr. Culver, you have no reason at all the suspect Mr. Jones of anything," Clark said.

"I have all the proof I need. He only returned half of the money stolen from me," Cincy said. "He and that shootist Fitz are in this together. Cole and Travis stole from me. Then Jones and Fitz killed 'em. They took half and gave me half my money back. I ain't given' you nothin' until all of my money is returned to me. Do you understand me?"

"But, Mr. Culver," Clark said.

"I bid you good day, gentlemen," Cincy said. Cincy snatched his revolver from his open desk drawer and drew a bead on Jones. "I said, good day, gentlemen."

"I have a warrant, Mr. Culver. Are you forgetting that?" Clark said.

"I don't give a hang about yer warrant and I'll thank you if you'd find your own way out," Cincy said. He cocked his pistol to emphasize his point.

"But..." Clark said.

"There will be no more buts," Cincy said. "And I'd appreciate it if you'd take yer butts outta here. If you don't 'ol doc's gonna have a hole to fix in Jesse's heart.Now, get yer thievin' carcasses out of my office and don't come back."

CLARK and his entourage stepped into the street.

"Jones!" a voice yelled at them from behind.

Jesse Jones turned to face the voice.

"I'm calling you out, Jones !" Cincinnati yelled.

Jones stood in the street facing Cincy. The others moved aside.

"Clear the street, everyone," Blanton shouted. They did.

"Cincy, there is no reason for this. We can settle it without gunplay," Blanton said.

"No, we can't," Cincy said to Blanton. "I'm calling you out, Jones. Do you hear me?"

"I hear ya, Cincinnati," Jones said.

"I got this, Jones," Fitz said. He stepped into the line of fire.

"I'm not fighting you, Fitz," Cincy said. "This is between me and Jones."

"Fitz, this is my fight," Jones said. Fitz stepped aside. "I will take your gun though. This LeMat is too cumbersome on the draw."

Fitz and Jones traded revolvers.

"I've got ya over a barrel, Jones," Cincy said.

"How so?" asked Jones.

"Kill me and you'll never know the identity of my contact back east, and if you don't kill me, I'll kill you," Cincy said. "Wound me and you'll still be dead."

"Gentlemen, please," said Clark. "Can't we come to some kind of agreement?"

"Better step back, Mr. Clark," Potter said. "You might get hit by a stray bullet."

"I'll count to three and we'll both draw. Agreed?" Cincy said. Jones nodded.

"One. Two. Three."

Two guns fired. One gun was faster.

Jones remained standing. Cincy did not.

Jones knelt in the street beside Cincy.

"Am I hurt bad?" Cincy asked. Jones nodded.

"Then I win, Mr. Jones," Cincy choked out. "I wi. . ."

Cincy was dead.

CHAPTER THIRTY-TWO

The death of Cincinnati Culver did not go unnoticed. Martha Belt likened it to a thunderstorm giving way to sunshine. 'A cleansing' is what she called it. She even went so far as to call it cathartic. The grass looked greener. The air smelled fresher. Martha even noticed a lilt in Jesse's voice. Cincy's death was like a great weight lifted from his shoulders.

She noticed, however, that Horace Clark, the President of the Union Pacific, wasn't nearly as elated by the previous day's developments as she was.

"We still aren't any closer to finding out who tipped Cincinnati off about the trail north into Dakota Territory," Clark said that evening at the Abel's home.

"No, we aren't," Jones said with a sigh. "But, I wasn't about to let Cincy kill me so you could find out." Martha reached under the table, found Jesse's hand, and gave it a squeeze.

"There isn't anyone in this room who would have traded Jesse's life for that information," Parson Abel announced. "We've seen a sad example in Cincy's life of what happens when the god of money replaces the One True God."

"Oh, you can't let that go for one evening, can you?" said Doc.

"Nope, I don't see how that's possible," Parson Abel said. "Witnessing is as essential to me as breathing."

"Well, while you're doing all that breathing, would you mind passing the mashed potatoes?" Doc said.

"I suppose it is too much to ask that we learn the name of Cincinnati's contact before my train pulls out tomorrow morning," Clark said.

"That would be nothing short of a miracle," said Henry Clarke, who was seated directly across the table from Horace Clark. "But, I've come to learn miracles have a way of happening in this town. Jimbo should be back in town tomorrow morning as well. With your help, Jesse, we'll take another load of supplies up to Camp Clarke. Oh, and I have to tell everyone that Jimbo has agreed with the name for the little town springing up near Camp Clarke."

"He has?" Martha said.

"Yes, he has," Henry Clarke said. "I'm pleased to say that we've all settled on his name for the town. We're going to call it Bridgeport."

"I like that," Horace Clark said. "I like that a lot. Bridgeport."

A knock at the front door interrupted the festivities. Parson Abel excused himself and went to the door. He returned a few minutes later carrying a saddlebag.

"It was Otis from down at the livery stable," Abel said. "He was going through Travis' tack and found this." He held up the saddle bag Otis had given him. "Otis said there's money inside."

"Well, I'll be," said Potter. "I'll bet it's the rest of Cincinnati's money." He looked over at Jones. "The money he thought you'd stolen from him."

Jones walked over to the doorway where Parson Abel stood.

"Let me have a look at it, will ya?" Jones said.

Parson Abel handed the saddlebag to Jesse, who cleared a spot on the table and poured out the contents.

Martha watched as money fell on the table. Lots of money, more money than she had ever seen in one place in her life. Then, when the money was all poured out, a black notebook fell to the top of the pile.

"Mr. Clark," Jesse said, "this may be the answer to your prayer."

Jones opened the notebook. "It's filled with a lot of numbers," he said. "I saw writing like this during the war when I found a Confederate spy doll. This is code. You simply take the message you want to send and convert it into numbers and symbols. At the other end all you need is a code-book like this to decipher it."

JONES NOTED THAT THE LOCOMOTIVE, though motionless, seemed to have a life of its own. The engine seemed to breathe in and out as it built up steam for the return trip to Omaha.

Jones, Henry T. Clarke, and Fitz were invited into Horace Clark's private train car. Clarke was at his desk, flanked by his U.S. Marshals.

"Welcome aboard, gentlemen," Clarke announced. "I've got good news. These marshals have deciphered the code using Cincy's codebook. We now know the identity of his contact back east. I've already telegraphed President Grant apprising him of the situation."

"That certainly is good news," Jones said.

"It is indeed," Clark said. "There are some in his administration that would like to treat the Native Americans in our country with contempt. They want to force them off their land and onto reservations under the guise of Manifest Destiny."

"I think Cincinnati Culver was one such person," Jones said.

"And he was not alone. Several men back in Washington D.C. feel the same way," Clark added. "They feel that because the French sold us the land, that it's ours and we can do what we please. But the Native Americans were here first and never gave their consent to the buying or selling of their land."

"That's an excellent point sir," Fitz said.

"That brings up an important matter, Mr. Fitzpatrick. On my trip to D.C., I plan to meet with Allen Pinkerton of the Pinkerton National Detective Agency and recommend that he train you to be part of my staff. What do you say to that?" Horace Clark asked.

"Thank you, sir. I would be honored," Fitz said.

"Your sister Sarah would be so proud," said Jones.

"For your help in putting an end to this matter, Mr. Jones, I'd like to present you with a reward of one thousand dollars," Horace Clark continued. "I've also consulted with Henry and it is his recommendation that we rely on you to supply us for our adventure known as the Camp Clarke Bridge. Do you think you can do that?"

"Yes, sir. Swede's Mercantile is ready to do that."

"You are doing a fine job, Henry. I've reviewed your specifications for the bridge and I will sign off on them right now." Horace Clark removed a fountain pen from its stand and affixed his signature before handing the document back to Henry T. Clarke. "Can you think of anything that I may have forgotten, gentlemen?"

All three men shook their heads.

"Very well, then," Horace Clark said. "If you will excuse

yourselves, I will make my return trip back to Omaha and then on to Washington after that. We will stay in touch, gentlemen."

Jones stepped down from the train, Clarke and Fitz followed. They joined Martha, Doc and the Abels on the railroad platform to offer their goodbyes as Horace Clark departed.

Two long whistles sounded from the engine and the drive wheels slipped a couple of times before taking hold to lurch the train forward. Horace Clark stepped out onto the landing of his car and waved farewell. His train was soon only a speck on the eastern horizon haloed by a bit of smoke.

"Well, we've got a lot to be thankful for," Parson Abel said. "Other than a few bumps and bruises we're none the worse for wear, are we? If everyone would like to stop by the house for a few minutes, Martha and Adeline made a couple of pies this morning that are ready to eat. One is fresh gooseberry and the other apple."

"When it comes to pie," Jones said, "there are only a few people who can make them like Adeline can."

"And Martha's pies are as good as mine," Adeline said. "Jesse, you are one lucky fella." She smiled. Jones looked at Martha and received the same loving smile.

"WELL, DOC," Parson Abel said. "It looks like we all survived one of the toughest years yet. Very little in the way of crops because of the lack of rainfall, but the gooseberries and apples are good."

"It's all seasonal," Doc said over a slice of apple pie. "Doesn't the Good Book say something like that? What is it? A season for everything? Or something like that?

"I didn't know that you've taken to reading the Good Book, Doc," Parson Abel said.

"Well, I've found I gotta read somethin' while yer up front at the church 'a ramblin' on like a magpie, ya know," Doc said.

"Why, you old hypocrite," Abel said. "All along I thought you weren't interested in the Bible."

"I ain't really, but since it's the only readin' material available in yer church, I gotta read what's available," Doc replied.

"Well, it looks like everything is getting back to normal," Adeline reflected.

"Yep," said Jones. "Two old friends engaged in verbal fisticuffs. It's just like old times."

"And that certainly is the case," Adeline said. "We are all getting just a little bit older." Adeline paused a moment before she continued. "But we're not all getting a bit wiser, you know?"

"What do you mean by that?" Jones asked.

"Well for one thing," she whispered, "Martha's been waiting all this time for you. She said you promised her that the minute this was all over, you would marry her. She's waiting for you to keep your promise, Jesse Jones."

"This whole thing only ended yesterday," said Jones.

"And she's been waiting since yesterday," Adeline replied.

"She has?"

"You men," Adeline said. "Why is it that you can see the anger in another man's eyes, but you can't see the love in the eyes of a woman?"

WHILE DOC and Parson Abel continued their verbal sparring in Parson Abel's den, Jesse Jones took Martha Belt by the hand and led her out onto the veranda. They sat in the porch swing.

"I've been thinking about you the past few days," Jones began. "Now, that the conflict is over, maybe you and I should revisit my house along Lodgepole Creek. After all, I told you I would. I like to keep my promises, you know?"

Martha hugged him. "Oh, Jesse," she said. "I've been waiting for you to say those words."

"You have?"

"Yes," she said. "Every since we traveled out there the first time. I know this has to be hard for you, losing your first wife and all, but I really would like spending my life with you. I've been waiting for you to ask me ever since Cincy was shot in the street."

"That was only yesterday."

"And today is yesterday's tomorrow," Martha replied. "And who knows for certain how many tomorrows we will have together. I want to spend all my tomorrows with you. I love you."

"I love you, too," Jones said. "Here's what I'm thinking. I'm thinking I'll rent a surrey and pick you up first thing tomorrow morning and we'll ride out to my place. And we can talk about how we will spend our tomorrows together.What do you think?"

"I think that's a wonderful idea, Jesse," Martha said. She kissed him. "Jesse, you've made my tomorrow a whole lot brighter."

"And I promise that I will work real hard to make each tomorrow better than the yesterday before it," he said. "I think the thousand dollars that Henry T. Clark gave me will get us off to a good start."

"Jesse," Martha said. "It's not about money; it's about us."

They kissed.

THE NEXT MORNING Jones drove a rented surrey to the Abel's home. He escorted Martha from the house to the surrey and helped her in.Martha noted that he seemed very somber, very resolute. She'd ask him questions but instead of carrying his weight in conversation as he usually did, his answers came out as one word or a nod.

As he had done the only other time they spent time at the cabin, Jones steered the surrey south until it met the road that went west along Lodgepole Creek.Martha talked. Jesse mostly listened.

The specter of the past is overpowering and haunting him, she thought. *My only hope is that his love for me will chase the specter away.*

When at last they arrived at the little clearing where the cabin he had built with his own hands sat, he tugged the horses to a stop and climbed out.Jones came around to the other side of the surrey to help Martha step down.

"Are you alright, Jesse, or is this too hard for you?" Martha said.

"It is hard. A lot harder than I imagined it would be," said Jones. "There are so many memories of happier times, and also too many shattered dreams."

"Whatever it is, Jesse, we'll face this together," she said and took his hand."Adeline has told me a little about your first wife, how you loved her and cared for her. She told me about a man named Custus who was filled with hate, who manipulated people, disregarded the Sioux, and stole gold right from under their watching eyes."

"Did she tell you that I had a chance to kill Custus early on, but didn't? Did she tell you that?"

"She did. She told me that each time you had a chance to kill him, you did the honorable thing and let him go," Martha said.

"And because I was so *honorable* Custus and his men followed me out here, waited until I left for town, and killed her," he said.

"Even after her death you honored your wife," she said. "Adeline told me Sarah circled words in her Bible in her own blood 'vengeance is mine, says the Lord.' You did not kill Custus although you had him in a strangle hold. Your friend Red Hand did. He put an arrow through Custus when he was about to throw his Bowie knife into your back. Jesse Jones, you are an honorable man, a man I want to spend the rest of my life with." She looked into his eyes and saw a tear make its way to the corner and run down his cheek. "I love you, Jesse Jones," Martha said. She kissed him.

"You shouldn't see me like this," Jones said. "My father taught me that a man isn't supposed to cry."

"I think that's happiness rolling down your cheeks," she said. "Besides I'm not about to tell anyone." She giggled a nervous giggle.

Jesse kissed her.

"A few weeks ago I couldn't take you inside the cabin," Jones said. "I wasn't ready then. I am now."

Jesse Jones held Martha's hand as they went room to room. He told her his dreams. Later, as they crossed the threshold on the way out again, he went to his knees and said, "Martha Belt will you marry me?"

Her answer came out firmly, "Yes, Jesse Jones. I will marry you."

He held her tightly and Martha heard the words, "It was here that my happiness died and it is here that my happiness is reborn."

CHAPTER THIRTY-THREE

The announced marriage of Jesse and Martha was the talk of the town. Everyone was interested in doing what they could for the man who saved them from evil men, not once, but twice.

When word leaked the couple planned to make their home in the cabin Jones built a few years back, volunteers came forward to restore the place. Colonel Englewood sent troopers to lead the restoration, all under the supervision of the soon to be Mrs. Jesse Jones.

A community work day was announced for the Saturday ahead of the wedding, setting the whole town abuzz. When that day arrived, all manner of conveyances brought the citizenry to the Jones' home. Some of the women busied themselves with the interior of the cabin, which now included two additional rooms in anticipation of a family. Others readied the luncheon they would serve at noon.

Some of the men cleared rocks away and tilled up the old garden spot. Others were led by Brody Belt in the construction of a cellar much like he'd built on his homestead; one that could save lives when needed against attackers of any kind or against tornados which had a nasty habit of destroying everything in their path. A third group of men stood watch over three pits they had dug and filled with charcoal. In these pits three hogs roasted to provide the evening meal.

Jones watched as the day unfolded before him. He had removed his shirt, grabbed a shovel, and joined Brody Belt's cellar construction crew.

Parson Abel and the most senior members of his congregation walked around the cabin. They halted every thirty feet or so and placed their hands on the structure and prayed. Jesse was pleased to see that Doc and his wife were among those who walked and prayed.

At noon the women stopped what they were doing and made sandwiches for everyone, and sliced and served the numerous homemade pies brought for the occasion. Makeshift tables were set up and two serving lines were readied. Everyone stopped working for a time.

"Heavenly Father," Parson Abel prayed. "Send your blessing upon the couple whom I will soon marry. Bless those who have volunteered today as an expression of their appreciation. Bless the food we are about to eat and bless the hands that have provided this food from your generous bounty. May this food nourish us as we faithfully do as you have asked us to do; to make disciples of all nations. This I pray through Christ Jesus. Amen."

All those present offered a resounding 'Amen'.

"The ladies ask that you form two lines. There are two tables of food and both are alike, so form up and come and eat," Parson Abel announced.

The hour lunch break passed quickly and everyone returned to their respective projects.

Work continued unabated until the evening meal was

served. At the end of the day everything was finished except the storm cellar.

"We're about three or four days away from giving you a cellar like ours," Brady Belt told Martha. "I want you to know that we are so proud of the man you are about to marry. You could not have made a better choice."

"Thank you," Martha said. "Had it not been for your move west, I would never have met him."

Those who completed a day's worth of work were treated to a feast of spit-roasted pork and all the fixings after Parson Abel offered a blessing.Additional pies and baked goods were served for dessert. When the meal was finished and the clean-up completed a convoy of buggies snaked their way back to Sidney.

THE WEDDING of Jesse Jones and Martha Belt occurred on October 24, 1874 in the church where Parson Abel served. Not a pew remained unoccupied. Many of those who had prepared the Jones cabin for the couple returned now to see them married.

Martha entered the sanctuary on the arm of her brother Brody.

"How are you doing? Any second thoughts?" Brody asked her as they prepared to come down the center aisle.

"The only thought I have right now is that it's a little too late to have second thoughts," Martha smiled.

"You are marrying a good man," Brody said. "You are getting a fine husband and I'm getting a very reliable brother-in-law."

Martha smiled at him and looked about the church. It was

a comfortable feeling to know that she was on a first name basis with everyone gathered there.

"Please rise," Parson Abel announced. The congregation did.

Martha and Brody moved forward into the sanctuary. Along the way she saw smiles on familiar faces. Seated about half way up the aisle she saw Bill Hickok and Bill Cody both of whom had journeyed in from North Platte. In front of them sat Henry T. Clarke and his new assistant Jimbo Livingston. Next to them sat Horace Clark and Fitz, no longer a hired gunman, but a Pinkerton Detective. In the front row, in her customary spot, sat Adeline Abel along with Doc Hardesty and his wife.

Martha felt Brody leave her side and she put her right hand in the left hand of Jesse Jones. She had never felt happier in her life. She tried to keep her eyes facing forward but could not help taking a quick glance at the man she would share her life with.

"The congregation may be seated," said Parson Abel. After they were seated he continued.

"We have gathered today before God and this congregation to unite this couple in Holy Matrimony. Marriage was instituted by God back in the Garden of Eden. It was instituted so that a man and a woman may delight in one another. That they may serve one another and, if God should permit it, to raise God-fearing children."

Martha became lost in the events of the day and the joy she felt. She came back to reality when she heard the words "I do" come from Jesse.

"And do you, Martha, take this man to be your wedded husband, to love and to cherish in sickness and in health, for richer or for poorer, as long as you both shall live? If so, then say, I do."

"I do," Martha said.

"Then by the power granted to me as a called and ordained servant of Jesus Christ, I pronounce you man and wife," Parson Abel said. "Jesse you may kiss your bride."

Martha was swept into Jesse's arms, and to loud cheers of those gathered there, he kissed her.

A wedding reception followed. Even more attended the reception than could fit within Parson Abel's church. Beer flowed freely.

At last, Jesse whisked Martha away. They climbed into a surrey with a wooden placard that said JUST MARRIED on the back.

"It's time for us to go home, Mrs. Jones," Jesse said.

Martha liked that. *Mrs. Jones. Now that has a nice sound to it.*

Before long, Jones pulled the reins tight and the lone horse pulling their surrey stopped. Jones lifted her from her seat and carried her across the threshold of the home they would share.

"Welcome home, Mrs. Jones," Jesse said. "I want you to know just how much I love you."

"I love you, too," she said. "You have made this the happiest day of my life."

MARTHA AND JESSE rode into town together early Monday morning.

"There is no school today," she had told him over breakfast. "The children are needed on the farm with harvest. We start school again in a few weeks. I can help you in the store, if you'd like."

"That would be wonderful," he told her. "That way I can keep my eye on you, Mrs. Jones."

Swede's Mercantile was a busy place and today was no exception. Townsfolk had delayed their shopping last Saturday to attend Jesse and Martha's wedding and the celebration that followed. They were making up for lost shopping time this morning.

Jesse and Martha came to the aide of Adam Potter and Adeline Abel who were doing the best they could to keep up with the bustling business.

"Didn't expect to see you this morning," Potter said.

"And why not?" Jones asked.

"Thought you might take a day off as a honeymoon day," Potter replied.

"We did plenty of honeymooning yesterday," Jones said. "Besides, we knew you'd be swamped in here today with the wedding and all."

"We can use your help in here, that's for sure," said Potter.

There was a lull in business about three o'clock. That was about the time when Henry T. Clarke arrived.

"I've been watching all the activity coming in and out of this place from up the street at the Moore Hotel," Clarke said. "Been waiting for the right time to come by for a little chat."

"Ladies," Jones said. "Would you excuse us for a few minutes?" Jones led Clarke into the storeroom. Potter joined them.

"Jesse," Clarke began, "I received a telegraph this morning from Horace Clark. He's in Washington D.C. He's officially authorized me to tell you that he's selected Swede's Mercantile to be the outfitter for the Camp Clarke Bridge.Now, there will be other suppliers in Sidney, but the bulk of the business will go to you.

"This is not going to be an ordinary project," Clarke continued. "The bridge itself will be about two thousand feet in length, spanning the north fork of the Platte River. I'm thinking that maybe I'll start a Pony Express of my own to connect Sidney with army outposts further north, and if a deal can be worked out with the Sioux, perhaps with mining towns that spring up in Dakota Territory. There's going to be a city to build by the bridge. I've mentioned that to you before. A city named Bridgeport. I've got big plans, gentlemen, and I'm pleased to tell you that you'll be right in the middle of them."

"Ain't this gonna be something?" Potter said. "We're smack dab in the middle of all of this. I wish Swede was still alive to see it."

"Me, too," said Jesse. "I'm sure this is way more than he ever dreamed of when he moved west and started this store. He and his wife were dirt poor."

"Now, you are the beneficiary to what he started," Clarke said. "Much like further generations will benefit from the work we're doing by providing cities, churches, schools, universities, along with roads and bridges."

"That's as it should be, isn't it?" Potter said. "One generation builds on the foundation of another."

"Well, that's certainly the way I see it, gentlemen," Clarke announced. "Provide goods and services for others, be honest in your dealings, and you'll be rewarded for it."

"And as often as not," Jones added, "it may not come in the form of money, but in the ability to sleep well at night."

"I could not agree with you more," said Clarke.

TRUE TO HIS word Henry Clarke placed order after order for supplies which Swede's Mercantile supplied. Jimbo Livingston recruited teamsters to transport the supplies north until the road met with the Mormon Trail. From that connection point the wagons traveled to the northwest until coming to the site of the Camp Clarke Bridge. There they unloaded and made the return trip to Sidney for additional supplies.

Money soon flowed in abundance into the coffers of Swede's, enough so that the owners could take a handsome salary. When that happened in the spring of 1875, Jones sat down with Parson Abel. Having seen what the love of money had done to Cincinnati Culver, Jones feared the same might happen to him.One day he and Martha sat down with the Abel's in their study.

"Let me take you to another place in Scripture," Parson Abel said. "One that I think will help you put things in perspective."

"That sounds like a good plan," Jones said. He looked over at Martha who nodded.

"It is said that Solomon was the wisest man who ever lived. He wrote down some of his wisdom in Proverbs. In Proverbs chapter thirty, he has a message that speaks to us about money." Parson Abel opened his family Bible to Proverbs. "Ah, here's what I was looking for; right here in chapter thirty, verses eight and nine. Give this a listen," he said. "Remove far from me vanity and lies: give me neither poverty nor riches; feed me with food convenient for me; Lest I be full, and deny thee, and say, Who is the Lord? or lest I be poor, and steal, and take the name of my God in vain."

Jones must have had a puzzled expression on his face for Parson Abel continued. "In other words, Solomon realizes that excess is not good. Neither an excess of poverty, nor an excess of riches, and he asks God to give him enough riches to be happy, but not too much. He also asks God not to let him fall into poverty, lest he be driven to steal and take God's name in vain. Does that make sense?"

"I think so," Jones replied. "Am I correct in saying that if we carry Solomon's words into our lives, we should keep only what we feel is necessary to live on and no more."

"I think that's the gist of what Solomon is saying," Abel

replied. "Take care of yourself and those who work for you. Make sure they have enough to live on so they don't resort to stealing."

"And anything above that, we should give away? Is that what you are saying?"Jones asked.

"That's always a good idea," Abel said. "There are many in town who could use a hand-up instead of a handout. Adeline and I can help you with that. That's the mission of the church."

Jones noticed something different about Martha in the light of the Abel's room. There was an aura about her that made him easily return her smile with a smile of his own

"Jesse?" Martha asked. "I'm glad we added onto the cabin."

Adeline gave Parson Abel a knowing smile.

Jones saw it. "Am I the only one not in on this little secret?" he asked.

"Jesse," Martha said. "You're going to be a father."

"I am?" said Jones.

"You are," Martha replied.

EPILOGUE

My great-grandmother is expecting a child. How wonderful is that? I'm glad I could end this book as I did. The baby she was carrying is my grand-father. Yes, I have read far enough along in my great-grandfather's diary to know that. She's carrying Jesse Jones Junior. When I shared this news with my wife, so said she was thankful for that fact. "Otherwise," she said, "I'd be married to the wrong man."

How was I to take a remark like that? I decided to take it at face value and tell her thank you in return. I said, "For the sake of our children I am glad you ended up marrying the right guy."

There was a hint of sarcasm in my delivery and she saw through it. She rolled her eyes and went into the other room.

That left me free to snoop even further into great-grandfather's diary. So far I have determined enough excitement exists for a third book leading up to the centennial year of our nation —1876. As I found when digging deeper, the celebration in Sidney was interrupted by three events. First, the startling announcement of the sudden death of General George Custer put a damper on the celebration. Second, a cattle stampede through the heart of Sidney during the centennial parade. And lastly, a gunfight between hundreds of armed men known as Night Riders, and the U.S. Army along with my great-grandfather and his friends at a place north of town called Camp Clarke Bridge.

I must read further.

Jesse Jones IV

DEAR READER

Thank you for reading **At the Point Of A Gun,** the second book in the Man With The LeMat series. Jesse Jones' story begins in book 1, **Death Rode To Lodgepole Creek** and concludes with **Gunfight at Camp Clarke Bridge.**

Reviews are lifeblood to authors. Please consider leaving a review of this book at your retailer's website or at places like Goodreads and BookBub.

ALSO BY ZACHARY LANE

Death Rode To Lodgepole Creek

Man With The LeMat book 1

There are many reasons settlers came west after the Civil War. Jesse Jones came to escape his past but the haunting memory of revenge for a friend's murder stays with him. He now wields the man's LeMat pistol. Stationed with the army at Sidney Barracks, Jesse uses his skill with the unusual pistol to guard the railroad from attack by the native Cheyenne.

After a vicious attack by Union soldiers, Sarah Fitzpatrick plans to become a singer but ends up working as one of Madam Roger's girls. With each encounter she despairs of ever being free of the memories. After a chance meeting with Jesse, her life takes a turn for the better.

Custus Leverette controls Sidney, 'the wickedest town in the west', and no one dares cross him. When he decides he wants Sarah, he'll destroy anyone or anything standing in his way.

Who will survive the battle between Custus' knife and Jesse Jones-The Man with the LeMat?

Gunfight at Camp Clarke Bridge

Man With The LeMat book 3

The promise of Black Hills gold is drawing prospectors and greedy men to Sidney. Plans are made for a bridge to span the Platte River, cutting days off travel time to the Dakota Territory. Jesse Jones and Swede's Mercantile are chosen to supply the materials needed to build the Camp Clarke Bridge.

Jesse leases a warehouse from banker Swan Holmes, a cheerful man who often claims, "God helps those that help themselves." When the phrase is repeated by the one armed man, Bill DuFreeze, and the town is overrun with shady men all wearing black bandanas, Jesse takes on the job of acting sheriff. In his search for answers he faces rustlers, accusations, destruction, and fear. What price will he have to pay to finally bring peace to Sidney, Nebraska?

ABOUT THE AUTHOR

Zachary Lane is a native Nebraskan; a small town kid who has always had a big imagination. A family vacation to a battlefield sparked his interest in the Civil War. The 'old shed' in his back yard soon became an officer's quarters or a fort. Lane fueled his imagination by reading books about this epic war that pitted brother against brother. His personal library is filled with books. Lots and lots of books. So many books that an ultimatum has been issued in the Lane household—if a new book comes in, an older one must be boxed up and put on a shelf in the garage.

Zachary began writing seriously after visiting a rest stop near Sidney, Nebraska. Observing and reading a historical marker overlooking the railroad and town in valley below set his imagination free to tell the story of life there in the 1860's and 1870's.

He still lives in Nebraska where he enjoys walks with his wife, playing with grandchildren, grilling on summer's evenings, smoking ribs and pork butts and stretching his imagination by writing new stories about early Nebraska.